CW01660713

All characters in this book are fictitious, apart from Winston Churchill.

Photo Attributions

"Bletchley Park" by Draco2008 is licensed under CC BY 2.0.

This is for the picture of the BP building

Enigma sign

"Bletchley Park - Block B - The Bletchley Park Story - Enigma machines - Enigma" by ell brown is licensed under CC BY 2.0

Created with Vellum

CHAPTER ONE

'No air raids for a week now,' I said to Bronwyn as we walked towards our flat. We struggled against a wind so fierce it almost blew my hat off. I had to ram it on my head to avoid losing it.

'Don't speak too soon, Cariad, or you'll bring those damned bombers back sure as eggs is eggs!'

We were on our way home from the Army Depot where we worked, and for a change had no voluntary work to do that evening. The sun had set over the rooftops, but there was enough light to see the flattened buildings we passed. I never got used to seeing them, always imagining the deaths and disruption to the innocent people who once lived or worked in them. But there were daffodils too, reminding us that life goes on and Spring was here, even if there was a chill in the air.

'What shall we do this evening?' Bronwyn asked with her Welsh lilt, 'Pictures? Dancing?'

I shook my head, 'Something to eat and a quiet evening reading my book and knitting. That'll do me.'

She play punched me. 'Not kidding nor nothing, but sometimes you're really boring.'

We turned into our street and smiled to see a group of young lads playing football in the road. There wasn't much traffic and they seemed canny enough to keep an eye on cars coming even while shouting encouragement or curses at each other.

But one was smaller than the rest. Probably two years younger. His baggy shorts hung well below his knees, a sure sign they were hand-me-downs, and his jumper had holes in each elbow. His light brown hair was cut in a pudding basin style that didn't do him any favours.

'Car!' shouted one of the older lads, and another grabbed the ball as they ran onto the pavement.

All except the little lad, who was inspecting his grazed knee.

The car, a black and cream Austin, moved far too fast for the road, and despite the noisy engine, the lad didn't hear it.

Bronwyn squealed, glued to the spot. An older couple, walking on the opposite pavement, froze too.

With no conscious thought, I darted into the road and grabbed the boy, aware the car was bearing on me rapidly. Heart beating fast and breathless, I yanked him onto the pavement without a second to spare. The driver beeped his horn and shouted abuse at me as if it was my fault. Petrol fumes were soon all that remained of him.

I put the boy down with trembling hands. 'Thanks, Miss,' he said, pulling his clothes straight. Then he joined his mates without a care in the world. I stood looking at him, hands clammy, shaking so much my teeth chattered.

'Coo, Lady, you was brave,' an older lad said. 'Mum would've given me hell if they'd knocked him down.' He turned and gave his brother a quick swipe round the head, then the pair of them ran to catch up with the others.

'Blimey, Lil,' Bronwyn said, coming over to me. 'I thought you were a gonna, for sure.'

I was still breathing so hard I could barely answer her. I put my hands to my heart. 'I'm not sure I'd have done that if I'd had time to think.'

The couple opposite were applauding me and calling 'Well done!'

Bronwyn put her arm round my shoulder. 'Come on, nice deep breaths. That's it. Not far to go. We'll take it easy so you can get yourself together.'

We reached our flat - the bottom half of a house - and went up the four steps to the front door. Using a shielded torch, I managed to fit the key in the lock and noticed the paint was scratched around the key-hole. The door was stiffer than usual and needed a good push. It groaned as if it was in pain when I shoved it open.

There, on the mat, were two envelopes that were to change the course of our lives forever.

But we didn't open those envelopes straight away - we didn't realise how important they were. The need for a cup of tea and a biscuit were much more pressing, so I threw them on a chair and headed for the kitchen. I put the kettle on then sat down on our rickety kitchen chair to get control of my wobbly legs. My mind was racing. What had I been thinking, running in front of the car like that? I could have died. The boy could have been killed too if I hadn't been quick enough. I'd never thought of myself as brave, and this wasn't courage, it was pure instinct.

The kettle whistling bought me out of my gloomy thoughts. The kitchen was cold, and I shivered as I reached for our old brown teapot with its knitted cosy.

'What are you doing this evening?' I called, trying to act normal even though I still felt shaky.

'Same as you, I suppose. Those air raids and the ambulance work are terrifying sometimes, but at least they're not boring.'

I only remembered the envelopes when I almost sat on them. Frowning, I noticed they were identical, apart from our names. I tossed Bronwyn hers and ripped mine open.

REPORT BLETCHLEY PARK BY 1500 HOURS MARCH 20.

ACCOMMODATION AVAILABLE.

My frown deepened, and I looked up at Bronwyn. 'What does yours say?'

She shrugged, 'Report Bletchley Park by 1500 hours on March 20. Accommodation available.'

She turned the paper over as if expecting something on the back. 'Nothing else, but it's from the Ministry of Defence, so I suppose it's genuine.'

I walked over and sat on the arm of her chair, comparing letters. 'That's exactly the same as mine. It's got to be a new posting, but Bron, that's only three days' time. How on earth are we supposed to get everything ready by then?'

Bronwyn nodded. 'And where the heck is

Bletchley Park, anyway? And what do they do there? Is it another depot?'

I shook my head. 'It can't be. I'd have heard of it if it was. We'll ask the boss tomorrow, but do you think we should start packing?'

She gave me a nudge so hard I almost fell off the chair. 'Have you lost your marbles? What it is, is like this. We've got so little stuff, we can get packed in half an hour. Getting bombed out twice wasn't fun, but at least we've learned to do without much.'

~

The station was crowded, as they always were since the war started. More than half the people waiting restlessly on the platform were in uniform. They had given us travel warrants, although the man in the office took ages changing them for tickets. I wondered how many people went from that station to Bletchley. The civilians were a real mixture - mums with little ones hanging on their arms or trying to escape; an elderly couple with their walking sticks; two lads who looked like they should be at school: and a few men wearing bowler hats and carrying briefcases.

The wind from a passing train blew so hard I

had to clutch my hat again. I went to the kiosk to buy a newspaper. The man serving had a cigarette hanging out of the side of his mouth and a droopy moustache. Without looking at me he muttered the price, and I put the coins into his grubby hand. The floor near the kiosk was covered in cigarette ends, and a drunk sleeping on a nearby bench snored loudly. Behind him a poster on the wall shouted 'Dig for Victory.' The picture was of a smiling, portly man in shirt sleeves, his braces showing. He held a wicker basket full of the fruits of his work: leeks, carrots, and a cabbage. In the other hand he held a rake. I smiled thinking of my mum's back garden. It was small, but she had made a superb job of growing vegetables. The front garden she kept for flowers apart from runner beans which had pretty red flowers themselves.

'What time did that letter say we had to be there, Lil?' Bronwyn asked, coughing from the smoke of a passing train.

'Three o'clock.' I looked up at the station clock, and took a step sideways to avoid the water dripping from the roof. 'If our train doesn't come soon we'll never get there on time. It's an hour overdue already. I wonder what happens if we're late?'

She shook her head and sighed. 'Who knows? Probably get shot. Not joking, but this is the biggest mystery of my life.' Her Welsh accent got more noticeable when she was emotional. 'Couldn't they even tell us what the job is? And what's Bletchley Park anyway? A fair ground? Why would they want army girls on a fairground?'

We stopped speaking for a while as the station announcement blared out, but it was hard to make out what they said over the rumble of porters' trolleys and people talking. A train toot-tooted as it approached the station, making everyone look alert, pick up their bags and grab their children.

'Bletchley! Anyone for Bletchley?' the guard shouted, tugging his uniform jacket over his bulging stomach.

I nudged Bronwyn. 'Quick, that's ours. Let's try to get a seat.'

She shoved her letter into her pocket and we picked up our battered third-hand suitcases and slung our kitbags over our shoulders where they bashed against our gas masks. The train belched smoke and black specks that made us rub our eyes as we struggled past all the other passengers.

Our last boss, Mr McDonald, had been as clueless as we were about what we were going to. 'We're going to miss you two girls,' he said when we told him we were leaving, 'but I expect you're hoping for something more interesting than typing in an army depot.'

He wasn't wrong there. We'd worked with lovely people in our office, and I was going to miss them, but no-one would call the work exciting. Anyone with basic office skills could have done it. It certainly didn't need any army girls.

Bronwyn tugged my arm, bringing me back from my little daydream. 'Come on, let's see if there's anywhere to sit further down the train.' But every carriage we went past was packed. Some had a mixture of civilians and military people, others were one or the other. One had an entire family enjoying a picnic meal. Three little ones sat on the floor, hankies tucked under their chin. The older children, parents and grandparents filled up the seats. They had hankie bibs, too. Their wicker basket was mostly filled with sandwiches, although I saw a cake and a few apples in there too.

'Look at them,' I said to Bronwyn. 'my stomach's rumbling. Let's get our sandwiches out when we find somewhere to sit.'

The train slowed as we approached the next station, and I saw the family gathering their stuff together. 'Come on,' I said to Bronwyn, indicating their carriage, 'let's get a seat when they go.'

We were soon seated in a corner, one each side

of the window, our kitbags and cases on the luggage rail over our heads. The carriage filled up quickly a mother and baby, an elderly man in a well-worn flat cap carrying a bag of vegetables, a middle-aged man in a beige raincoat, and a WAAF. Those RAF women sometimes thought themselves better than us ATS girls and their uniforms were a lot smarter, that's for sure.

'You going to Bletchley Park?' I asked the WAAF who was getting a cigarette out of her bag. She nodded, but otherwise didn't answer.

I gave it another try. 'Do you work there? What sort of place is it?'

She took a deep drag of her cigarette and filled the carriage with smoke before she answered in a posh voice. 'Awful old Manor House. Ghastly. Absolutely monstrous. But the grounds are okay, I suppose, and the lake's nice.'

'What do they do there?'

Cigarette clasped between two fingers, she wagged it at me. 'Careless talks cost lives, even you must know that,' she said, and unrolled a newspaper, held it in front of her face and totally ignored me and everyone else.

Okay, I thought, I hope they're not all like her or we're going to have a miserable time.

The train ground to a halt, and we all looked up,

knowing we weren't near a station. 'Oh, not again,' the woman with the baby said, jiggling it up and down, attempting to stop it crying. 'My mum's waiting for me and I'll get a right earful if I'm late.'

'But it's not your fault. Surely she'll understand,' Bronwyn said.

The woman snorted again. 'That don't mean a thing to her, I can tell you.' Then her eyes slid to the middle-aged man sitting next but one to mean a smile made her lips twitch. The elderly man in between us was fast asleep, still clutching his veg, so I couldn't see what had caught her eye without bending forward. Her eyes moved from the middle-age man then back to me a couple of times. Then she gave a little grin and raised an eyebrow. Curious, I leaned forward and looked across the sleeping elderly man. It took me a minute to realise what the she was trying to show me.

One hand in his pocket, the middle-aged man in his beige mac was playing with himself. He certainly wasn't counting his coins. My jaw dropped, I'd never seen such a thing before. Then I saw the funny side and stifled a giggle. I gently kicked Bronwyn's foot to get her attention. She looked at me, and quickly twigged what was happening. Without a moment's thought she said, 'I'll get those sandwiches now.'

She stood up, stepped in front of the man and reached above his head for her kitbag.

Then she dropped it on his lap.

He yelled and jumped up, thrusting the kitbag off his guilty lap with a loud curse. The woman opposite and I fought to keep a straight face as we heard Bronwyn give the most insincere apology you could ever imagine.

The man's face was scarlet, but I couldn't tell if it was embarrassment or anger. Spluttering, he stood up, grabbed up his bag and stormed out of the carriage slamming the door behind him. The woman, Bronwyn and I burst into loud laughter waking up the old man. He looked around befuddled. 'What's going on?' he said. 'Did I miss something?'

The WAAF merely raised an eyebrow. Then she reached into her handbag, got out a powder compact and powdered her nose.

As the train slowed for Bletchley, the WAAF dug into her bag again. She sprayed herself with Chanel No. 5, and put on some bright red lipstick without using a mirror. I watched her enviously, I've never been able to manage that. I remembered an article I saw in a Vogue magazine someone lent me. It said, "To be as attractive as possible is almost our civic duty. When there are so many sad and ugly things in the world, women should say to themselves humbly, 'I will do my best to be as pretty as I can, so that when people look at me, they will feel refreshed. Make an effort to be easy on the eye.'"

That was easier said than done when lipstick was scarce. Sometimes we even stained our lips with beetroot, although it never looked right.

Bronwyn and I picked up our stuff, said goodbye to the young mum and went into the corridor. We had to step over several soldiers sitting on the floor to get to the door.

There were only a few people on the wet platform. The snooty WAAF walked straight past us as if she'd never seen us before. More of a surprise was a grubby urchin who shouted ''ere Miss, I'll read your secret writing for ya!' He scampered off, leaving us bemused.

We looked around, wondering what to do next. 'I suppose we'd better follow everyone else,' I said, stepping round a puddle and hitching my kitbag and gas mask higher on my shoulder. But Bronwyn spotted a sign on the station wall. 'On Arrival at Bletchley Station go to the phone box, ring this number and await instructions.' Another sign said

'Take the exit from the arrival platform, go to the station forecourt and report to a hut on the far right-hand side marked RTO (Railway Transport Officer). DO NOT GIVE him your envelope. He will direct you.

The hut was gloomy, its windows painted blue for the blackout. A portly man with red cheeks was sitting inside bashing away at the typewriter and muttering under his breath. The keys were so well worn, there were no letters left on them, and the table bounced with every keystroke. He was making so much noise he didn't hear us until I coughed loudly. He jumped, then looked up and smiled. 'Let me guess, you're newcomers. Going to the madhouse, is that right?'

I swallowed hard. 'Do you mean Bletchley Park?'

His smile got wider. 'That's right, me ducks, the mad house. Hang on a mo, and I'll ring them to tell them you're here. Have a seat while you wait; they won't take long.'

There was only one other seat in the little hut. I let Bronwyn have it and put my gear down on the dusty wooden floor. The once-cream walls looked like they hadn't been painted this century and were covered in railway notices, maps and timetables.

There were two empty cups on the man's desk, one with a thick coating of mould.

He finished speaking and turned to us. 'Your transport'll be here in about fifteen minutes. Hope you like it there.'

'Why did you call it the madhouse?' I asked.

He gave a brief grin. 'Well, by all accounts, there are some odd types up there. Harmless, just a big odd. We see them at the station here and in town. Walk around like their heads are somewhere else, they do. Jump a mile when they realise you're speaking to them.' He lifted his uniform cap and scratched his head. 'One of 'em always wears his gas mask when he rides his bike! Bonkers! Mind you, I've heard tell he's a genius.'

'What sort of genius? What does he do?'

'No idea, Love. We don't ask and they don't tell. Where have you two come from then?'

'Deptford, in London, army depot,' I said. 'from what I saw out of the train window, this is going to be a bit different.'

He laughed. 'You're not wrong there. We don't get bombing round here, or not so far anyway.'

He paused and listened. 'Sounds like that's your transport, me ducks. Best of luck.'

When we arrived at Bletchley Park, we looked around in amazement. The Manor House the snooty WAAF hated so much was impressive. It was long, with six big windows at the front and a grand front door off centre. Either end had windows that curved round, although they weren't identical. In front of it was a gravel path, then a grassy area, then the lake the WAAF mentioned.

Near the big house was a load of huts. They were dreary wooden things with pitched roofs and metal framed windows - not much better than a long garden shed. Each hut had a number on it. A few people walked between the huts or round the lake, some in uniform, some in civvies.

Bronwyn gave a low whistle. 'The house may be nice, but those huts are downright horrible. Hope we won't be working in one of them. Or living in one.'

The driver of the van overheard her. 'No-one lives in them, they're all for work. They'll have found you digs in Bletchley or somewhere else nearby.'

'What? In the town?' I asked, 'how will we get there?'

He braked outside the side of the main house. 'You go on in there and they'll explain everything.'

Curious, we stepped out of the van with our bags. To our surprise, we could hear a piano being played somewhere near. Later we learned the park was stuffed full of musical people, some quite well known.

'I don't know about you, Lil,' Bronwyn said, 'but I feel a bit nervous about all this.'

I looked around some more. It was a world away from the grimy, inner-London, bombed out area we were used to. 'Me too, Bron, me too, I've got butterflies in my stomach.'

A fierce-looking woman stood up from behind a desk inside the Manor House when we walked in. She was tall and thin with short wavy pepper and salt hair. She wore an immaculate WAAF sergeant's uniform. Not a crease in sight. I wondered if she took the skirt off and hung it on the back of the toilet door while she did her business to avoid it being rucked up.

'Names!' she demanded without so much as a smile or hello. Her pen was at the ready as she turned the page in a massive book on her otherwise empty desk.

Once satisfied we were who she was expecting,

she closed the book and without looking up said, 'Room 14 upstairs.'

The hall was spacious, with rooms on either side and the staircase ahead and to the right. Gawping like a couple of kids, we tiptoed along the patterned carpet, expecting any minute we'd be told we were in the wrong place. The staircase was wide, with a mahogany banister and a lovely chandelier overhead. On the landing were more doors either side, but we found the right one without trouble. We knocked, waited for a response, and went in.

There were three desks in the room. Two had typewriters on them and all had phones and desk lamps. A woman was typing at one desk. She looked up and smiled before carrying on with her work. The second desk was unoccupied, although a cardigan hung over the back of the chair showed its owner was usually there. The biggest desk was in front of the enormous bay window. Behind it sat an older man who wasn't wearing a uniform. He had no typewriter, but his wire in-basket was stacked high. When the door shut behind us, he looked up. He had the biggest moustache I'd ever seen. There was probably more hair in it than on his head.

'New arrivals? Names?' His voice wasn't unfriendly, but it was very businesslike.

'Lily Baker,' I said.

'Bronwyn Jones.'

We went through the rigmarole of our details all over again.

'Right, Soldiers,' he said. 'Now listen to me very carefully indeed. I'm going to explain the Official Secrets Act to you. You must sign it to work here.'

'But what work will we be doing?' I asked before he could go on.

He brushed aside my question with a flick of his hand. 'You'll be told about that when you report for duty. Now listen and listen well. You don't breathe a word about what goes on in Bletchley Park to anyone. Anyone. And you don't even tell each other what your work is. You don't tell anyone else either.'

Bronwyn was balling a fist. 'But what is the work here?'

'As I said, you don't need to know at this stage. You'll soon learn not to ask questions. When you are assigned your duties, they will be all you need to know. Now, let me explain the details of the Act. I must warn you that if you break it, the consequences will be very serious. Very serious indeed. Prison at the very least.'

I paled. Prison, at least? Did that mean hanging was a possibility?

For the next ten minutes he drilled into us the need for total secrecy. My mouth went dry as I listened to him. In fact, he scared us so much with threats of prison or worse, we both vowed never to breathe a word about anything. 'And you need to know...' he hesitated as the phone rang on his desk. He picked it up, then put his hand over the receiver and spoke to the typist. 'Joyce, show these two where everything is, then bring them back here.'

'Can we work together?' I asked as we gathered our stuff.

'You can ask, but I can't guarantee it.'

He waited until we had left the room before speaking again. Joyce got her cardigan and bag and ushered us out of the room. 'Let's go outside first, while there's still plenty of light.'

It was late afternoon, and the light was fading a little. It struck me how peaceful it was after London. The depot where we'd worked bordered on a railway line on one side and a busy road on the other. Here, instead of the hooting of trains and the rattle of traffic, what we heard were birds and the footsteps of people walking between the mansion house and the huts. Then, to my amazement, the beautiful sound of choral singing carried from the house. Joyce saw the surprise on my face.

'There are a lot of social activities you can get involved in here. Not just singing, but games, sport, quizzes, cinema trips and goodness knows what else. The trouble is fitting them round your shift work.'

I stopped walking. 'We'll be doing shift work?'

She nodded. 'Yes, everyone does. Midnight to eight, eight til four, or four to midnight. It plays havoc with planning a social life.'

'You're not in uniform,' Bronwyn said. 'Are you a civilian? I expected to see everyone in uniform.'

By now we were walking by the lake. A tall thin man with thick brown hair and a fair-isle hand-knitted jumper was standing looking at the water, deep in thought. He was holding a cup, but still as a statue. Then he stamped his foot, shouted, "Got it!" threw his cup in the lake and strode towards one of the huts.

My jaw dropped open, and I looked at Joyce, a question in my eyes. She grinned. 'He'll be some brain-box trying to work out something. Half of them are crazy as a box of bats, but brilliant.'

'But the cup...'

She laughed. 'It's a bit of a thing here. Rumour

has it the catering department is running out of crockery and we'll have to provide our own. One genius has a tin mug, and he chains it to the radiator in his hut! You couldn't make up some of the stuff that happens here.'

I shook my head in disbelief, but also relief. This place was going to be more fun than the depot.

Joyce clapped her hands. 'You were asking about uniforms. People here are a real mix of military and civilians. Few people mind if you wear a uniform or not. Up to you.'

My eyes widened. 'Goodness, I've never heard of such a thing. It'll be lovely to wear our own stuff for a change.'

'The only time we might ask you to wear a uniform is if someone very important is coming. There are rumours Churchill is thinking of paying us a visit. That'd be a uniform day for sure. Come on, let me show you the important bits of the house, like the canteen.'

As we walked back, the throaty roar of a motorbike interrupted the peace of the scene. It turned left beside the house and the rider walked into a little cottage.

'Messenger,' Joyce said, nodding towards where he'd been. 'They come at all hours from all over.'

I opened my mouth to ask more, but remembered we weren't supposed to ask questions, so shut it again.

Joyce looked at her watch. 'This time of day, people often gather in one of the big rooms in the house for coffee or tea. Come on, we'll grab a cup, then I'll finish the tour.'

The room was crowded, mostly with women, all standing. I caught snatches of conversation. 'What film is on in town this week?' 'What shift are you on tomorrow? 'I wonder if there's any chance of a decent meal in the canteen tonight.' 'How did your date go?'

Seeing all the women made me realise I'd seen a lot more women than men so far. I thought it safe to ask about that.

'You're right. Loads more women than men. This isn't a great place to work if you're looking for a husband.'

'Not joking nor nothing, but I'm not looking for a husband,' Bronwyn said, 'not even someone else's.'

That made Joyce raise an eyebrow, but she said nothing. She guided us to the tea urn and told us more about what to expect. 'After you've finished speaking to the boss, you'll be taken to your digs.'

'Where will they be?' I asked.

'They might be in Bletchley Town, but if nothing is available, it could be further afield. Anyway, whoever takes you will explain you have to stay there until they collect you and brought back here to be assigned to your new work.'

Bron and I looked at each other, frowning. 'How long's that going to be? What do we do for food?'

Joyce refilled her cup and reached for one of the few biscuits left in a huge tin. 'It's all taken care of. If your new landlady doesn't provide meals, you'll find a stock of food there.'

'But you haven't said how long we'll have to wait.'

She shrugged. 'It shouldn't be more than two days. But I must emphasise you mustn't leave your digs. They could need you any time. And, of course, not a word to anyone.'

I squashed down a chuckle. We knew nothing, so there was no fear of us giving secrets away.

CHAPTER TWO

The Bletchley Park transport dropped us outside our new digs in the middle of Bletchley town. We threw our kitbags over our shoulders, picked up our cases and gas masks and stood outside looking around. Happy Days Guest House was a double-fronted house with bay windows on either side of the central front door. Set back was a newer extension. The street was busy with buses, cars, and the occasional horse and cart.

The white painted wooden gate groaned as I opened it, and I noticed the small front garden had a pretty display of tulips. We could smell the yellow and red Stock even over the stink of the traffic. As Bron and I reached the front door, we heard a furious argument going on inside. We couldn't make out the words, but the tone was pretty clear.

'Not being funny, but what the heck have we come to?' Bronwyn said, plonking her case down. 'Do we knock or wait until they've finished rowing?'

My heart sank. We hadn't asked if we could change digs. Was it likely we were going to have to live in a really miserable place for ages?

A door inside slammed, and a woman's voice bellowed, 'Good riddance!'

I waited a second, then knocked on the door, my heart in my mouth. It was pulled open so quickly she must have been standing very close. Her breathing was noisy, and her eyes bulged. But only for a second. Then it was as if she registered we were there and her face was transformed. The muscles relaxed, and she smiled and held her arms open.

'You must be the new girls from Bletchley Park. Come in, come in, lovely to see you.'

She stepped aside, and as I walked past her, I noticed she smelled of spirits.

'Come into the lounge,' she said. Her voice had become more refined than when she was arguing.

The room, one of the front ones with a bay window, would have been light and airy but for the criss-cross tape to protect against bomb blasts. The floor was polished wood with a large moss green rug with pale pink roses in a diamond pattern. There was a small upright piano, a two-seat settee, and two armchairs. They were a little shabby, but clean and with spotless white antimacassars. A low table held a vase of daffodils and a local newspaper.

Our landlady stood in the centre of the room. Short, like me, she wore a flowered dress with a hand-knitted cardigan over the top.

'My name is Gladys Wilson, Mrs Wilson, but you're welcome to call me Mrs W. I own and run Happy Days. My husband, Donnie and I live in the flat annex ...'

Something outside caught her eye, and she looked up and pursed her lips. 'Oh dear, there's Carolyn, about to come in. She arrived yesterday and she should not be out. I'll have to have a word with her.'

The door opened and the most beautiful girl I'd seen outside of films walked in. She was tall, about five foot nine inches, and slender, with long golden hair that fell in loose waves. She looked racy in high waist, wide legged trousers topped with a flower-patterned blouse and a bright red jacket. As she saw Mrs W, the smallest frown appeared on her forehead. She speedily covered it up with a smile that didn't reach her eyes.

Mrs W stepped towards her. 'Carolyn,' she began. 'You've been told not to leave the house until you're collected by someone from the Park.'

Carolyn smiled and patted her arm. 'Don't worry yourself about it, sweetie. I'll take responsibility. Anyway, I only went for a teeny walk to the shop to get some Craven As.'

She sat in an armchair, crossed her long legs and took out her cigarette packet. She held them out to us. 'Anyone join me?' she asked. Bronwyn and I shook our heads.

Carolyn turned to Mrs W, who was looking at a loss to know what to say next. 'I can show these two round if you want to get on. I presume they're having the big back bedroom.'

Even though she was already smoking, Mrs W helped herself to one of the cigarettes, put it in her pocket, then turned to leave the room. Her lips were puckered so tight the surrounding skin was white.

As soon as she'd gone, Carolyn chuckled. 'I'm so wicked, teasing her like that, but it's so much fun, why would I want to stop!' She took a long drag of her cigarette and blew impressive smoke rings. Admiring her work, she poked a finger through one of them, then turned to us. 'I'm so sorry. I haven't even asked you your names. I'm Carolyn Mortimer.'

Within minutes, we were chatting as if we'd known each other for years.

'It's so smashing to be sharing with you two, and there's another girl expected this evening, Peggy something. She'll have the box room next to yours.' She put her cigarettes away and stood up. 'Come on, let me show you your room then we'll make some tea.'

'Are we allowed to use the kitchen?'

She gave a little laugh. 'Yes, there's a list of rules on the back of the door that'll take you a week to read. And an honesty box if you use any of her food, like tea leaves.'

The bedroom was decorated in exactly the same way as the living room, or lounge, as Mrs W called it. It had the same rose patterned wall paper, and the same moss green curtains, but there was a wall-to-wall carpet, albeit a threadbare one. Bronwyn and I dumped our bags on the beds and followed Carolyn to the kitchen.

As we walked downstairs, we saw Mrs W waiting for us. 'Settled in, Girls?' she asked. 'I know how difficult it is on the first night, so I've made a little salad and left some bread. You'll find the price under the plate. Please leave your money in the honesty box.'

'Thanks very much, Mrs W,' I said, 'but if we're not collected tomorrow, what do we do for food if we can't go out?'

She followed us to the kitchen as we spoke. 'There's toast for breakfast and you can cook yourself a boiled egg. And I'm an excellent cook, if I say so myself. I can provide a meal at midday and supper time any time with appropriate notice. You'll need to pay, of course.'

'That sounds lush,' Bronwyn said, 'but we'll be working shift work so it might be difficult.'

Mrs W peered at her as if she was seeing her for the first time. 'Welsh, are you? Bit dark skinned for a Welsh person, aren't you, fuzzy hair too?'

Bronwyn's eyes narrowed and her jaw tightened. 'We come in all colours, just like the English.'

Mrs W took a step back. 'Okay, okay, I didn't mean anything by it! All the same to me as long as you pay your rent on time. By the way, we're expecting another girl, Peggy.' She looked at her watch. 'She'll be here any minute.'

She was a funny old stick, but I was grateful for her forethought about food. She glanced at the clock again. 'My goodness, you girls must be starving. You can eat here in the kitchen if you like. The salads are in the cold store, and bread in the bread bin. I must go now. WI meeting tonight. Please look after Peggy when she arrives.'

When she'd left, Carolyn laughed. 'Women's Institute, my derriere. Pub more like. Talking of which, I've got some cider in my bag, I bought it with my cigarettes. Want to share it?'

While we were fetching our food, there was a thundering knocking at the door. There stood the blondest girl I'd ever seen. A pink ribbon tied in a bow on the top of her head made her look sort of cute. She wore a green, slimline dress that stopped daringly at her knees and a grey coat over the top. She was a sight to behold.

''Ello, sorry I'm late. Bloody trains is 'opclcss. Can I come in then, or are you all going to stand there gaping at me 'til I drop?'

We almost tripped over our own feet as we stood aside to let her in.

'Sorry, come on in. You must be Peggy.'

She dropped her suitcase down just inside the door. 'I'm busting for a wee. Where's the khazi?'

We gave her directions and glanced at each other, open mouthed.

'Well, what an interesting mix of girls we shall be,' Carolyn finally said.

Peggy came back down, smiling broadly. 'Sorry

'bout that, Girls, but when you gotta go, you gotta go. And I went. So, what's up?'

'We're heading for the kitchen. Mrs W, the landlady, has left us some food.'

'Jolly good, lead on then.'

As we fetched our modest salads and bread, it started to rain heavily, the drops so big they beat against the windows. Peggy looked at her salad and lifted a limp lettuce leaf. 'What the blinking 'eck is this? It's been dead at least a week. Not fit for nothing but rabbits, is it?' But she ate it just the same. 'You all army girls?' she asked.

We nodded, 'Yes, but we don't always have to wear uniforms at the Park, apparently.'

She giggled. 'Just as well, 'cos I'm a Civvie, see. I'm gonna work in the Beer 'ut whatever that is. Sounds like someone's shed. Been a barmaid for a year, so I know what I'm doing.' She put down her fork. 'I'll give you extra if I serve you!'

We soon learned a lot about Peggy's experiences of working in a bar, and more besides.

'But 'ere's me talking about meself again. Tell me all about you three.'

We gave edited versions of our life stories. 'Cor, is that all you're gonna tell me? Still, plenty of time. What're you gonna be doing up there?'

'We don't know, Peggy,' Carolyn said. 'We haven't been told.'

'Blimey, that's a turn up for the books. I'm one step ahead of you lot then. Where you from then?'

'Surrey,' Carolyn said, her accent very clear.

'We both lived in London before we came here,' I said, indicating Bronwyn.

'Me too! I'm from Battersea, thought I'd better get out before the cops find me...'

She stopped and looked at us, no doubt alarm written all over our faces.

She hooted. 'Just kidding! You should see your faces! I came 'ere to be near me boyfriend, Ken. 'E's some sort of maintenance man at the Park. You 'ave to meet 'im, 'e's lovely, always wanting to look after me. Mind you, I 'aven't known 'im that long so it's early days and all that.'

'It's nice to have a man who cares. I hope it goes well for you. Bronwyn and I are boyfriendless at the moment.'

'Me too,' Carolyn said.

I changed the subject. 'I do miss being able to see out of the windows at night,' I said. 'One of the many things I'm looking forward to when this damn war ends is taking down the rotten blackout blinds.'

'Let me see,' Bronwyn said. 'What am I looking forward to?'

We spent a happy ten minutes listing all the things we hoped to see and do. Lights in the streets at night; the end of food rationing; bananas; being able to travel abroad, although Carolyn was the only one who ever had, for a holiday.

'Cor, you been abroad? Lucky bugger!' Peggy said, eyes wide.

Bronwyn grinned. 'We have too. Paris. We worked there for a while, but I can't tell you any more than that. Top secret.'

Mostly, we looked forward to not worrying if a bomb would kill us or the Nazis'd invade us.

We washed the dishes and put them away, then went to the living room. Carolyn opened the piano lid. 'Mummy always said well-educated young ladies should be able to play the piano. Or piahno as she pronounces it. It's probably the only way I didn't disappoint her. Fancy a sing-song?'

She was amazing. She could play anything without sheet music. We sang *Over the Rainbow, Walzing in the Clouds* and a load of songs from the Great War. To our surprise, we discovered all four of us had decent singing voices.

'We could start up a trio like The Andrews Sisters!' Bronwyn said with a sparkle in her eyes.

‘’ay, don’t forget me!’ Peggy said.

I laughed. ‘There must be some sort of singing club we can join at the Park or in the town.’

Carolyn was topping up our glasses when we heard the creak of the front gate. It was followed by a thud and the sound of someone cursing.

‘Do you think that’s someone trying to break in?’ Carolyn whispered.

I laughed. ‘They’ll have to be a lot quieter about it if they want to be successful.’

Uncertain what we’d find, we turned off the lights and opened the front door a few inches. The rain had stopped, and it was dark as a dungeon. Then a cloud moved away from the moon and we could just make out what the noise was about. There, picking herself up from the flower bed, was Mrs W, still cursing, although more quietly. She spotted us, brushed herself down, said ‘Oops a daisy,’ waved and called, ‘Good night, Girls, sleep well.’ over her shoulder. Then she wobbled her way round to her flat at the side of the house.

We closed the door and leaned against it, struggling to stifle our laughs.

‘She a boozer?’ Peggy asked. ‘’ad enough of them with me dad.’

‘Do you think that’s going to happen every night?’ Bronwyn said.

'If she's like me dad it will be,' Peggy said with a groan.

We headed back into the living room, and I realised how tired I was. It had been a stressful few days, what with packing, leaving our London home and seeing our new workplace and digs. But the future looked promising.

I lay in bed next morning struck by the silence. London is never quiet, especially when there's a war on. Traffic, drunks, accidents, air raid alarms and the noise of other people's radios and rows all competed to make sleep difficult. But Bletchley was different. So far there'd been no bombing at all here, and the only sound I heard at night was the occasional footsteps outside and Bronwyn's gentle snoring.

I woke up before her and snuck into the bathroom to avoid having to wait. There was one between the four of us - Mr and Mrs W must have had their own in their flat. It may have been Spring, but it was jolly cold in there and I shivered as I had a good wash and brushed my teeth. In the mirror, I could see my face already looked more relaxed than it had for months. As well as my work in the army depot, I'd volunteered as an Air Raid Warden and it would take a long time before the memories of some of the awful things I'd seen faded.

I'd finished washing and was picking up my things when there was a gentle tap on the door. 'Can I come in? I'm busting for a pee!' When I opened the door, Bronwyn rushed past me as fast as a cat chasing a mouse.

I went into the bedroom and looked at my small collection of clothes. Should I wear my uniform or civvies? I didn't want to spend all day in my uniform if we weren't collected, but if we had to go to the Park in a hurry, I didn't think I should go in civvies. Carolyn said we could, but what if my new boss didn't like it?

In the end, I wore civvies and laid my uniform on the bed, ready for a quick change if necessary. Then I went downstairs to the kitchen. Mrs W was there, humming as if she had a clear head and hadn't been blind drunk the night before. She coughed and put her cigarette on a saucer.

'Morning, Lily,' she said. 'It is Lily, isn't it? Have I got the right name?'

'That's right, it's Lily. Okay if I make myself some toast?'

She put a cup of tea in front of me. 'Go ahead, and it's sandwiches at midday if they haven't picked you up before. You happy with your room? Getting on with Carolyn okay?'

I got the bread out of the bread bin and began cutting myself a couple of slices. 'The room's fine and we're getting on really well with Carolyn and Peggy. I think we'll be very happy here.'

She wiped down the table and got out a knife for me. 'I'm glad to hear that. I found an empty cider bottle in Carolyn's rubbish bin. I hope she won't prove to be a drinker. They're always trouble.'

I almost choked on my tea.

I had nearly finished my second cup when the others appeared. Mrs W had gone by then and they hooted when I told them her comments about drinkers.

We sat for ages round the kitchen table, wondering what to do with the day.

'We can't go for a walk,' Carolyn said, 'but any of us can nip to the corner shop. It's only about a hundred yards away. Better go separately though.'

Between my army work and the ARP work, I wasn't used to having more than the odd day to myself. Living in London, it was easy to fill the time if I had the energy to go out.

'I don't know about you three, but I feel fidgety what with not knowing when we'll be collected.

Makes it hard to settle to anything, even reading my book.'

I looked out of the window. 'It's not a bad day. We could offer to do some gardening.'

They looked at me as if I'd lost my mind. 'Any other ideas? Better ones?'

Suddenly, there was a loud bang in the street outside, followed by a scream and the sound of running feet. We rushed to the front door and flung it open. A car had driven into the back of a bus and overturned, ending up on one side. There weren't many people about and luckily not many passengers on the bus. The conductor, an elderly man, was frantically trying to open the car door, which was horizontal. Gravity and the weight of the door were against him.

'Someone help me get this man out!' the conductor shouted. 'He's unconscious and bleeding!'

Carolyn stood unmoving, wide eyed. 'What shall we do?' she asked, looking pale.

'Go inside and phone the ambulance and police,' I ordered. 'We'll deal with this.'

I'd had first aid training with the ARP, and Bronwyn had volunteered on the ambulances, so we confidently tackled the dreadful situation. It was impossible to get him out with the car on its side. I looked around at the spectators, who were a mixed bunch. What we needed were a few strong men. The problem was quickly solved when an ancient fire engine arrived, siren blaring. The firemen looked past retirement age, but that didn't stop them getting the car right way up. The poor passenger got thrown about a bit, but it couldn't be helped.

We pulled him out and lay him down on the pavement. 'Peggy, go and get a cushion, a tea towel, and a blanket,' I said. I checked his breathing and his pulse. Both seemed okay, although he was still unconscious. He groaned as we moved him though, so he was hurt somewhere other than his head. I gently squeezed his arms and got a worse groan near the top of one. I touched the shoulder and his reaction was stronger. I thought he probably had at least a broken shoulder, but I was too scared and inexperienced to do more.

As soon as Peggy bought the tea-towel, I pressed it against the cut on his head. That made him groan again. We put the cushion under his head and covered him with the blanket. One fireman took over. 'Leave it to me, Missy, we're trained for this sort of thing.' Then, to my relief, an ambulance arrived too.

The tension in my shoulders released. I'd been kneeling and I sat back on my heels and let out a long breath.

Bronwyn took control and moved all the people away so the ambulance crew could park and do their job. Their brakes squealed as they stopped a few feet away from us, and one of them jumped out and ran over. 'What's happening?' he asked, breathless.

His navy-blue uniform with a white sash was spotless, and I wondered if we were his first call of the day.

'He was unconscious when we got him out of the car. Cut on head, pulse and breathing steady. Maybe a broken shoulder. I haven't checked anywhere else.'

He bent down beside me, as his driver joined us. 'Okay, you can go now, we'll take over. You did a good job. Thanks.'

'Get a stretcher,' he said to his colleague and continued checking the man over.

We went back into the front garden, where Carolyn still stood looking shocked, and Peggy was biting her nails.

I put my arm through Carolyn's. She'd been watching all this as still as a rabbit in the headlights. 'Never seen anything like this before?'

Her bottom lip trembled. 'Never. Have you?'

Bronwyn laughed. 'Just a bit. Nothing much shocks you after weeks of the blitz in London.'

Her eyes widened, and she looked at me. 'You, too?' she asked.

'And me,' Peggy said. 'You think you'll get used to it, but you never do.'

I nodded. 'We'll tell you about it some time, Carolyn.'

She wiped a tear from her cheek. 'Before I did my square-bashing, I'd lived a very sheltered life. Mummy and Daddy were very protective of me. The worst I've ever had was falling off my favourite horse, and then I only sprained my wrist.' She sniffed and blew her nose on her lace-edged hankie. 'I think I've got a lot to learn.'

Bronwyn took Peggy's arm and together we watched as they put the injured man in the ambulance and the fire engine drove away. I walked forward and picked up the tea-towel and other things we'd used. Luckily, only the tea-towel had blood on it.

'Soak it in cold water straight away!' Peggy said. 'I 'ad to do it loads of times when my bleeding little brothers and sisters fell over and cut themselves open.'

Carolyn turned to her. 'How many brothers and sisters have you got?'

Peggy laughed, 'More than we 'ad money for,

that's for sure. But let me see to this and I'll join you.'

Mrs W was preparing our sandwiches, oblivious to the drama going on outside her front door. 'Fish paste and tomato, okay?' she asked. Silently I swore I'd never have fish paste again once this damn war was over.

'Fine,' I said. 'Thanks. I'll tell the others to come through. By the way, there was an accident outside. I'm afraid we used one of your tea-towels to stop the bleeding from a man's head. We've put it in to soak so it should be okay.'

She whirled round, spinning on the spot. 'Who was it? Not my Donnie, was it?'

I stared at her in surprise. 'I don't know what he looks like. What sort of car does he have?'

She clutched my hand. 'A green Morris Minor. It wasn't him, was it?'

I held her hand in both of mine. 'Don't worry, it was a black car, so not your husband's.'

She let go of my hand and turned back to cutting bread. 'That's okay then. Someone else's worry. Not that I'm sure I'd miss him, come to think of it.'

The others appeared, and we sat at the table eating our sandwiches. Mrs W joined us, although I noticed she had cut her bread thicker and had one more sandwich than us.

'So, how are you girls getting on? Bet you miss your old lives, all those boyfriends! I know what you girls get up to when there's a war on. I certainly did in the last one, but don't tell my Donnie! You don't want to let those young boys die a virgin, do you?'

There was a deadly silence as the four of us looked at her, our jaws hanging open.

She blinked hard. 'What? What? Cat got your tongues? Did I speak out of turn?'

'She'd fit in well where I come from,' Peggy muttered.

Mrs W turned and put the kettle on again, her back to us. 'Any roads, Mr Butcher, the butcher down the road, isn't it funny that he's a butcher and his name is Butcher? He says there's not many men up there at the Park, so that's not going to be something you need to worry about.'

As she spoke, we looked at each other, shaking our heads, wide eyed. I decided the best thing was to talk about something else. 'How long do people like us have to wait to be collected from the Park?'

She turned back to us and grinned. 'Don't like talking about you-know-what then? Whatever's the world coming to? But to answer your question, it varies, but I doubt you'll wait beyond tomorrow afternoon.'

That evening there was a knock on the door and Peggy surprised us by rushing to open it.

'Must be her boyfriend,' Carolyn said. 'Let's see what he looks like.'

We went to the bay window and peered at the man standing on the doorstep. He was short, but not as short as Peggy, and although it wasn't that warm, he only wore trousers and an open-necked shirt. We must have made a noise because he turned and looked in our direction. We ducked down like naughty children, giggling.

Peggy had left the door to the living room open so we could hear their conversation.

'Come on,' he said. 'Surely you can come out for a pint. I miss you.'

'I can't. I told you, I've got to stay here until I'm collected and taken to the Park. There's four of us waiting.'

There was a pause, then Peggy spoke again. 'I've told you, I can't go out.'

Carolyn surprised us by standing up. She went out of the living room to into the hall.

'Are you having trouble, Peggy?' she asked in her most haughty voice. 'Do you need any help?'

By now Bronwyn and I were watching out of the window again.

'Can I help you with anything, young man?' Carolyn asked, even though he was probably older than her. 'I'm sure you wouldn't want Peggy to get in trouble before she's even started her new job, would you?'

We saw him let go of Peggy's arm so suddenly she almost fell backwards.

'I just want to spend time with my girl!' he muttered. Then he spun on his heel and strode off.

Carolyn and Peggy came back into the living room together.

'You didn't need to do that,' Peggy said. 'He just wants to be with me because he cares.'

I spoke up. 'It didn't sound like that to me, Peggy. It sounded like he didn't see your point of view at all.'

'That's right,' Bronwyn said. 'He sounds like a bully to me. If you've got any sense you'll get rid of him double quick.'

Peggy's face dropped. 'You're wrong, it's because he wants to be with me!'

Then she ran upstairs to her bedroom without another word.

'Did I do wrong?' Carolyn asked.

'No,' Bronwyn said. 'She needed rescuing. Daft thing can't see when a bloke is trying to control her rather than care for her. My mum had one like that once. It was like he got inside her brain so she couldn't see what was going on.'

'Do you think we should go after her?' I wondered.

'Let's give her a few minutes, then one of us can go up,' Bronwyn said. But half an hour later Peggy came down, and called from the hallway. 'I'm making some tea. Does anyone want some?' as if nothing had happened.

~

Still reeling from Peggy's quick change of mood, we went into the living room.

'Right, Girls, what shall we do this afternoon?' Bronwyn asked.

'I noticed there's a jig-saw puzzle on the book-shelf,' Carolyn said, 'and I've got a book.'

Peggy had a better idea. 'Let's play Truth or Dare.'

'Brilliant!' Bronwyn said. 'I haven't played it since I was a kid. Dangerous game though.'

'I'm not sure I can remember how it works,'

Carolyn said. 'We played it when I first joined up. Had to pass the boring evenings in the army huts somehow. We learned a lot about each other, I can tell you, sometimes more than we wanted to know.'

'So what do you do?'

I searched my memory. 'We get some slips of paper and each write six questions the other people have to answer. Then we write six dares written on other slips of paper. They're all muddled up and face down. If someone refuses to tell the truth, they have to pick up a dare from the pile and do it. Oh, and we draw straws to decide who goes first, then go round clockwise.'

Carolyn frowned. 'I think this is the sort of game where it would help to be a bit tipsy. We'd better not though in case they come to collect us.'

We found some paper, and each went to a different chair to write our truth questions and dares. It took me a while to think of any, and my mouth was dry as I remembered the game could end up being very embarrassing. Eventually, I wrote six questions:

When was the last time you lied?

What are you most afraid of?

What's the most embarrassing thing you've ever done?

What's the worst thing you ever said to anyone?

What's the best bit of advice you've ever been given?

What was the worst thing you ever did at school?

For dares I wrote:

Give a foot massage to the person next to you.

Pretend to be the person on your right for two minutes.

Tell the others three things about you - two truths and one lie. They have to guess which one is the lie.

Try to lick your elbow.

Show off your secret talent.

Tell a ghost story.

When we'd all finished writing, we put our questions and dares into two piles.

'Right. I've made some pretend straws out of paper. Who's taking one first?'

'I will!' Carolyn said, and got a long straw. So did I, and Peggy squealed with relief when she got a long straw as well.

'Looks like it's me then,' Bronwyn said. The questions had been shuffled so she wouldn't know if she was getting her own or not. Without hesitation, she picked one question from the middle of the pile.

She read it and grinned. 'I don't know which of you wrote this, but it's mean.'

We looked at her expectantly.

'"Tell us about your most awkward date."' That's what it says. You'll have to give me a minute. There's so many to choose from.'

I laughed. 'I believe you!'

She grinned and pointed at me. 'Wait! I know what it is, and it's your fault!'

'My fault? What did I do?'

'Last Christmas you gave me some fancy French knickers. You'd sewn them by hand because you didn't have a sewing machine. Remember?'

I remembered sewing them in secret when Bronwyn was on her ambulance duty and I had an evening off. They were lovely knickers, especially when you compared them to the awful army regulation ones. I'd got some parachute material from the market, and my mum had enough pink lace to go round the legs.

'Of course I remember,' I said. 'What about them?'

She grinned. 'Well, I never told you 'cos I didn't want to seem ungrateful, but...'

I held my breath. 'But what?'

She laughed. 'I was with a date in a queue

waiting to get tickets for a film and the knickers only bloody fell down, didn't they?'

We laughed so much our sides ached.

'What on earth did you do?' Carolyn asked when she could catch her breath.

'I kept a straight face, stepped out of them without a word and put them in my bag as if that sort of thing happened every day. My date didn't even notice, but the people behind us did. I heard them sniggering. Good job it was too dark to see my red face!' She pointed to me. 'And you'd better use stronger elastic next time!'

'Girls round our way often don't bother wearing them at all,' Peggy said, 'Saves time on a night out.'

The door opened and Mrs W poked her head round the corner. 'I heard laughing and thought I must be missing something. What are you all doing?'

The four of us looked at each other, silently hoping she'd go away. But we were too polite to say so.

'We're playing truth or dare,' I said.

'Oh, I love that game. Can I join in?' She sat down with us without waiting for an answer, her ciggie hanging out of the side of her mouth. 'Wait a mo,' she said and leaned over to grab an ashtray, knocking almost an inch of ash into it.

'Who's turn is it next?' she asked.

'We're just going round clockwise,' Carolyn said.

Mrs W got up. 'That's not fun, hang on,' she said and left the room.

'What's she up to now?' Carolyn said. 'Bet she's gone for a swig of gin.'

Two minutes later, Mrs W was back with two bottles of beer. One was already opened. She took a swig from it, then hiccuped. 'Naughty, 'scuse me!' she said with a grin. Then she placed the second on the floor and sat down again. 'We spin the bottle and when it stops we see where the neck is pointing. That person goes next.'

'I'm not going next!' Bronwyn said. 'I just had a turn.'

Mrs W raised an eyebrow. 'Okay, Miss Stroppy. If it stops at you, we'll spin it again.'

It stopped at me and my heart sank as I reached for one of the paper slips.

Then I sighed with relief. 'Mine says "pretend to be the person on your right for two minutes!"' I looked at Bronwyn and grinned. 'That's you!'

I'd never tried copying someone's accent before and had no idea if I could do it, but I'd shared digs with Bronwyn long enough to hear her Welsh accent in my head.

I stood up. ‘It’s like this, see, Cariad. Not telling a lie nor nothing, but us Welsh people are full of mischief, not kidding but we likes a bit of fun... and that man is so lush...’

I was amazed that my accent wasn’t half bad.

Bronwyn stood up and thumped my shoulder. ‘I’m not telling a lie nor nothing, but that’s just plain mean!’

The rest of us fell about laughing.

Bronwyn had her hands on her hips, ‘Okay, enough poking fun at my wonderful accent. Who’s next?’

We spun the bottle, and it stopped at Peggy. She took a piece of paper. ‘Okay, this says “What’s the best thing you’ve ever done?”‘

She bit her lip as she thought, then clapped her hands. ‘Well, there’s one I’m not telling you, but the one you can know about might not have been legal, strictly speaking.’

We all looked at her wide eyed.

‘It was like this, see. Pubs round our way are a bit rough. I was at the bar getting the next round for me and me mates when this bloke comes up behind me and only put ’is 'and right up my skirt, didn’t ’e!’

‘Wow, what did you do?’

‘There was a beer bottle near and I picked it up

and smashed it over 'is ’ead. Went down like a log, 'e did. Well deserved, too.’

There was a pause as we all looked at her in amazement. She was small, but she knew how to look after herself.

Carolyn shook her head. ‘Nothing like that ever happens in the Dog and Drake where I live. It’d be more interesting if it did. What happened?’

‘Dunno, walked out, didn’t I?’ She grinned at the memory, ‘but I ’eard ’e was still around so ’e can’t have been too bad.’

Next it was Carolyn’s turn. She picked up a paper slip and read ‘What’s the worst thing you ever did at school?’

She put her hand on her heart. ‘I hardly dare tell you.’

‘That sounds juicy,’ Mrs W said, blinking as ciggie smoke went into her eyes. ‘Come on, spill the beans! I do like a bit of gossip.’

Carolyn bit her bottom lip. ‘Well, there was this girl in my class who bullied me. Tore up my homework, called me names, told lies about me. That kind of thing. So I... well I... I was sitting behind her in class, looking at the back of her head. She was very proud of her long blond hair. That day it was in a plait and well... I... leaned over and cut several inches off.’

There was silence for a few seconds as we took that in, mouths open, then we all asked questions at the same time. 'What did she do?' 'Did she punch you?' 'Did you feel pleased?' 'How come you had scissors handy?'

Before she had time to answer them, the doorbell rang.

We looked outside. There was the van that had brought us to Happy Days. I looked at it and got butterflies in my tummy again. What was it going to be like working somewhere like the Park? It seemed so different from anywhere else we'd been before. What work would I be doing? What if I hated it?

Mrs W sauntered to open the door as we three dashed upstairs to get changed into our uniforms.

'You'll have to wait a minute,' we heard her saying in her best voice, 'They're just getting their things together. Go on into the lounge and they'll be with you in no time.'

By the time we came down, she was standing at the bottom of the stairs with a packet of sandwiches for each of us. She'd only been in the kitchen briefly, but she smelled of gin again. Somehow it didn't seem important.

'That's very kind,' I said, and squeezed her arm in thanks.

Then, with the others behind me, we walked towards the van and headed to our new workplace.

They took all four of us to an office in the big house. It was a small office that seemed filled with just one desk, a chair and a filing cabinet. The room smelled faintly of Lily of the Valley perfume. There was nowhere for us to sit. The woman behind the desk smiled as we walked in. 'I'm Gladys North. You are?'

We gave our names.

'Can we work together? Well, me, Bronwyn and Carolyn,' I asked.

She held up her hand. 'Hold your horses. I need to look at your paperwork.' She shuffled some papers and read in silence for a couple of minutes. Then she looked at Peggy. 'I see you're going to be working at the Beer Hut. You can head off there now while I speak to the others. You can't miss it, it's well signed.'

Peggy's face dropped. 'Oh, okay then.' She turned to us, 'See you later, Girls.'

When she'd gone Miss North turned back to us. 'So Carolyn, you speak German, is that correct?'

'Yes, I went to a boarding school there for a couple of years while Daddy was posted to India.'

The woman nodded. 'Are you fluent? We have need for your skills.'

Carolyn let forth with a long steam of German which could have been Greek for all I knew.

The woman held up her hand again. 'Okay, that sounds impressive, not that I speak more than a few words. You'll be working in hut three.'

My spirits dropped. Neither Bronwyn nor I spoke German, so we wouldn't be working with her. 'We both speak French,' I said.

She looked again at her papers and shook her head. 'We have no need for French speakers at the moment but that situation could change any time though, so we may need you in the future. I see you both have typing and clerical skills so I'll put you in the office in the main building.'

She still hadn't told us what these language skills would be used for.

'So Lily and I will be together, then?' Bronwyn asked.

'That's right. It's pretty routine stuff, but keep in mind that everything we do here is vital to the success of the war effort.'

She shuffled her papers some more. 'I see you three will be on the same shifts. That's lucky.'

She stood up and handed each of us a sheet of paper. 'Good luck with your new roles, Girls.'

CHAPTER THREE

Bronwyn, Carolyn and I started our new jobs at eight the next morning. Although it was early spring, we shivered as we waited at the bus stop and had our greatcoats over our uniforms. The weather had been up and down for a while, snowing sometimes, mild others. Peggy was still in bed. The rest of us had eight til four shifts that week, but as a barmaid, she worked different hours.

There were plenty of people around, hurrying on their way to work. A coal lorry stopped next to the bus stop, its brakes squeaking. The coal man jumped out and lugged a big bag of coal over his shoulder as easily as I picked up my handbag. He vanished out of sight between Happy Days and the house next door.

'Perhaps we should walk,' I said when no bus appeared when it should. 'Mrs W said it's only a mile.'

'You two going to the Park?' a lady standing near us asked.

'We are, and it's our first day. We don't want to be late.'

She looked down the road. 'Hang on, here it comes, it's not often very late, but you young things can easily walk once you know the way. Or get a bike. Save money on the fare.'

If what we saw from the bus was anything to go by, Bletchley Town was a let-down after the hustle and bustle of London. We passed a cinema that looked like it had seen better days, several shops, a library, a British restaurant, four churches, and a church hall. There were a variety of houses, many with Spring flowers in their gardens. A park we passed had a big lake and several trees with crab apple and other blossoms.

'If we end up doing different shifts, we'll have to get used to going to the cinema on our own,' Carolyn said, tucking a stray curl behind her ear. 'I've never done that in my life. I always go with my friends or Mummy.'

I remembered a job I used to do. 'I'm used to it. I used to be assistant manager at a cinema. I loved it. Met my fiancé just outside.'

She looked down at my hand. 'But you don't wear a ring.'

Edward and I had wonderful times together, but long absences caused by the war meant we'd drifted apart. 'I'm not engaged now, but it's fine. I'm okay with it. So is he.'

Carolyn looked at her ringless hands. 'I've had three proposals, but didn't take to any of them. They all wanted me to be a stay-at-home wife waiting on them hand and foot.'

I smiled. 'Let me guess, that wasn't your cup of tea.'

'Nor yours, I imagine. Mind you, they were all rich enough to afford staff. But I still didn't want them. Money's not everything.'

I was tempted to say she wouldn't see it like that if she didn't have any, but before I could speak, the bus pulled into the Park, right outside the manor house.

I thanked my lucky stars I was going to be working there with Bronwyn, and we wished Carolyn good luck as she walked towards her hut.

My new title wasn't very inspiring - Assistant Secretary - but I wasn't complaining. Bronwyn's title was even less inspiring. She was a Clerical Officer. But when I met my new boss, the Senior Secretary, I wondered if I was right to be pleased.

We were shown into the room we would work in. It was medium size, big enough for four desks, two filing cabinets, and a small table. There was a shabby rug on the wooden floor and the inevitable blackout blinds. A window looked over the gravelled path at the side of the house. There was also an inner window that looked over a hallway, it was about as big as a serving hatch in grand houses. A woman stood up as we entered the room. She was tall, taller than a lot of men, and so thin my dad would have called her lucky legs. That was because her legs were so thin it was a wonder they didn't break when she walked. Her hair was cut in a style twenty years out of date, one side held back with a hair clip. She wore a dreary brown dress and sensible brown shoes. Her knitted stockings wrinkled round her ankles.

'Lily Baker? Bronwyn Jones?' she asked. 'Come in. I'm Miss Mary Abbott, Senior Secretary. Unlike you, I'm a civilian. You may wear civilian clothes at weekends, but I expect you to be in uniform on weekdays. You may call me Miss Abbott. We share the room with Iris Brand, but she actually works for another manager. She's a civilian and works nine to five as do I. I have not had an assistant before and I really don't need one. I'm perfectly capable of completing all the work myself, but I expect I can find you something to do. Which one of you is Bronwyn?'

'I am,' Bronwyn said, trying to smile.

'We have a big backlog of paperwork for you to make a start on.' I thought that was puzzling when she just said she could cope with anything. She spoke again. 'Lily, you'll be typing.'

I swallowed hard, and my stomach clenched.

'And this week,' she went on, 'you'll be on an eight til four shift, but next week you'll be four to midnight, then midnight until eight am. Rotating. If I'm not here any time, go to see Miss Smyth from the next office. She will help you. You may go to her with any queries. Any questions?'

I hesitated, not wanting to look stupid. 'When do we have a break? I was told the hot drinks were served in this building. I didn't have time to have a cup of tea this morning.'

A deep frown made speech marks between her grey eyebrows. 'Break? You've only just got here. You have twenty minutes at ten o'clock and forty-five minutes at twelve thirty. And you should know I am very strict about time-keeping.'

Her words gave me a sour taste in my mouth.

'Right, I assume you both have decent skills,' she said, indicating the smaller desks. They both had a typewriter, in and out trays, and a pot with pencils in it. 'Those are your desks. I don't mind which way round you sit. There are letters and other things to be typed in the in-basket, Lily. One carbon copy, no mistakes. You'll find a supply of stationery in your bottom drawer. Let me know if you need more. You can get on with those letters now. Bronwyn, come with me and I'll make a start teaching you what you need to know.'

As I sat down, I realised I still had no idea what Bletchley Park was for; what sort of war work went on here. I was no wiser by the time I'd typed the letters - they were all just making arrangements to see people. I didn't even know who the man was, whose name I typed at the bottom. I triple checked them when I'd finished, sure that Miss M. Abbott would be super critical. Sure enough, when she came back in with Bronwyn, she looked at them so hard it's a wonder she didn't get a magnifying glass out.

'Humph...' she said, lips pressed tightly together. 'Well, you'd better get on sorting these invoices, I suppose if you've finished the typing. Alphabetical and date order.'

Twenty minutes later, she finished explaining

what I'd grasped after ten minutes. The work was similar to what I did in the depot where I'd last worked. I stretched my arms above my head, and then sorted the papers, concentrating hard. Miss Abbott was at her own desk, bashing away at her typewriter.

I looked up when there was a gentle tap on the door, a triple tap. Miss Abbott leapt from her chair as if her bottom was on fire, and opened the door with a big smile. The first smile I'd seen. The visitor was a man about her age wearing a brown cotton coat with 'Porter' written on the top pocket.

He grinned at her. 'You okay, Mary? Got time for a tea break?'

To my amazement, she giggled and blushed, stroked her hair, and moved a step closer to him. 'Of course, if it's you. Let's go before all the biscuits vanish.'

'I'm going for my break now,' she said, turning to me. 'You can have yours when I get back.'

I sat back and folded my arms, smiling at what I'd just seen.

'So there is a heart behind that stern exterior,' I said to Bronwyn. 'Think she'll ever warm to us?'

Thirty-five minutes later, Miss Abbott came back. Never a word about her having the same length break as us. She was pink and glowing, even as she reminded us we could only take twenty minutes.

The break room was packed and the queue to get drinks proved that a twenty minute break would mean no time to even drink my drink, never mind meet some people. We weighed it up. To obey her or not? After all, she couldn't put us on a charge - she was a civilian. So we queued for a drink and chatted to the people near us who were friendly and obviously took more than twenty minutes for their coffee break.

The room smelled of coffee and occasionally of men's cologne. One or two of the men we passed were sorely in need of a bath, and I wondered if they neglected their toilet or had been working non-stop for several days and nights. The bags under their eyes suggested the latter. None of them was talking about work - it was obviously true that we couldn't even discuss our job with each other. But I overheard conversations on the weather, the awful meals in the canteen, the films currently on in Bletchley and how hard it was working nights.

I was pleased to see Carolyn walking into the tea room soon after us. She joined us in the queue. 'How's it going?' I asked.

She raised her eyes to the sky. 'It's like anything new. A lot to learn.'

I shrugged. 'I don't think that will be true for us.'

The room was pretty noisy, but I thought I heard someone talk about putting on a play.

'Shhh,' I said. 'Let's listen.'

'So when are we meeting to decide what's in the next Review?' a tall thin man with Billy Bunter glasses said, pushing them further up his nose. They promptly slid down again.

'Some time next week, Tuesday I think,' the other man said. He was older, almost completely bald, and wore a thick tweed jacket with leather patches on each elbow.

'Excuse me,' I said. They didn't hear me over the general hubbub. I leaned over and touched the bald one on the arm. 'I heard you talking about putting on a play. I'd be interested in knowing more about that.'

'Do you have acting experience?' he asked, looking from one of us to the other, his eyes resting on Carolyn.

I shook my head. 'No, but I've been in a variety show and I'd like to give it a go.'

'So would I,' Bronwyn said.

'I can play the piano,' Carolyn said.

'Keep an eye on the noticeboard in the main hall. Someone will post the date.' He smiled at us. 'Look forward to seeing you all.'

We thanked him and collected our tea. It was bright orange, with lumps of milk powder floating on the top. I stirred and stirred, but it made no difference, nor did squashing the lumps with my spoon. Carolyn looked round. 'Mrs W was right about not many men here. Those who are are much older than us or look like they're a million miles away all the time. Wouldn't notice a woman if they tripped over one.'

I remembered the time and looked at my watch. 'Damn! We'd better get back, the Miss A will be after us.'

'Who the hell...?' she called after me.

'Tell you later!

When we got back, the woman we were to work with was at her desk, busy with some papers. Miss Abbott wasn't there, thank goodness. The woman stopped what she was doing and stood up, moving towards us with a smile.

'You must be Lily and Bronwyn. I'm so pleased to have someone to work with. I'm Iris,

Iris Bland. Bland by name, but not by nature I hope!'

Iris was a fair bit older than us and soon told us her three daughters had all left home, two to get married and one in the Land Army. 'She always did like being out of doors.'

'So you're a local person then?' I asked.

'Bletchley Town born and bred, so if you want to know anything about the town, I'm your woman.'

Miss Abbott came back in then. She looked at us. 'I see you two have introduced yourself. Time to get on with your work now.' She looked from one of us to the other. 'As it's your first day, you may all go to lunch at the same time. Iris can show you the ropes. After today, I expect you to alternate.'

When she turned her back to get something out of one of the filing cabinets, Iris poked her tongue out at her. My eyes widened, and I spluttered - I'd never seen anyone older than fifteen poke their tongue out at someone. She definitely wasn't going to be bland.

At one o'clock, we headed for the canteen. It was a long, low brick building with windows on either side and a wooden floor. The smell of boiled cabbage mingled with the smell of cigarette smoke, made it difficult to breathe until we adjusted. The noise from people talking and cutlery scraping on plates was loud enough to make it difficult to hear each other as well.

From our place in the queue, we couldn't see the food.

'Don't eat the sausages, whatever you do,' Iris said. 'Heaven knows what's in them. Sawdust, I reckon. The food's terrible, but it fills you up and you don't have to use your food coupons. You'll soon learn what's worth risking.'

I grimaced. 'Oh dear, I hope it's not awful because we've already paid for a month's worth. They wouldn't let us do anything else.'

'That's normal, and tough on you people who work shifts. I hear the food's even worse at night. Dried to buggery. Excuse my language.'

As we moved along the long counter to get our food, other smells made our noses wrinkle: boiled meat and fried liver and onions. The servers bellowed instructions to the cooks behind them when they got low on some dishes, making our ears ache. I noticed they definitely gave the men bigger portions. They got bigger smiles, too.

We took our food and stood wondering where to sit. In the army, lower ranks were never allowed to sit with officers, but with the mixture of people here, it was impossible to tell who was who.

'We can sit anywhere,' Iris said. 'No-one knows or cares what your rank is. Loads of us are civilians, anyway.'

There weren't many places left, but we squeezed ourselves round a table near a window.

I looked at my meal. 'Tell you the truth, I can't remember what I asked for, and I sure as hell can't tell what it is from looking at it.'

Iris laughed. 'You'll get used to it. It is filling. I'll give it that much, just as well, because you can't go back for seconds. One of my friends tried to disguise herself to get more, but they spotted her and shouted at her in front of everyone.'

My jaw dropped open, it may not have looked like an army camp, but some bits were familiar from training.

'What's it like working here?' Bronwyn asked.

She shrugged. 'No-one talks about their work, of course, but there's nothing to stop us talking about people. I suppose it's like anywhere else. Some people and some jobs are okay, others bore you silly,' she chuckled. 'At least we're doing something useful.'

I began to eat and guessed it was supposed to be Shepherd's Pie and cabbage. I would soon learn that every meal came with cabbage.

'So, where are you living?' Iris asked. 'Did you

get somewhere in Bletchley or did you have to go further away?'

I swallowed a grisly bit of meat I'd been chewing for ages, strange when most of it was mince. 'We're in Bletchley. Happy Days Guest House. It's me and Bronwyn and two other girls.'

She stopped eating and put her knife and fork down. 'Happy Days, did you say? Well, that'll be interesting. I look forward to hearing all about it.'

I frowned. 'What do you mean?'

'Let's just say Gladys and Donald, or Donnie as she calls him, are well known in town, especially in the pubs. But they're harmless enough, as far as I know. You could do worse.'

Without warning, there was the sound of a plate being smashed on the floor. The room went silent, and all faces turned towards the source of the noise.

A WAAF girl was standing up, her face so tense it was scary to look at. She was looking toward the serving area. 'A cockroach!' she screeched. 'A bloody cockroach in my meal. What is it with you bloody lot?' Then she swept her cup and saucer onto the floor, burst into tears and ran out. Someone near her called 'Wait!' and hurried after her.

I looked at Iris, who was quite unperturbed by this outburst. 'She should worry, I found a dead mouse in the gravy boat one day!'

I pushed my plate away and decided once I'd used up my month's worth of food, I'd bring sandwiches. Or maybe I'd start the next day.

~

Bronwyn, Carolyn and I were dropped off in the town centre. Mums were walking their kids home from school, trying to keep them under control while pushing prams with the latest addition to their family. Elderly people walked their dogs, stopping frequently so the dogs could sniff every lamppost and tree. Older school-children walked past in groups, laughing and shouting to each other.

'Come on,' Carolyn said. 'Let's go for a drink to celebrate surviving our first day. I'm buying!'

'Lush,' Bronwyn said, 'but they won't be open just yet, and I'd like to get out of my uniform.'

A while later, we explored the High Street. The greengrocer's shop had potatoes, carrots, turnips and leeks, but not a lot else. The striped awning over his display flapped in the wind, applauding his efforts. Next we passed a post office, the library, and a clothes shop whose window display showed clothes no-one under eighty would wear. The Moon and Stars pub stood between a chemist shop and a butcher.

'You two grab a table, and I'll get them in,' Carolyn said. She took our orders and headed to the bar. Three men were already there, all of them wearing bowler hats and tweed coats. In the public bar, most of the men wore flat caps. The men gaped at Carolyn as if she was a Hollywood star. She noticed and wiggled her hips provocatively while giving us a sardonic grin.

It was a pretty basic sort of place, with wooden floorboards and furniture that had seen better days. Where most pubs had Toby jugs or something else distinctive hanging over the bar, this had nothing. But there was a darts board, and a domino set sat at the end of the bar, along with two packs of playing cards.

Carolyn came back with three drinks and three packs of Smiths' crisps on a battered tin tray. She took off her coat and hat and sat beside us. 'So, how was your first day?'

Somehow, without ever mentioning the work we did, we still talked for an hour about it. Bronwyn and I weren't clear about what we were doing and how it fitted in with the war effort, but we decided not to worry about it. 'It's got to be useful somehow, or they'd never pay us,' Bronwyn said.

Our rumbling stomachs moved us on.

'Let's go to the fish and chip shop,' Carolyn said. 'Anything but that damned canteen. They should be ashamed of themselves.'

Bronwyn looked surprised. 'I thought it was okay - must be you two being used to better food than I ever had in Swansea. Mind you, that cockroach that WAAF found was a bit much. But the chippy's a good idea. Tomorrow we need to get ourselves organised for food to cook in our digs.'

'Can either of you cook, then?' Carolyn said, sidestepping some dog-business on the pavement. 'We have a cook at home. Mummy never learned to cook, and the nearest I got was sitting in the kitchen to keep warm in winter.'

Bronwyn looked at her as if she was from outer space. 'Well, it's high time you learned then, that's the truth. We can teach you if we're ever on the same shifts again.'

I laughed. 'We can teach you what you can cook on two rings and no oven. Mind you, I helped mum a bit before I joined up. I can make jam tarts, so that's a start.'

Back in Happy Days, we ate our fish and chips straight from the newspaper, making the kitchen smell of malt vinegar.

I put my paper in the pile by the door. 'I'm

going up to get a cardigan,' I said, washing my hands and wiping them on a tea towel.

As soon as I walked into our bedroom, it felt different. I stood in the doorway looking round, unsure of what had changed. Everything looked the same. Then I realised what it was. It smelled different. When we left, it smelled most of cold air and talcum powder. Now there was something else, and I couldn't work out what it was. My heart beat fast and, without thinking about any danger, I looked under our beds; behind the curtains and in our wardrobe.

Nothing.

I shook myself, telling myself my imagination was playing tricks on me.

Then I went to my bedside cabinet.

It was a well-used wooden one with two drawers, scratched around the handles and with water stains on the top. I opened the top drawer where I kept my undies and a few personal things, still telling myself off for being a scaredy-cat.

But when I looked in the drawer, my heart beat fast again. Things had been moved. I'm not the tidiest of people, but I always roll my knickers up and put them, like sausages, next to each other. Two pairs were the wrong way round. I looked closer.

That meant someone had not only noticed my knickers, but unrolled them and rolled them back up again. They'd all been touched. Not wanting to handle them, I threw them on the floor to be washed again. It can't have been much of the thrill to inspect my knickers because they were very plain and boring. I didn't own much jewellery and what bits I had weren't worth stealing, but I kept them in a knotted hankie. Now they lay on top of the knickers. None missing, but it proved someone had been in my stuff.

I rushed downstairs to the kitchen, where Carolyn was putting on the kettle. I was so put out I could hardly speak. 'Someone's been looking through my stuff!' I said, my voice shaking.

They turned to me with matching frowns. 'What do you mean, Cariad?' Bronwyn asked. 'You look really shook up...'

'I went to get something out of my bedside cabinet and someone's been in there. Things have been moved around.'

Her eyes widened. 'Oh my word. Is anything missing?'

'Not that I can see. You'd better check your things.' I sat down heavily, my head in my hands as they left the room. If someone had snooped, why hadn't they put things back as they were? Or stolen something? Not that my well-worn undies and cheap jewellery were worth much. I tried to calm my breathing, telling myself not to be silly.

Bron was the first one down. 'Someone's been poking in my stuff, too,' she said. 'There's nothing missing that I can see.'

Carolyn was next. 'One of my pairs of knickers is gone. A pink silk pair, they were folded up with the others, and a gold bracelet is missing too.' She dragged her fingers through her hair and looked pale.

The kettle whistling got our attention, and I got up to make the tea. 'What are we going to do about it?'

'What, the tea?' Carolyn asked.

'Don't be daft. Someone poking around in our stuff, and stealing your bracelet. We don't have a lock on our door and even if we got one, we'd have to give Mrs W a copy…'

'... And she's the most likely culprit,' Bronwyn said. 'But what do we do? Accuse her? We definitely need to go to the police and report it.'

As she spoke, we heard the front door opening. We looked at each other, then walked into the hall.

It was Mrs W. She was taking off her coat and hat and putting down bags of shopping. 'Hello, Girls, just been getting rations in for you. How was your first day at work?'

We were silent for a minute and she looked from one of us to the other. ‘What is it? Is something wrong? Has the electricity packed up again?’

My stomach sank as I tried to think how to tell her, but luckily Bronwyn was more direct than me.

‘Someone’s been through our stuff, and Carolyn is missing a pair of pink knickers and a gold bracelet.’

Mrs W blinked several times and leaned back. ‘Are you sure?’ She paused. ‘You don’t think I did it, do you?’

‘Come into the kitchen so we can talk about it,’ I said.

The silence was so heavy I was sure I could hear my heart beating. I hate conflict.

Mrs W picked up the shopping again and followed us. We sat round the table like members of a jury.

‘Did...’ Carolyn started.

Mrs W held up her hand. ‘Before you say anything else, I did not go through your things. I have never, ever done such a thing to any of my guests. It must have been someone else.’

‘Who else comes into the house?’ I asked.

She sat back and folded her arms. ‘Let’s see. There’s May, the cleaner, of course. But she’s been with me for years, and I’d trust her with my life. An electrician came this morning. It's true I left him to it. I had things that needed doing.'

'Anyone else?'

She scratched her cheek. 'Well, Donnie was here earlier, but it won't be him, of course. The only other person I can think of is Fred, the gardener. But like May, he's been with me for years. He comes in every morning in the growing season and makes himself a cuppa.'

We sat back and looked at each other. 'How will we sort this out?' I asked. 'It's horrible thinking that someone has been poking through our stuff. Do you have keys to our rooms?'

She nodded. 'I do, but May has one as well. No-one else. But I must have some somewhere from my bed-and-breakfast days. I'll hunt them out for you.'

We heard the front door open and Peggy came into the kitchen looking tired. We all looked up as she walked in. She stopped in the doorway. 'What's 'appened? You all look... I dunno... weird.'

When we told her about the missing items, she rushed upstairs to check her stuff. Two minutes later, she was back. 'Nothing gone, thank goodness. Not that I've got anything worth nicking!'

Carolyn went to the police station and reported the theft next day. 'There's been a spate of thefts,' the desk sergeant told her, 'but this doesn't fit the usual way the thief works. We'll let you know if we find anything. I'll put the word out to the coppers on the beat to listen for any information.'

~

We were no nearer to finding the thief when our shifts changed the following week. We were all on nights. Peggy was still on two 'til ten.

Miss Abbott warned me that there would only be the two of us on duty in that section at night and we must arrive a few minutes before midnight so that whoever was before us would be able to leave promptly. She explained other people would work in the office upstairs, so we wouldn't be alone in the building.

The night was cloudless, and as we walked from the bus stop towards the big house, I looked up at the sky.

'I've never seen so many stars in my life,' I said, getting Bronwyn's attention. 'I reckon in London we only saw a tenth of the number we can see here.'

She looked upwards. 'You're not kidding. Often we couldn't see any because of the smoke from burning buildings. Hey, look! A shooting star, make a wish.'

'Please make this war end soon,' I whispered. As if to answer, a second shooting star shot across the heavens. 'It's never this dark in London, either, not even in the blackout.'

'You're right. Often the moonlight reflects on the barrage balloons. I don't miss seeing them in the sky. Like silver floating slugs, they were.' Bronwyn pulled a face thinking about them.

I looked around at the gardens and lake. There were no lights from any of the buildings because of the blackout, but overhead was what in London we called a bombers' moon. It was full with a halo, giving enough light to make out the shape of the buildings and the outline of trees round the lake. On the opposite side of the lake, I could make out the silhouette of a man. The tiny red glow told me he was smoking. Three hut doors opened and closed, and echoey footsteps followed. I assumed they were other people changing shift. A dog barked a long way off, and I heard machines whirling in one hut. I breathed in the cold, fresh air and we turned towards the big house, our footsteps loud on the gravel, then quieter on the grass.

A typist we didn't know was putting her coat on as we arrived in our office. 'I'm Sybil,' she said with a tired smile. 'It's pretty quiet. Miss Abbott left a pile of work for you, but I don't think it'll take you all night.' She buttoned up her coat and wound a bright red hand-knitted scarf round her neck.

'Is this your first night shift?' she asked, pulling on a matching hat with a blue and white bobble.

I nodded. 'It is. I was an Air Raid warden in London and Bronwyn here was an ambulance driver, so we're used to working nights, but that was a very different kettle of fish.'

She smiled again. 'Well, at least you don't have to worry about bombs here. Mind you, some people say this place is haunted. Seen nothing myself, but you do hear the house settling down as it gets colder. There's not so many people around at night as during the day.'

I hung up my coat and put my bag and gas mask next to my desk. 'What do you mean, settling down?'

'You know what old houses are like. The radiators rattle and the wood creaks as temperature changes. Nothing to worry about. We're not supposed to sleep on nights, but we all do if we run out of work. Camp beds and blankets are in the cupboard in the hall. Make sure you put them away before the next shift though.' She looked at her watch.

'I'd better get off or I'll miss the bus. Nice to meet you both, see you tomorrow night.'

The office was cold, so we turned on the little electric fire and fetched the blankets to put round our shoulders. Through the inner window we saw a few people leaving and some of them waved goodbye despite looking worn out.

'You got much work there, Bron?' I asked, seeing her sorting through a pile of papers.

'Two or three hours' worth, I'd say. Looks like we'll be able to get some shut-eye.'

As I began typing, I noticed again how quiet it was. No Miss Abbott thumping away at her type-writer, or Iris scratching away at her paperwork. A messenger went by the window on his motorbike, his tyres sliding on the gravel. I wondered if that was his last journey of the night. Bronwyn used to be a dispatch rider and often told me how hard it was riding through the countryside in almost total darkness, not to mention the lack of road signs.

I must have been working for about an hour when I paused to stand and stretch my legs.

'Come on, let's get a cuppa,' I said, dragging Bronwyn's attention from a list of figures she was trying to sort out.

No-one else was in the tea room and it was strange to see it empty. The water in the urn was hot, and I put tea-leaves in the smallest pot I could find - it would hold about fifteen cups. As I stood waiting for the tea to brew, I yawned and flexed my stiff fingers. I was miles away in thought when a loud noise made us both jump a mile. A man who'd been sitting with his back to us in a high-backed chair suddenly stood up, scraping the chair legs on the floor. He'd been invisible from where we stood. The noise jarred like fingernails scratching a blackboard, and I gasped and bit my lip as he walked towards me. He yawned and stretched his laced fingers over his head.

'Sorry, Love, did I frighten you? I didn't hear you come in. I must have nodded off. I'd better get back to my hut or they'll all be moaning at me.'

With shaking hands, I poured my tea and took a deep breath to let my heart calm down. I sat in a chair and picked up a local newspaper that had been left behind.

MORE HOUSE THEFTS IN BLETCHLEY

The headline screamed at me. Could this explain what happened to us? I read the article out loud to Bronwyn.

Police have reported another spate of thefts from houses and gardens in Bletchley. Superintendent Merry said, 'We have received reports of three house thefts in the last week. They appear to be similar to those reported two months ago. Small items and items of ladies' clothing have been stolen both from homes and gardens. We appeal to anyone who may know anything about these crimes to report them to Bletchley Police Station.

'Cor,' Bronwyn said, taking the paper from me. 'I bet it's Carolyn's knicker nicker. He's got to be some sort of pervert.'

She tore out the article. 'We'll talk to Carolyn about it on the way home in the morning.'

We took our tea back to the office, resisting the temptation to snooze in one of the armchairs. Miss Abbott was very strict about having someone in the office at all times in case urgent work came in. As I walked, I noticed the glass tear-drop chandelier inside the front door threw sparkles across the wide staircase and the hall, but left dark patches, too. I heard a creak and tensed, then remembered it was probably just the woodwork settling down. Then, just as I reached out for the doorknob for my office, I saw a movement out of the corner of my eye. My breath caught as I spun round, spilling a few drops of tea onto the faded hall carpet.

No-one was there.

I stood still, listening, and saw Bronwyn doing the same. Then we heard footsteps overhead, although not immediately above us. They sounded as if they were headed for a room at the back of the house.

'We're a daft pair of sods,' Bronwyn said with a grin, 'scared of noises in a house when we've both dealt with death and destruction without turning a hair!'

I laughed. 'You're right, there are people working upstairs. Come on, let's get the rest of our work done then we can have a sleep.'

I'd finished the typing Miss Abbott left and thought how the time went much more slowly at night. It was almost as if the clock on the wall and my watch were both on a go-slow, refusing to move time forward.

I sat back in my chair, pulling the blanket more closely round my shoulders. Bronwyn's pile of papers had gone down, so I guessed she'd nearly finished, but didn't want to break her concentration.

Rubbing my hands together to warm them up, I put a new sheet of paper in the typewriter and began writing to my mum. Our home was a two-bedroomed corporation house in Sunbury, a suburb of Oxford. Life had been rough on her for years. My dad was a bully and not above giving her the occasional swipe. But conscription had caught up with him and he was abroad, serving King and country as far as I knew or cared. He tried to worm his way back into Mum's favour. She was having none of it, and good for her.

All our letters were censored, of course, but I was careful what I wrote, anyway.

Dear Mum,

I'm sorry it's been a while since I wrote to you. You'll see from the address at the top of this letter that I've moved again - out of London this time. I am sharing a guest house with Bronwyn and two other girls. One is a Londoner called Peggy, and the other is Carolyn whose parents (Mummy and Daddy!) wanted her to marry someone from what she calls 'their set.' Lucky for us, she didn't. I think they'll both be good fun.

I'm doing routine office work, nothing much to say about that. I'm looking forward to having a little break when the weather is warmer. Me and Bronwyn are working together and would like to go to the seaside somewhere - somewhere where the beaches aren't covered in barbed wire if that's possible.

I hope you are keeping okay. Are you still at the factory? Have you got used to handling all that dangerous stuff? Does Margaret next door still snore enough for you to hear her through the wall?

I haven't been to the pictures here yet, but the

local one doesn't look half as grand at the Dream Palace.

If you have time, do write and tell me your news.

Much love

Lily xxx

I put the letter in an envelope, left it open for the censors, put it in my bag and visited the Ladies. Then I got the camp beds out ready for a sleep. Bronwyn finished what she was doing and followed my example.

The pillow was as soft as a rock, and I wished I had another blanket. I put my coat over it and snoozed in all my clothes. My thoughts drifted this way and that as they do when we head towards sleep. I heard the dog barking again, but it seemed further away, or perhaps it was a different dog. I half woke up when I heard someone snorting, but smiled when I realised it was me. Then I remembered nothing until I woke with a start when someone stroked my cheek.

Half dreaming, I thought it was Bronwyn messing about, but I looked and she was dead to the world. There was a faint trace of the scent of Pears Soap in the air, my grannie's favourite.

The desk light was on so I could see the room,

even though the corners were in darkness. Someone had stroked my cheek. I was sure of it.

But there was no-one there.

I swung round so I could see the room better. As well as the desk lamp, some light came through the internal window from the hallway. Even though my eyes told me I was the only one awake I got up, trembling, and tiptoed round the room looking under the three desks and behind the filing cabinet. Then I sat in my typist's chair and touched my face where I'd been stroked. It felt normal.

I took a deep breath and told myself it must have been part of a dream. There was no other explanation. Or someone opened an outside door, and it caused a draft.

But perhaps it was a ghost. I could almost hear Sybil saying that. But no, she'd never seen anything. It must just be my tiredness and the strangeness of sleeping somewhere so different. Then I remembered all the air-raid shelters I'd slept in, and the different digs Bronwyn and I had shared in London. Somewhere new to sleep had never given me strange dreams before.

That proved nothing. This was just a dream. I got up, looked around one last time and headed back to the tea room, hoping there would be someone there to talk to.

Two women were making drinks and cheerfully said hello even though they must have been as tired as me. One of them washed up some cups, muttering 'why can't people wash their cups when they've finished?'

'Better than throwing them in the lake!' I joked.

One of them, a tall thin brunette whose hair was in an immaculate Victory Roll, dried the cups. 'We were just talking about what to do with our spare time. These shifts are good one way, but it's not like we can see a film or go to a dance when we've got a morning off.'

The other one got out the milk. 'I volunteer at one of the junior schools. Listen to the kids reading for a couple of hours a week. It's fun and the teachers are appreciative. Mind you, some of them whiff a bit. The kids, not the teachers!'

I liked that idea. 'Are they flexible about us not being able to do the same time each week?'

She grinned. 'Trust me, they're so desperate they'd have you reading next day if you offered.'

I thought it was a great idea, but it slipped my mind for a few weeks.

CHAPTER FOUR

I went to fetch my cardigan and when I got back, there were half a dozen people in the tearoom, two men and four women. It was clear they all knew each other, and to my delight they were talking about what entertainments they could put on. At first they didn't notice me because they were so engrossed in their conversation, but the noise of me filling the kettle got their attention.

One woman, short and dumpy with a beautiful face and vivid blue eyes, looked over at me and smiled. 'Hello,' she said, 'haven't seen you before. Are you new?'

By now, they all turned to me and they looked friendly.

'Yes, pretty new and this is my first night shift.'

I wondered whether to ask them if they had had any spooky experiences. Trouble was, if they hadn't they'd have me down as someone crazy.

'I heard you all talking about entertainment. I'd be interested in getting involved in that. Can I join? Is that possible?'

The beautiful woman beamed. 'We can always use more willing volunteers. I'm Beattie by the way. You are ...'

'I'm Lily, Lily Baker, and I'm assistant secretary to Miss Abbott. My friend Bronwyn started with me, but she's still asleep at the moment.'

She frowned, 'Never heard of Miss Abbott. Where's your office?'

I indicated towards the front door. 'Off that corridor to the right. It's spooky here at night, isn't it.'

One man, a good-looking one with a dimple on his chin, grinned. 'You're not wrong there. But there will be people working upstairs, the Directorate is up there and some others. Still, I'm glad I work in one of the huts. We're busy every minute of the day and night over there. But never mind that. Do you have any performing experience?'

My heart sank. 'A little. I sang a solo song and was part of a duo, telling jokes at a charity variety show. That's all, I'm afraid.'

'No need to apologise, that's more than a lot of

us had when we joined. We're just looking at the review George here has written, with a little help of course.' The man speaking was tall, over six feet with thick dark brown hair and brown eyes. His hair was too long to be fashionable and curled up over his collar. He handed me a copy of the script. 'I'm Grant, by the way.'

I knew I'd remember his name because just looking at him gave me tingles inside.

'I've already had a look at the script and it looks fun, Grant,' Beattie said.

'That sounds interesting. Has it got a few songs?'

'Absolutely, a couple they'll know and can sing along to, and one George has written.'

A short, rotund man with a shock of brown hair laughed. 'I'm hoping one day someone famous will notice my song-writing skills and take me away from all this!'

Somewhere in the building, a clock chimed, making Grant start and look at his watch. 'Time to go, troops. Same time tomorrow night? Quick read through so you can decide what parts you want to audition for.' He looked at me, giving a heart-melting smile, 'Will you join us?'

I felt a foolhardy blush creep up my neck and hoped he didn't spot it. 'If I possibly can, and I'll be with my friend Bronwyn, she's interested too,' I said.

I resolved to get plenty of sleep before my next shift, so I didn't have bags under my eyes.

They all walked with me in my direction, but Beattie pulled me back a little way. 'Don't be taken in by his smile. I heard he has a bit of a reputation for being a heart-breaker. Never commits.'

'Thanks for the warning,' I said. 'See you tomorrow.'

Her words didn't break my heart, but they made it sink. I couldn't believe I was feeling like an empty-headed teenager about Grant, especially as women at the Park outnumbered men by goodness knows how many. If Grant was really a womaniser, he'd have plenty to choose from. Giving myself a mental slap, I walked back to my office. Bronwyn was awake, and we sighed when we realised there were still three hours of our shift left. I checked and double checked the work I'd done so that Miss Abbott wouldn't find anything to complain about.

'Hey, someone must have been here, there's some more typing in my tray,' I said, making Bronwyn look up from the camp bed where she was rubbing her eyes.

'Yes, some bloke came in. Never said a word, just put the papers down and left. I was half asleep.'

What would we do if whoever it was reported us to Miss Abbott?

I shrugged. There was nothing we could do about it now, but I decided that in future if we were out of the office we'd fold up the camp beds and blankets and hide them. The new letters only took half an hour to type, so I lay down again, trying to sleep. My thoughts spun around the ghostly stroke on my cheek, and meeting the Am Dram people. But I must have drifted to sleep because the next time I looked at my watch there was an hour and a half of the shift left. Birds were singing, and I thought again about how lovely it was to hear them without the background of heavy traffic. I pushed open the blackout curtains and saw the promise of a lovely Spring day outside. The leaves on the trees on the other side of the gravel path were opening, and daffodils and narcissi danced in the breeze.

Digging in my bag, I pulled out my knitting. Bronwyn had been trying to teach me to knit for a long time, but I took ages to get the hang of it. It seemed every female I knew was knitting socks for the troops, but I still wasn't up to that standard. I'd got a jumper at a jumble sale and unpicked and washed it. Then I'd wound the wool into balls, but it was still a bit crinkly.

'Blimey, haven't you finished that scarf yet?'

Bronwyn said, rubbing her face as she sat up. 'The war'll be over before you finish it at this rate.'

I grinned. 'Less of your cheek, or I won't do any sewing for you!'

After an hour, I went to the Ladies', washed my face and combed my hair, checking that my clothes didn't look too wrinkled. I bumped into Iris as I walked back to our office.

'Is Miss Abbott in yet?' I asked, relieved we'd hidden the camp bed and blanket.

Iris raised an eyebrow. 'I saw her outside talking to that porter she fancies, so I expect she'll be awhile yet. No accounting for taste.'

We went into the office and she took off her coat and hat. She got a comb out of her desk drawer and tidied her hair. 'Go on, you two, go and get your bus. I hope you get some sleep. Everyone says shift work plays havoc with your body clock.'

On the way out, I looked at a notice board in the corridor. It was items for sale or wanted. There were three bicycles, and we wrote down the details of those. Cycling here wouldn't take long from the town. There were some strange things too - a stuffed owl, a pair of black nearly new women's shoes size five, a grey woollen blanket and then, almost covered by the other notices. I saw something that interested me, a sewing machine. Taking no chances, I tore the notice off the board and put it in my pocket. Mum had shown me how to do dress-making so long ago, I couldn't remember how old I was when I first made something. I may not be much good at knitting, but I could sew.

The following evening, we went into work early so we could venture into the Beer Hut, where Peggy worked, before starting our night shift. As well as alcohol, there was a NAAFI that sold everything from stockings to cigarettes. I took a detour and walked round the lake while Bronwyn chatted to someone. There were always geese near the water, some preening their wings, others plucking grass. In the fading light, I spotted two or three fish lazily swimming near the edge and some spindly legged skimmers flitting across the surface. Further round I saw a couple sitting close, his arm round her shoulders. They never took their eyes from each other's face, oblivious to anything around them. Two men were rowing, their lack of expertise clear as they went haphazardly this way and that. The sound of their drunken laughter drifted across the water, competing with the splash of their oars. Then a frog croaked loudly, bringing me out of my daydream and I turned to go to the beer hut.

When I walked through the door of Hut Two, the Beer Hut, the air was full of cigarette smoke and the smell of beer. After the relative quiet of the lake, the hubbub was deafening. I headed towards the bar, where I knew Peggy would be on duty. She didn't notice me at first, being deep in conversation with a man who was looking down her blouse as much as looking at her face. She must have noticed, but seemed unfazed.

I caught her eye, and she grinned and took my order, but we didn't have time to chat because others were there, waving their ten bob notes for attention.

I turned back to the room, and there, coming towards me, was Grant. He beamed at me. I was surprised he even recognised me when we'd only met briefly.

'Hello, Lily, isn't it? I thought I recognised you.' He took a swig of his beer.

'It's my first time in here. Peggy, the blond barmaid, shares a house with us. Do you come here often?'

He laughed. 'I think that's my line! Yes, I come here two or three times a week so I hope to see more of you.' He gestured to a group nearby. There were three WRENs, smart in their uniform, and a jolly middle aged man with a thick thatch of grey hair.

Grant introduced me to everyone, but I forgot their names, apart from the grey haired man who was John. It didn't matter, it was hard to hear each other over the clamour, anyway. They were talking about a dance in the town, or the village hop as they called it. They sounded enthusiastic. I'd learned that for many people at the Park, their working days were hard because of the need for total concentration. Maybe that's why they took any chance to let their hair down.

Grant turned to me. 'The dance is tomorrow. Would you like to come with us? We'll get you back in good time for your midnight shift.'

I remembered he was supposed to be a bit of a ladies' man, but warmed to his smile and friendly eyes. 'I'd love to,' I said. 'My friend Bronwyn would want to come as well. How shall we meet?'

One of the WRENs overheard our conversation. 'We all meet in the Dog and Drake in the High Street about seven, and go on to the dance when we feel like it. Do come, the more the merrier.'

CHAPTER FIVE

'Can you start now? This afternoon?' Mrs Howard, the head teacher, said, her eyes looking hopeful.

I was taken aback as I'd only gone to enquire about listening to children reading. It was some time after I'd been told the school needed help.

'I haven't had any training or anything.'

'Younger brothers or relatives?'

'No, but I've sometimes let my friend's little ones read to me.' It was feeling like a job interview, not an enquiry about some voluntary work.

'Excellent. Why not have a trial run for an hour this afternoon? Will that be okay?' She was already standing and moving towards the door.

I'd slept for a while during my night shift and

managed a few more hours after I got in, so I wasn't feeling tired. And one hour wasn't committing myself. 'If you're sure.'

'I'm sure. Come with me. I'll take you to Miss Russell's class. She's told me she's got a few youngsters who need help.'

Miss Russell looked past retirement age, and so did her clothes. I'd read that with a lot of male teachers called up, a lot of older teachers were being bought back to their pre-retirement jobs. Her wiry grey hair was pulled in a tight bun and she wore brown lace-up shoes and a brown tweed skirt with a cream long-sleeved blouse. She should have been intimidating, but the smile she gave when the head-teacher told her who I was quickly dispelled that idea.

She grabbed both my hands. 'Oh, you're just what we need. If you can help, even if it's only for a couple of hours a week, you'd be an angel.'

She looked around the class. 'We have several children who need help. Let me think.'

The children were silently reading, pretending not to be listening to our conversation.

'Do you mind if it's a boy or a girl?' she asked.

'No, whoever needs it most. Will I always listen to the same child?'

She nodded. 'That's what we like to do unless

you don't hit it off.' She fingered the cameo broach at her neck. 'I think Tommy would be ideal. He's a lovely lad.'

She clapped her hands. 'Children, carry on reading, but Tommy would you come here please?'

He cowered in his seat, making himself as small as possible. Miss Russell went over and knelt aside him. 'It's okay, Tommy, you have done nothing wrong. This nice lady is here to help you read.'

He looked at her, wanting to believe it was true, but soon looked away again. I joined them. 'What's your favourite book?' I asked.

He opened his desk and took out Swallows and Amazons, handing it to me with a shy smile.

'I used to read this when I was your age,' I said, opening the pages. 'It's exciting!'

Miss Russell bent towards me and whispered in my ear. 'It's a simplified version for his reading level.'

I held out my hand. 'Right, Tommy, we've got the book. Let's see where Miss Russell wants us to go.'

Three minutes afterward, we were in a small storeroom. Tommy was short for his age. His hair was fair and cut badly. His clothes were a little too small and his shoes had a hole in one toe. He didn't dare look me in the eye. The few other children I'd read to were my friend's brothers and sisters. They knew me well and were real live-wires. The opposite to this little lad. My heart went out to him, and I wanted to give him a hug.

As I opened the book, I heard his tummy rumble. 'Are you hungry?'

He nodded, the corners of his mouth turned down. I opened my bag and took out an apple I'd bought to have later. 'Here, have this, I don't need it.'

His eyes lit up, and he snatched it out of my hands with a quick thank you. He bit into it as if he hadn't eaten for a month. Juice dribbled down his chin, and he wiped it on his sleeve.

When he'd finished he held out his damp hands, and I cleaned them with my hankie. 'Okay, let's get started. I need to see where you've got to. Why don't you read a little to me?'

He was eight years old, but I guessed he was reading at the same age as someone a couple of years younger. Every time he got a word wrong, he hung his head and muttered 'Sorry, Miss.'

I patted his hand. 'Don't worry if you get a few words wrong. We all make mistakes when we're learning.'

He said something I didn't hear, and I asked him to repeat it. 'Mum says I'm stupid if I get a word wrong.'

I didn't know what to say. I could hardly say she was being unkind. 'Soon you'll get all the words right and she'll be pleased as punch!' was the best I could do.

Every time he struggled with a word, he fidgeted, but I gave him full credit for trying. After an hour, I decided he'd had enough and closed the book.

'Have you got many books at home?' I asked.

He shook his head. 'No, Mum says there's not enough money for books.'

'Have you got any brothers or sisters?'

He shook his head. 'No, mum starts them, but things go wrong and she loses them. I don't know why she doesn't go looking for them if they're lost. If I lose my socks, we have to look everywhere for them. She's started another baby now.' His bottom lip trembled. 'She's not very well. My dad said I've got to be the man of the house now he's at war, so I try to look after her.'

I went back to the classroom with him, promising to hear him read the next week. Before I left, I knocked on the head teacher's door. She pushed aside an enormous pile of papers and greeted me with a smile.

'How did you get on?'

'I read with Tommy ... oh, I don't know his last name.'

'That'll be Tommy Gibson. Nice lad, but very lacking in confidence.'

I clasped my hands together. 'He said he doesn't have any books at home. Do you have a school library?'

Her face dropped. 'We do, but there's not many books in it. They fall apart or kids forget to return them, and we haven't got any money to replace them.'

As I walked back towards Happy Days, I saw Peggy getting off the Bedford bus. I hurried to catch up with her. 'Been shopping?' Only after I'd spoken did I notice she had no shopping bags.

She stopped to tie her shoe lace. 'No such luck. The Park doesn't pay me enough for new clothes even if I had any coupons.'

She straightened up and hitched her gas mask higher on her shoulder. Curiosity got the better of me. 'Have you been all the way to Bedford, then? Do you know someone there?'

She swallowed and put her hands in her pockets. ‘Just looking round. Never been there before. But what’ve you been up to?’

I recognised someone trying to change the subject when I saw it, and I wondered why she didn’t have any clothing coupons. What was she doing with them?

CHAPTER SIX

'It was Friday night and the Dog and Drake was crowded. Like me, lots of girls wore uniform, no doubt because they could get into the dance half price that way. I looked around and wondered if many local people went to the dance. Even if they did, with so many men being called up, there would still be a shortage of men to dance with.

'Penny for them,' Grant said. 'You looked miles away.'

I smiled. 'I was just wondering if there would be any men to dance with.'

He patted my hand. 'Never fear, I'll dance with you.'

Madge, one of the AmDram group who'd been

sitting near us, leaned over to him. 'You'll be dancing with me too, I hope.'

He frowned for a fraction of a second. If she noticed, she didn't show it. 'Of course, we'll have a dance,' he said, then turned to John and said something I couldn't hear.

Madge looked across at me next. 'Grant and I went on a bike ride in the countryside. Lovely day it was. We had a picnic and lay under a tree. He's got a soft spot for me, you know.'

Brenda, a girl on the other side of her, laughed, 'Well, you'll get his attention in that dress, that's for sure. Why didn't you come in uniform like the rest of us? You'll have to pay full price to get in.'

Madge looked down at her dress and smoothed the material. 'Perhaps I just wanted to look my best. After all, Grant's only seen me out of uniform once.'

The girl grinned. 'Strikes me you'd like him to see you out of civvies, too.'

Madge slapped her arm. 'Don't be so coarse. You know I'm not that sort of girl.'

Her friend looked at me and raised an eyebrow, but said nothing else.

'The weather forecast is good for the weekend. If me and Grant can get away, perhaps we can go to the flicks or something.'

'Does he know?' Brenda asked.

Madge smiled. 'He will, after this evening.'

A girl on the other side joined in the conversation. 'Hey, Madge, wasn't that bike ride with a group, not a date with just you and him?'

Madge paled, then glared at the girl. 'Sure, some others came along, but it was all about me and him.'

We got no further because someone called 'Come on. Drink up. Let's get to the dance before it's too late.'

Bronwyn had been chatting to some other people and joined me as we walked to the dance. I pondered on what Madge had said. It seemed like she was making something out of not a lot. But then I remembered the warning that Grant was a bit of a ladies' man. After Beattie's comments, I needed to be on my guard.

The village hall was like so many others. A stage at one end, with floor length faded maroon curtains pulled back, a Union Jack and a picture of the King on the opposite wall. The blackout blinds were already in place and the air was thick with cigarette smoke. The wooden floor bounced with the weight of so many people dancing. Grant, who'd been walking ahead of me, came back to find us. 'Would you like a drink, Lily?

Bronwyn?' he asked. Even through the cigarette smoke, I saw how attractive he was. Not typical film star looks, but a cute dimple and lovely brown eyes. He rubbed his forehead with his fingers.

'Are you tired?' I asked.

He gave a wry grin. 'I'm always tired. Even when I'm not at work, my brain won't switch off, so sleep is hard to find.'

I knew better than to ask what his job was, but guessed he was one of the scientists or mathematicians. If so, his job would be doing much more for the war effort than typing letters.

Madge sidled up to us. 'Tired, Grant? Come and sit with me, I'll massage your shoulders.'

'No thanks, Madge, I'm going to the bar. Can I get you anything?'

'A Cinzano, please.' She stroked his arm as she spoke. I wanted to smack her.

'A lemonade for me, please,' I said.

'Same for me, please, got to stay awake for our shift,' Bronwyn chipped in.

As Grant walked away, Madge turned to me. 'Lemonade? You're old for a kid's drink, aren't you? And I've seen you looking at Grant. Don't waste your time, he's mine.'

I gave her a half-smile and turned to talk to

Bronwyn. The band was playing Tuxedo Junction, and I tapped my toes, itching to dance.

Grant came back with the drinks, struggling not to spill them as he wove his way through the dancers. Beattie, the girl who had kindly welcomed me the first time I met the AmDram group, had joined us and we were busy chatting when Grant put the drinks down. We'd had several get-togethers since, and the plans for the review were coming along well.

He gave Madge her drink with a smile and joined me, Bronwyn, and Beattie. 'What are you girls talking about? Practicing your lines?'

'It's a bit too noisy in here,' Beattie said, speaking, 'but I had a thought about the review. Why don't we get this band to play one of our songs, then we can get up there on stage. We'll wow the dancers and it'll be good publicity for the review.'

I froze. Get up on stage? I'd only ever done that at the review in London and then only sang to cover for someone who was ill.

'You've gone white,' Beattie said. 'Are you okay?'

I shook my head, aware of a film of sweat on my brow. 'Terrified. I've only been on stage once.'

'And I've never been on one in my entire life,' Bronwyn said. 'but I'll give it a go. My voice isn't as great as Lily's, mind, but it'll do with you lot drowning me out.'

Grant touched my arm and sent a tingle through my body. 'You won't be alone, either of you. We'll pick a song we all know and there will be several of us. From what you told me, you did a solo before. It'll be a lot easier than that.'

'I thought we'd already chosen the songs,' Beattie said.

He shrugged. 'I'm sure we can change it. How about Chattanooga Choo-choo. Everyone loves that, and people can dance to it.'

Taking our drinks, we went outside to do a quick practice. Madge spotted us and followed like a lost puppy. It was a mild evening with a gentle breeze. The smell of beer and cigarettes followed us out of the village hall, but was soon replaced by the delicate scent of Spring flowers.

'Come on,' Beattie said. 'Let's go round the back and further away. We can run through it twice, that should be enough. We all know it.'

We went to a nearby park, and she took control like the conductor of an orchestra. 'Right, this will not be fancy, no solos or anything. We don't have time to sort all that out. Ready? One. Two. Three.'

'Hey there, Tex...'

We had three false starts, once because I'd always heard the words wrong, so sang them wrong, giving Madge a chance to poke fun at me. Then we got in our stride and before we'd even finished the first attempt, had a few people watching and tapping their feet. By the time we finished the third time round, we had fifteen people giving us a round of applause and calling for an encore. We grinned widely, bowed, and headed back to the hall.

'Right,' Beattie said. 'Ready for the stage?'

Beattie and I went to the band to persuade them to let us do the song. I'd been given the job of introducing it and giving a plug for the venue we'd just begun rehearsing. The thought of it made my mouth dry.

The band-leader checked his band knew the song - how could they not - and said we could go on after the next number. We went to the Ladies' on the way back, combed our hair, put on lipstick and tried to look our best. Or as good as you can in uniform. But when we headed back to Grant and Madge, I paused. He was leaning over, whispering in her ear, looking every bit as if they were together. I swallowed hard, pushed my shoulders back, and carried on walking, a fixed smile on my face. Madge gave me a triumphant grin.

Minutes later, we were on stage. Beattie spoke to the band and again acted as conductor. But before she started, she nodded to me to do my introduction.

The hall was small compared to the cinema where I'd done a solo in London, but it was still intimidating. In the cinema, I couldn't see beyond the first couple of rows. Here I could see everyone. The drummer did a drum roll to get attention.

'Ladies and gentlemen,' I said. 'We're five members of the Bletchley Park Review team and we're here to sing a song to encourage you to come along to the review. It'll be songs, jokes and sketches. We'll be letting you know the date as soon as it's agreed. Thank you very much. We hope you'll sing along with us.'

It was a short speech, but frightening enough to make me need to undo my top button and loosen my tie. Beattie looked at the band-leader, clapped her hands, and pointed a finger at us in a 'go' gesture.

And we were off, supported by the band, who were brilliant and made us sound good. I soon thoroughly enjoyed performing. I knew I'd never forget that moment and that song as long as I lived. We got a massive round of applause and left the stage, laughing and joking. Grant danced with me twice, but danced with several other girls, too. I tried not to notice.

After the band played God Save the King, we all drifted outside. Grant had been walking next to me and kissed me goodbye on the cheek as we separated. I realised I had no idea where he lived. 'You fancy that Grant bloke, then?' Bronwyn said as we walked the short distance home.

'No, I...'

She laughed. 'You can't fool me, Lil. I've seen that look on your face before. Mind you, there'll be plenty of competition. Good job he's not my type.'

We hurried back to Happy Days, changed ready for our night shift, and got on our bikes.

CHAPTER SEVEN

The next time I had an eight til four shift, it coincided with a jumble sale I'd seen advertised. It was in the Women's Institute building, and I cycled as fast as I could, keen to see if there was anything left. The sale had started at two o'clock, so I wasn't very optimistic. Peggy had a day off and planned to go, but she'd have been long gone. She didn't seem to have much and I hope she'd got there early enough to find some good bargains.

Clothes rationing had been going for a while, and people, myself included, longed for something different to wear. I promised Bronwyn I'd look out for something for her too. We still hadn't been able to replace all the clothes we lost in the bombings.

The WI hall was still busy, and footsteps of hopeful bargain hunters shuffling around the bare floorboards echoed from the vaulted ceiling. At the far end was a table selling home-made jam, cakes and pickles. Above it was a picture of the King and a poster with the word 'Food' in big letters at the top. Underneath it said,

Buy it with thought
Cook it with care
Use less wheat and meat
Buy local foods
Serve just enough
Use what is left

After years of food rationing, I couldn't imagine anyone not following these guidelines.

I hurried to the table, but it was almost bare. One small jar of strawberry jam, one dismal wonky Victoria sponge cake and four parsnips were all that was left. I bought the lot and hurried back to the tables selling clothes. It's sad, but true, that jumble sales have their own smell. It's hard to describe, but the aroma of clothes that either hadn't been washed recently or had been stored with mothballs was distinctive. My nose wrinkled as I pulled out garment after garment. I wanted enough material out of whatever it was to make two dresses; one for me, and one for Bronwyn. Carolyn had more clothes than either of us had ever owned in our lives, so there was no need to consider her. I found a man's jacket with a hole under the arm and several buttons missing. The collar was quite worn too, but I knew I could alter it to make a short jacket. Then I found three dresses that had belonged to women a lot bigger than me. I got those as well as a decent petticoat I thought I could cut up to make undies. Using strong elastic, of course.

Then I spotted Peggy at the other end of the hall. She didn't see me and it surprised me to see she was looking at children's clothes. I went over and said hello. She jumped as if a starter pistol had gone off behind her.

'Oh, Lily, it's you. You frightened me.' She glanced at the little girl's dress she had in her hands and then back at me. 'These are for my friend in Bedford,' she said.

'I thought you said you didn't know anyone there.'

She went pink and avoided my eye by looking at the stall again. 'I meant she wasn't in on the day I went there.'

She got her purse out and paid for the things she'd picked, then hurried out. I stood looking after her, confused. She'd said before she didn't know anyone in Bedford. It was very odd, but I couldn't think of a sensible reason except I must have misunderstood. I turned and went back to looking for things to buy.

I'd missed the best bargains. The other things I got were old fashioned and not in great condition. One blouse had two buttons missing and a tear at the hem. Another had a collar so grubby I knew it would never come clean, and a flared skirt had a torn zip. It was way too big for me, but that didn't deter me. I knew I could mend little tears, remove collars and put in a new zip. I was itching to try out my new sewing machine, even if it was at least thirty years old.

I reached for a white cotton man's shirt and grasped it at the same time as someone else. Laughing, we both let go, apologising. It was a girl about my age. She had mid-brown hair tied up with a red and white spotted scarf and her red dress was well worn but she made the most of it with accessories. She already had three items over her arm, and she looked at my collection. 'Those don't look like they'd fit you. Are you shopping for someone else or will you alter them?' she asked.

'I'll alter them for me and a friend. Do you do dress-making?'

She held up the white shirt. It was a man's one and big. 'Yes, I thought I could cut this up and make a blouse for the summer. I'm Doreen, by the way.'

After a few minutes talk about dress-making, we chatted like old friends. 'Shall we get a cuppa?' she asked. 'I don't know many people round here. It'll be good to have someone to talk to.'

We spent most of the time in the cafe inspecting our finds and swapping sewing tips. 'Do you know how to turn a collar?' 'How do you cover buttons?' And a dozen other such questions. I was happy to offer her ideas, and she did the same for me. Then we turned to more personal matters, like where we came from. She said she was from the north of England, although I didn't recognise her accent.

'What's your job?' she asked, stirring her tea.

I gave the usual answer. 'I'm just a typist, up at Bletchley Park. Routine stuff.'

She still stirred her tea. 'Oh, I've heard of that place, but never understood what goes on there.'

I shrugged. 'It's just a communication centre, very low key.'

She looked up. 'There's a lot of people work there for something low key.'

I shrugged again, deciding to change the subject. 'Where do you work?' I asked.

'Here and there. I'm a restless soul. I get bored being in the same place for long. At the moment

I'm cleaning for my landlady in return for my rent. I live on Sherwood Drive.'

I was still learning my way round parts of the town, but remembered that was next to the railway line. 'Doesn't it get noisy with the trains at all hours?'

'I suppose it's like anything else, you get used to it.'

I nodded. 'You're right, our place are on a main road, but at least the bedroom is at the back.'

She gave me her address so we could drop each other a line and arrange to meet again. Although my digs had a phone, hers didn't.

When we separated, I was pleased to think I had a new friend, and someone I had something in common with. After saying goodbye to her, I stepped outside with my jumble haul and bumped into Carolyn. She wrinkled her nose at the jumble smell.

'You're going to be busy washing,' she said.

'I certainly am. You going anywhere in particular?'

'Not really, just out for a walk.'

We walked past a clothes shop. Like all the shops, it was difficult to see the display because of the criss-cross tapes on the window. Carolyn peered in and shook her head. 'Even my granny wouldn't be seen dead in the stuff they sell in there. This town's hopeless for shopping.'

We walked on further and went past a pawn-broker with the usual three brass balls over the doorway.

'I sometimes go in these shops,' Carolyn said, heading for the door. 'You occasionally find unusual antique jewellery that my grandmother would like. It solves the Christmas and birthday present problem.'

I'd never been inside a Pawnbroker's before, but I knew all about them. When me and my mum and dad lived in rooms in Coventry, a lot of our neighbours were poor. Really poor. They'd go off to the Pawnbrokers when they were broke with anything they thought they could borrow money on. I even saw one woman take her husband's winter coat. Anything to get money to put food on the table for the kids.

But sometimes people didn't have the cash to redeem their stuff and after a while it got sold. This shop was full of an amazing mix of stuff - cameras, clothes, a telescope, three long-necked vases, assorted shoes, and various tools.

'Come in, come in,' the man behind the counter said. 'Looking for anything in particular?'

Carolyn gave him one of her dazzling smiles.

She was dressed in a royal blue summer dress with a narrow skirt that showed off her long legs. A white cardigan was slung over her shoulders. I wished I had half her style.

'I'm just looking for jewellery. Something suitable for my grandmother.'

'Then you've come to the right place, that's for sure,' he said with a smile. The counter in front of him had a glass top displaying jewellery. Carolyn spent a minute or two looking at them, then shook her head and sighed. 'Nothing quite right, I'm afraid.' She made to turn away, but he stopped her.

'Hold your horses, Miss, that's not all of it. I've got two more tray fulls under the counter.'

Grunting with the effort, he pulled one out. It was three feet by about eighteen inches. Like the top display, the contents were divided into categories - necklaces, rings and so on. Within seconds, Carolyn gasped and reached forward. 'My bracelet!' she exclaimed.

I'd been looking at some cameras, wishing I had the money to buy one, and I rushed over to her.

'Look!' She held it up. 'This is definitely my bracelet.' She looked at the man. 'This was stolen from my room. Who bought it in?'

His smile turned to a frown. 'I hope you're not accusing me of receiving stolen goods, young lady.'

Carolyn narrowed her eyes. 'I'm not accusing you of anything, but I'm telling you someone stole this bracelet from me. From my room.'

He blustered and thrust his hands into his brown overall pockets. 'You must be mistaken, it's probably just like yours. Happens all the time.'

Carolyn pointed out a tiny mark on the outside of the bracelet. 'See this mark? That's identical to mine and I'm sure you'll agree that proves it. Now, who bought it in?'

He busied himself putting the tray away, avoiding her eye. 'I can't tell you that. What goes on between a pawnbroker and his customers is as secret as the confessional.'

Carolyn put her hands on her hips. 'You can either tell me now, or tell the police. Which is it to be?'

He went pale. 'Look, I'm no fence. I never take no stolen goods. I thought that bracelet was on the up-and-up or I wouldn't have taken it in.'

Carolyn tapped her toe. 'Who was it?' Her voice was sterner than I'd ever heard before.

He blustered again. 'Now look here ... '

'Just bloody tell me!' I'd never heard her swear before, and she looked ready to jump across the counter and grab him by the throat.

He backed up until he was against the wall behind him. 'Keep your hair on! Keep your hair on! I'll get my book if you stop shouting.' He turned to a cupboard to his right and took out a big green book that, when opened, was wider than it was long. He licked his thumb and flipped through the pages. 'Let me see, when was it...'

'Never mind the date, the deal number is here on the bracelet,' Carolyn said, thrusting it towards him. 'It's 658.'

He clenched his fist, but his shoulders sagged in defeat. He turned one more page and ran his finger down the lines. 'Here it is. A J. Watson bought it in. I don't remember him at all. Could have been a woman for all I know. Whatever. Whoever it was didn't come back.'

I whispered in Carolyn's ear. 'Watson. Maybe it's Wilson. Could be our landlord. Donnie.'

She turned to him again. 'Was it Mr Wilson from Happy Days Guest house? I bet you know him, everyone does.'

He caught his breath. 'No, it wasn't him, I'm sure it wasn't. He hasn't been in for ages.'

'Right,' Carolyn said. 'I'm going to the police station with this now. Do you want me to sign for it?'

'I want you to pay for it! What do you think I am, a charity?'

'A fence? Taking stolen goods? The police'll be interested in that.'

He gave the biggest sigh I'd ever heard and put his hands up as if he had a gun in his back. 'Okay, okay, you can take it away with you, but you gotta sign for it, and one way or another I want my money.'

He got a small notebook out of his cupboard and scribbled something on it. 'Sign here!' he said, his podgy finger leaving a damp mark on the paper.

She signed, spun on her heel, grabbed my arm and we left, slamming the door behind us.

Going into the police station reminded me of some trouble I'd had with a bloke some time before. They hadn't been very helpful. But that was in a different town, and this time the desk sergeant looked more businesslike.

He took the bracelet from Carolyn and turned it over. 'And you're absolutely sure it's yours?'

'I'm certain.'

He nodded. 'You'd better have a word with my boss.' He indicated some chairs in the waiting area. 'Sit there and I'll fetch him.'

Five minutes later, an older man came from a back room. 'Carolyn Mortimer? Come with me, please.'

He was whippet thin and tall, his uniform

trousers not quite reaching his shoes. He showed us into a small interview room.

'Please sit down,' he said. 'The desk sergeant has told me what's happened. May I see the bracelet in question?'

He inspected it. 'Hmm, excellent quality gold.' He cleared his throat. 'We know the pawnbroker who had this. He's not a crook, but he's perhaps not always as careful as he could be about checking the identity of the people he deals with. I expect this is what's happened here.'

Carolyn leaned forward. 'He said a J Watson bought it in and I wonder if it's Mr Wilson, our landlord at Happy Days Guest House. After all, it was stolen from my room.'

His head jerked up. 'That's interesting, very interesting. I'd like you to give us a statement, and we'll get one from the pawnbroker as well.'

'Do I have to give the statement now?' she asked.

'My colleague can take it now, or arrange a date and time that suits you.'

They kept the bracelet for evidence, so Carolyn wasn't likely to get it back in a hurry.

As we walked back to our digs, I said, 'It could be Donnie's brother, you know. He snoops around sometimes.'

She bit her lips. ‘I hadn’t thought of that. Still, I’m going to leave it to the police, there’s no way I can prove anything. Are you going to wash that stuff you got at the jumble sale? I can smell it from here.’

CHAPTER EIGHT

I saw Grant a couple of times in the tearoom before the Review meetings. He came over and chatted for a few minutes each time, seeking me out. I still wondered if I imagined there might be some spark between us. I certainly felt one. But he'd never behaved in any way I'd call romantic. Naturally, he was the first person I looked for when I went to the Review read-through.

I was thrilled when he came and sat next to me, but disappointed when Madge sat on the other side. As we waited for everyone else to arrive, she monopolised him, leaning towards him and touching his arm regularly.

George, who'd written the review, called us all to attention and explained what to do. It was quite simple because it was the first read-through, so no acting was expected.

'This is my first chance to check how the Review reads,' he said with a gentle smile. 'We can find out if the wording is too stiff or sloppy or just plain wrong. And if the jokes work, of course. So I'm expecting you to be honest about what you think.'

'How long is the Review?' I asked.

'About an hour and a half, longer if we get heaps of applause after each section. And we'll have a raffle in the interval, of course. They're always good for raising more money. Everyone agree?'

We all nodded. 'Although no acting is required, please try to say your lines as you would in the real thing if you can. Okay, let's get started. If you have a song to sing, just say the words now, and I'll teach you the music another time. We'll sing the songs we all know through once so I can work out timing. Oh, and I've added another song, Tommy Dorsey's 'When they ask about you.' We can't reproduce the Big Band Sound, but the audience will love it. I thought Lily and Grant could sing it.'

'Me?' I squeaked. 'Won't that mean sometimes I'll be singing and sometimes Grant?'

He nodded. 'That's right. You can do it! You've got a great voice.'

Grant smiled at me. 'Come on Lily, it'll be fun.'

Before I could respond, there was a huge thunderclap, and the room flashed bright with lightening. I looked out of the window to see rain pelted down. Big raindrops splashed off the roof of a car outside and dripped off leaves on the trees as if they were crying. The thunder and lightening came again, making us jump. I saw Madge pretend to be frightened and clutch Grant as if he could save her. I wanted to choke her.

George clapped his hands and shouted. 'We haven't got time for this to pass. We'll just have to carry on. Shout your lines if you have to.'

Several people hadn't had time to even read their parts, much less make a good fist of them.

Bronwyn had a cold, so she hadn't joined us, but I passed on the message that she was more interested in behind-the-scenes work. George was delighted. 'Just what we need,' he said, rubbing his hands together. 'Tell her to contact me as soon as she's better.'

As he spoke, Carolyn walked in. She smiled at me and gestured to George, who was in charge. 'Am I too late? I'd be thrilled to play piano if you haven't already got someone. I'm Carolyn, by the way. I house share with Lily. I'm sorry I haven't made it to other meetings.'

George looked delighted. 'Don't worry about that. It will be wonderful if you play the piano. Nigel was going to play as well as do stage management, but if you relieve him of that, he'll have less to cope with.' He turned to Nigel. 'Is that okay with you?'

'Terrific,' Nigel said, 'You go ahead. Makes things easier for me.'

She gave him one of her dazzling smiles and came to sit next to me. We'd all got away for the late afternoon get-together, so when we finished our session we headed to the Beer Hut.

For once, it wasn't too busy, because it wasn't between shifts. Peggy was behind the bar, polishing the top as if it hosted killer germs. She wore a low-cut blouse that showed off her curves to best effect, and a blue spotted scarf tied her bouncy curls back. As we walked in she looked up, gave a wide grin and shouted, ''ello, all, come on in!'

She got some glasses ready and began pouring a pint, confident that at least one of us would want beer. She leaned over to me. 'I'll slip you a packet of crisps,' she whispered.

I grabbed her arm. 'No, don't, I don't want you to get in trouble.'

'Nothing compared to what the others do,' she said with a raised eyebrow.

Madge, whose part in the review was even smaller than mine, grabbed Grant's arm. 'Come on, sweetheart, I'll buy you a drink for a change.'

Most of the conversation at first was about the read-through, but after a drink or two some people left and the rest of us split into three smaller groups. I was with Madge, Grant and a WAAF called Emily.

Emily took a long swig of her beer. 'Sorry if I haven't been on form tonight. My rotten boyfriend just dumped me.'

I put my hand on her arm. 'I'm just so sorry, that's horrible.'

She turned to me, fighting back tears. 'Has it happened to you?'

'No, but I was engaged once. What with the war and everything, we drifted apart.'

Grant looked at me. 'You never said. Did you find someone else then?'

'No, it wasn't that, just distance not making the heart grow fonder. He had someone else in mind, but was too honourable to ask her out while we were together.'

Emily sighed. 'Honesty, integrity, that's what I've got to look for in the next bloke.'

She turned to Grant. 'What about you? Do men have these problems, too?'

He laughed. 'I can't speak for all men. We're not all rotters, you know. I was engaged once...' He stopped. 'Anyone else fancy another round? My shout.'

As he walked to the bar, I watched his back, noticing his shoulders were tense. I wondered what happened about his engagement. Did she die? Run off with another man? I guessed they didn't drift apart like me and Edward did, or he'd surely be more willing to talk about it. Could what happened to his engagement explain why he was so reluctant to get close to anyone.

~

I tried to sleep after a night shift, but woke up far too soon. Giving up the attempt, I got up and made myself some tea and toast. I spread the toast with the usual fish paste and found a wrinkled tomato to slice on top. When I'd finished, I looked at the clock. Still hours until I had to leave for work again.

It was a nice day, so I went for a walk in the park. There was a light breeze flirting with the pink blossom on trees that lined the two major intersecting paths. An elderly couple walked arm in arm, holding each other close. Two boys walked with their dog, shouting 'Stop it, Rover! Bad boy!' They struggled to control the dog when it saw a squirrel. I reached an ornamental pond where the two paths met. Sparrows bathed in the elaborate fountain, chirruping as they hopped about, their song barely heard over the sound of the water.

My energy soon flagged, and I dropped onto a bench. My bag and gas mask slid off my shoulder and wobbled on the edge of the seat. I lunged for them and caught them just in time. After my lack of sleep, my eyelids burned. I shook myself upright and noticed a child feeding the ducks. He ran away screaming when they came towards him, hoping for more. His mum looked at me and we smiled in acknowledgement of his terrified reaction.

As I walked back, I saw Iris, who worked in my office. Even though we worked together, we got little chance to talk with Miss Abbott monitoring us non stop and not letting us have breaks at the same time.

'I'm so glad I've bumped into you,' she said. 'I had a thought about that bracelet that was stolen from your friend.'

My heart leapt. 'Do you know something about it?'

'Not as such, but I remembered that the family next door is very close to your landlady. And the lad, Timmy, he must be just a bit too young to call up. Well, he's got a reputation for being light-fingered.'

'So it could be him?'

She shrugged. 'I'm not making any accusations. But I wonder if your Mrs W gives his mum a spare key in case something happens and she's out. Possible.'

It gave me something to think about as I carried on walking home. I made myself a hot drink and read the script again, having resolved to tell Carolyn when I saw her. I fell asleep on the sofa half way through reading it, and when I woke up, Bronwyn was in one armchair looking through a magazine.

'You look like an angel when you're asleep,' she said. 'Shall we go to the chippie?'

I yawned and stretched. 'Yes, let's.'

The smell of vinegar drifted up from the newspaper, making my mouth water. If I kept eating chips at this rate, I thought, I'd have to be letting out my clothes.

~

Once again, Miss Abbott hadn't left us eight hours' worth of work. We both worked through what she had left, concentrating hard. Then I stood up and stretched my stiff shoulders.

'Do you mind if I go outside for a while to get some fresh air?' I asked. 'We can't both go at the same time in case someone brings some work in.'

'It's okay with me. I'll go now after,' she said in her confusing Welsh way.

It was about two o'clock in the morning, so I put on my coat and threw my blanket over my shoulders. To my amazement, I could see by the light of the moon that three or four other people were walking around the lake. The air smelled fresh, and I could just hear the footsteps of the others as they walked on the gravel. The only other sound was a faint whirring from one hut. I had no idea what that was about.

I began walking round and, to my surprise, I bumped into Grant. Literally. He was walking in the shadow of a shrub and I didn't see him, so I walked straight into him.

'I'm so sorry,' I said, feeling an absolute fool.

He held my arm to make sure I didn't fall over and then peered at me. 'Oh, it's you, Lily, what's a nice girl like you doing out at this time of night?'

'Hoping to bump into you!' I said, without thinking. I could have bitten my tongue off.

He laughed and linked his arm through mine. 'Well, bump into me you certainly did. Let's do one circuit of the lake, then I should get back.' He paused. 'I don't seem to know much about you. What did you do before you joined up?'

Maybe it was the dark, or the silky air, but I told him all about working in a shirt factory and then in the Picture House. 'And that's without all the excitement since I joined up.'

He pulled my arm to his side. 'You can tell me all about that another night. Well, as much as you can without giving away secrets. Do you like your work here?'

'It's pretty boring, to tell you the truth. I've worked in Paris for the British Expeditionary Force, so doing routine typing seems a bit of a comedown. I've let it be known I'd like to be a translator, but they didn't need any more French speakers.'

'Don't give up hope, Lily. Bletchley is expanding so fast, they may need more in the future.'

He stopped and looked around. 'Right, I'm back, and I'd better get into my hut. Let's meet at the same time tomorrow night. We can walk round and practice our song. By the end of the week we'll be perfect.'

My heart thudded so much it was difficult to speak. 'Same time tomorrow,' I finally said.

He squeezed my hand, ''Til then.' And he was gone. I stood for a minute watching him walk to his hut, then, light as air, I turned back towards the big house.

As soon as she saw me, Bronwyn knew something was up. 'You look like the cat that got the cream, all starry eyed!' she squealed. 'What's been happening out there? Whatever it is, I want some.'

I pretended to swoon. 'You'll never guess what. I bumped into Grant and strolled round the lake with him.'

'You what! Did he kiss you?'

'I wish. But he put my arm through his as we walked and said to meet him again same time tomorrow night. He's a good listener too, kept encouraging me to tell him about myself.'

'Can't be a real man then,' Bronwyn said, 'but I'm happy for you even if you did lie and say you weren't interested in him when I asked you.'

She put her coat on and draped her blanket as I had. 'I'm off to see if I can pick up a handsome man in the dark!'

Dead on the dot of two next night, I headed back to the lake and was delighted to see Grant standing waiting for me. 'Glad to see you remembered,' he said.

As if I'd forget.

He put my arm through his again. 'You mentioned last night you'd worked for the BEF in Paris. That must have been interesting.'

I told him how I'd discovered one of the other telephonists was a spy and how she'd killed herself by walking in front of a bus.

He clutched my hand. 'That must have been so awful.'

'It was. After living in London in the bombing, I got used to all sorts of deaths and injuries, but this was different because I knew her. Not only that, I liked her.'

We got to the section of lake where he had left the night before, but he kept walking. 'I've got time for one more circuit.'

'You keep asking me about myself, but I don't know anything about you.'

He was quiet. 'I'm not a very interesting person. I'd much rather hear about you.'

I tried asking in different ways, but he was very adept at bringing the subject back to me or talking in general terms about the war.

We walked round the lake once more, and I expected him to leave, but instead he said, 'Let's sing our song. I presume you know it.'

'I do, it's lovely, but I'm not sure I can sing it.'

He tucked my arm in his again. 'Come on, as we go we'll decide which of us will sing which bit and which we'll do together.'

We ended up going round the lake three more times, once almost tripping over a couple who were laying on the grass kissing. We had a lot of false starts with the song and we'd need plenty more practice, but I felt less panicky about it.

By the next night, our voices were firmer even though we sometimes forgot our words. By the third, we stopped occasionally to sway to the music together, followed by Grant twirling me round. The remaining nights we went over and over our routine. His hand in mine felt magical and went we swayed together, I was in his arms and wished it would last forever. Most nights we got a smattering of applause from other people walking in the dark.

But he never kissed me goodbye, not even a peck on the cheek. That didn't seem to tie up with being a Ladies' man. I tried to keep my feelings in check, but each time I saw him, my heart sang, and I spent too much time thinking about him in between our meetings.

CHAPTER NINE

Like all of us, Carolyn looked forward to getting letters from home. But this one was extra special and when she'd read it, she waved it around as if we could see what it said.

'Lily! Bronwyn!' Her eyes shone with excitement. 'Guess what! It's my birthday soon and my parents are planning to have a party for me. In London. At the Savoy! You will come, won't you?'

It wasn't really a question. Carolyn was used to getting her own way. It should have made her unlikeable, but somehow it didn't.

I remembered the few parties I'd been to. All modest affairs in someone's house to celebrate a birthday or anniversary. The food wasn't luxurious, but we had a good old knees-up. A party at the Savoy would be miles away from those.

I shook my head. 'I'd love to, but Carolyn, it will be a posh dress do, and I don't have anything like that.'

Bronwyn nodded. 'It sounds lush, but I don't have anything suitable to wear either.'

Carolyn came and sat on the arm of my chair. 'You've got to come. You and Bronwyn. There must be a way round it.'

As she spoke, the door opened and Mrs W came in, a cigarette hanging out of the corner of her mouth as usual. She looked from one to the other of us. 'What's up? You look like you've lost a pound and found ten bob.'

'Lily and Bronwyn need posh dresses for a party and they haven't got anything grand enough.'

'Even if I had enough clothing coupons, I couldn't use them on something I'd only use once,' I said.

Mrs W raised her eyebrows, and an inch of ash fell on the rug. She ground it in with her shoe. 'Keep the moths off,' she muttered. 'A posh party, then. Well, I never. Let me think. I always say where there's a will, there's a way.' She paused and bit her thumb, then she clapped her hands together. 'Got it! I've got some old dresses that belonged to my mother when she was a young wife. I never had the heart to throw them away. My granddad had the sort of job where they went to some grand events, so she had some long dresses.'

'But...'

She held up her hand. 'No buts! They'll be old-fashioned, but I've seen you on that sewing machine, Lily, and I reckon you could make something out of them. She was a fair bit bigger than you as she grew older, so lots of material. Want to come and have a look?' She took the cigarette out of her mouth and blinked as the smoke got in her eyes.

Carolyn nudged my arm. 'You'll do a wonderful job! We all have to make sacrifices while this wretched war is on. I'm not going to have a new gown. Mummy is getting her dressmaker to remodel the one I wore to a ball a couple of years ago and add some trimmings so it looks different.'

I tried to suppress a smile at her 'sacrifice' and we followed Mrs W to her bedroom. It was a little bigger than the room Bronwyn and I shared and decorated in a style that must have been fashionable when her mother was a young woman. The wallpaper was pale green with a pattern like long strands of leaves climbing up it. The double bed had a very elaborate velvet padded headboard in darker green and the blanket box at the bottom of the bed matched. The wardrobe and two dressing tables were all perfectly preserved and there was even a plant stand with an aspidistra in one corner.

Mrs W swept her arm wide as we looked at the room. 'Lovely, isn't it! I know it's like it's frozen in time, but it's not. I had it completely redone five years ago. I love this style.'

She walked to one of the wardrobes and started pushing clothes aside. She threw a very wrinkled dress on the bed, then reached under the wardrobe to a big cardboard box. There were three more dresses in there. We shook them and particles of white dust, probably talcum powder, drifted in the air. The dresses smelled faintly of mothballs. I gasped when I saw beyond the musty smell and wrinkles. They were from mid to late Victorian era and absolutely beautiful; like something you'd see in a museum.

Carolyn smiled. 'We've got old photos of my aunts wearing dresses just like these. They're fabulous.'

Mrs W ran her hands over the one nearest her. It was a pale lemon with a delicate sprig of flowers pattern. The neckline was scooped with three fabric flowers on one side. Sleeveless, ribbon bows sat on the shoulders. The bodice went down to an impossibly tiny waist. No way I'd ever get into it. Then it gently flared out again and even had a train adorned with more of the fabric flowers. It was lovely.

'Your grandmother must have had some very special events to go to,' I said in a hushed voice, in awe of the work the seamstress must have put into it.

Mrs W pulled her bright pink knitted cardigan closer round herself and gave a sad smile. 'She did. She was a debutant, you know.'

I frowned. 'What's one of those?'

'You must know, we still have them. They're girls who are presented to court. Their parents had to be well off, and they had to apply to the Lord Chamberlain to present their daughter or son to the King. It was a sort of marriage market, where people hoped to find a suitable partner for life. Rich partners, of course, preferably with a title.'

I picked up the dress and held it against myself. 'And your mother wore this? How can you consider letting me alter it? It has such a history.'

She shrugged. 'It's not doing much good where it is. But I have one request. When you've made yourself something and worn it to Carolyn's party, give me the dress back. And I'll want a photo of you wearing it, mind. I've got one of my mother in it somewhere and I'll put the two together. Same for you, Bronwyn, of course.'

I did something I never thought I'd do. I hugged her. She was stiff as a flagpole, and patted me on the back as if I were a child she was humouring.

'Come on,' she said, backing away. 'Good luck with it. I've got to go to the shops.'

I took the dresses into our bedroom and laid them out, trying to work out what I could do with them.

'Hey, Lil, look how the dresses get bigger. Must have been as she grew older.' Bronwyn ran her hand over the fabric. 'this one is so elegant. I wonder if you could just make it fit so one of us could wear it just as it is.'

I studied it with a fresh eye. 'It'd be different, that's for sure, but I like your idea.'

Carolyn nodded. 'That one, the blue one, would be stunning. It's vintage, but so classy.'

'You starting work on it now, Cariad?' Bronwyn asked, her eyes shining.

I looked at the time. 'No, we're on duty tonight, but we can get ourselves something to eat, then sit and unpick the ones we decide to use.'

'I'll leave you to it,' Carolyn replied. 'I'm going for a walk. Need some fresh air, and some more Craven As.'

Bronwyn and I went into the kitchen and got out our food.

'I've got some news,' Bronwyn said with a little smile.

I stopped chopping an onion and turned to her. 'What's that then? Got promotion already?'

'Better. I've got a date.'

I started chopping again. 'That's fantastic. It is someone from the Park?'

She grabbed another knife and began cutting up some carrots. 'No, but I met him there. He's a supplier. Supplies fruit and veg to the canteen.'

I laughed. 'I hope he doesn't know what a mess they make of his food.'

She chuckled and put the carrots in a pan. 'I'll have to ask him. We're going to a pub, then to the flicks. His name is Jim, and he's a bit of a looker.'

I stopped what I was doing. 'He's not married, is he?'

'I didn't ask, but he wasn't wearing a ring. Not that it means much. I'm guessing if he's willing to be seen in town, he must be free.' She paused for a minute. 'Unless he lives somewhere else, of course.'

We put a stew on to cook low and fetched the dresses. Then we went into the living room and started unpicking two of them.

Carolyn came back in from her walk, sat, and

got her packet of cigarettes out. 'You girls look busy. What are you doing with those dresses?'

'Unpicking them, so Lily can get to work on them,' Bronwyn said, waving her tiny scissors in the air.

I snipped a set of perfect pearl buttons off the back of one dress, and put them in an empty jam jar, 'Have you invited anyone else from the Park to your party, Carolyn?'

She blew one of her perfect smoke rings. 'Just a handful of people. I don't think they'll all come though.'

'Pity, we might have known someone. But perhaps I'll find myself a posh beau.'

'Lily's really trying to find out if Grant is coming,' Bronwyn said.

Carolyn looked up. 'I did ask him, but he said he'd be away.'

Bronwyn swore as she snipped a bit of fabric on a seam. 'Maybe I'll find someone better than a fruit and veg man.'

'Let me help unpick,' Carolyn said. 'My nanny used to show me how to cut up old sheets. She made hankies from some of the material and she taught me how to hem them. I even did a little embroidered flower on one corner!'

'You devil!' I said with a grin, 'Have you ever been a Deb?' I asked her.

She sat next to me and began unpicking the train of one of the dresses. 'I wasn't a Deb, but my older sister, Frances, was. Mummy was a Deb herself and she went crazy ordering new dresses, making the right contacts. She loved it, but Frances hated it, especially as Mummy was so set on finding a titled husband for her. But I remember her Deb dress, ivory with short sleeves and long gloves. And they had to wear three feathers in their hair when presented to royalty.'

'Feathers? That's just plain crazy. Did she snag herself a Duke?'

Her face dropped. 'No, but she got a Knight of the Realm, a Sir, not quite what mummy ordered, but good enough. Unfortunately, he was rather too fond of booze and gambling. And other women, of course.'

Bronwyn turned round the dress she was unpicking, looking at it this way and that. 'Poor sod. Not kidding nor nothing, but that Deb business sounds like a right fussy palaver. Round our way we meet our blokes down the pub.'

'Aren't you going to be a Deb, then?' I asked Carolyn.

She gave a harsh laugh. 'I am not. Mummy

went on and on at me, but I absolutely refused. I joined up to get away from it all. She was furious, she even threatened to cut me out of her will. Several of my friends are going to be Debs, though.'

Just then, a movement near the front window caught my eye. I looked up and frowned. 'Hey, look, there's a man going in the side door to Mrs W's place.'

They followed my gaze. 'Never seen him before, but he looked like Mr W, doesn't he? He might be Donnie's brother.'

I remembered Carolyn's missing bracelet and knickers and began to put two and two together. 'And I wonder if he's got a key to this place.'

Half an hour later, we went to check the stew and to make ourselves some tea. There, sitting at the kitchen table reading the racing pages of the Telegraph, was the man we saw earlier. He looked up and smiled, and his smile reminded me of someone I used to know who turned out to be a slimy crook.

'Hello, Girls,' he looked us up and down as he spoke. 'I 'eard Gladys 'ad some new talent, and she wasn't joking. I'm Ernie, Donald's brother.'

'Pleased to meet you,' I said, wishing he would go away. 'Excuse us. We're just getting a drink and checking our meal. We'll be out of your way in no time.'

He leaned back in his chair and put his hands behind his head. 'Don't 'urry on my account. I love 'aving a bit of girly company, me.'

'Well, don't get used to it,' Bronwyn said, turning to stir the stew.

'You work up at the Park then?' he asked. 'What do they do up there, anyway? No one ever says.'

'And we won't either, there's a war on in case you didn't know.' Carolyn said, not looking at him.

I shrugged. 'Careless talk costs lives as the posters always say.'

He got some American cigarettes out of his pocket and held them out for us. 'Fancy a ciggie? These are the real deal.'

'No thanks.'

We busied ourselves with our meal and tea and left the kitchen as quickly as we could.

'I wouldn't be surprised if he's our thief,' Carolyn said.

'Sure as day follows night, that man is a black marketeer,' Bronwyn said, balancing her cup on the arm of her chair. 'Wonder if he's got any stockings?'

CHAPTER TEN

'Have you thought about cutting it this way?'

Doreen, the girl I'd met at the jumble sale, was round at Happy Days having a sewing session with me. Her dress making ability was about the same as mine, but she had some different ideas and they were good ones. She was helping me decide how to remodel the dresses Mrs W had given me. They were already unpicked, so I was laying pattern pieces on them, seeing what fitted where. I'd found the patterns at the jumble sale too. They were very old-fashioned, but easily altered.

'Where do you come from?' she asked.

'A suburb of Oxford called Sunbury, but originally from Coventry. What about you? Have you got family?'

She took a pin out of her mouth. 'No, all alone in the world.'

I sat back on my heels. 'I'm so sorry, that must be hard.'

She bit her lip. 'It was at first, but you learn to live with what life throws at you. It makes you adaptable.'

'Can I ask questions or would you rather not talk about it?'

She looked at the pattern piece she'd picked up. 'I don't mind. Do you think this one would do for the back?' She folded one side over. 'You could have a low back dress. It would be very glamorous.'

I took the piece from her and studied it. 'You're right, that's a brilliant idea. Do you remember your parents?'

'Yes, thankfully I do, but they died in a car crash several years ago. I was an only child, so no brothers or sisters either.'

'That's tragic, poor you. It must have been awful.'

She turned another pattern piece this way and that. 'Mmm, it was. The end of my family life. How about this piece for the front?'

She stretched her arms. 'I need to go to the WC. Where is it?'

'Upstairs, first door on the right.'

When she left the room I decided to make a cuppa and while I was in the kitchen, Carolyn came in. We chatted for a few minutes as I made the tea, then I remembered Doreen.

'Oh, goodness, Doreen went upstairs to the WC a while ago. I haven't asked her if she'd like some tea.'

'She's probably back fitting pattern pieces from what you've said.'

She wasn't in the living room.

'I hope she's okay,' Carolyn said. 'Maybe she's ill.'

We went to the bottom of the stairs and I called up. 'Doreen, are you okay up there?'

I heard a drawer close and, to my amazement, we saw her coming out of my bedroom. She gave a little smile and walked towards the stairs.

'Wouldn't you know it, Aunt Rosie visited today and I was looking for a present for her. Have you got one I could have?'

I had no idea what she was talking about. 'Your aunt Rosie? Is she here? I haven't heard her come in.'

'You'll find what you need in the bathroom cabinet,' Carolyn said, and I turned to her in amazement.

'Why would there be something for Aunt Rosie in the bathroom cabinet?'

Carolyn grinned. 'It's a euphemism for a monthly.'

By now, Doreen had gone back into the bathroom and closed the door.

Carolyn paused for a minute. 'Strange though, I've only ever heard that expression…'

Before she finished what she was saying, the front door opened and Mrs W came in, very red and flustered.

'So glad you're home, Lily, I only forgot my blooming key, didn't I!' She held her cigarette so the smoke wouldn't go in my eyes and looked upstairs. 'Is there someone else here?'

'It's just my friend Doreen, using the bathroom.'

Mrs W flicked ash on the carpet again, her usual form of moth deterrent. 'Well, I hope she leaves it clean. Right, I'm off now, lots to do. See you later.'

Mr W, Donnie, was cleaning the outside of the kitchen windows. Within minutes, we could hear her telling him he'd missed this bit and that bit. I thought I heard a faint 'Yes, Dear, sorry Dear.'

Carolyn and I went back into the living room. 'Bit odd, Doreen poking around up there,' she said.

The living room door opened and Doreen reappeared. 'Thanks very much, Lily. I should have been better prepared.' She got down on the floor and began moving pattern pieces around again. 'Do you dress-make as well, Carolyn?'

'No, I can only just manage to sew on a button, but I like watching other people do it. Did you make the blouse you've got on?'

Doreen smiled. 'I'll tell you a secret. It was a man's shirt I got at the jumble sale. He must have been a big man, because there was plenty of fabric for someone my size.'

'Talk about make do and mend,' Carolyn said, admiration in her eyes. 'Who taught you to dress make?'

'I was in a boarding school for orphans. They thought it was very important that the girls learned practical skills.'

'Gosh, so much more practical than my school. Our head teacher thought learning languages was the be all and end all.'

I adjusted another pattern piece. 'I know you speak French and German, Carolyn. Do you speak any other language?'

She shook her head. 'That's enough to be getting on with.'

Doreen stopped what she was doing and looked up. 'Do you use your language skills in your job now?'

Carolyn opened her mouth to answer, then paused. 'I'm afraid I can't talk about my work. I'm sure you'll understand.'

CHAPTER ELEVEN

'Right,' said George, 'you know who you'll be with in each sketch and have a rough idea of your words. Is that okay?'

This was the latest rehearsal after a couple of weeks' gap. We were in the ballroom of the big house. It was mock Tudor with dark wooden beam criss-crossing the ceiling and eight chandeliers. The floor was wood and at one end was a set of windows, while on the longest wall was a pair of doors. It wasn't hard to imagine a ball being held there.

George clapped his hands. 'Attention, all of you!' He paused until we stopped chatting. 'As you know, the performance will be in the village hall in Bletchley. Unfortunately, we can't rehearse there yet because they have other things on. But look around...' he swept his arm to show where to look. 'See those markers on the floor? They show you the actual size of the stage, so when we're rehearsing in a minute, make sure you keep inside those parameters.'

Instinctively, we all shuffled outside the markers, leaving space for people to perform.

'As we go through the numbers, we'll need to place markers on the floor for where each of you will stand.' He flourished some sort of sticky paper.

He looked around at us performers. It was a title I was trying to fit on for size, performer. Me, a performer! There were a dozen of us, plus Bronwyn and Nigel, who were doing all the backstage stuff, and Carolyn as a pianist.

'Pity there's no proper spotlights!' Bronwyn moaned. Nigel was in charge of moving the props in between sketches where they were needed. I mentally went through the list of sketches and songs, hoping I'd remember what I had to do.

There was a jolly song to start with. We would all take part in that, including Bronwyn and Nigel. I tried to persuade her to do more, because her singing voice was pretty good and strangely, her Welsh accent wasn't noticeable at all when she sang. Not that it would matter. A couple of sketches came next. I was in one with Beattie, a second song, two comedy acts, another song, another sketch and then the grand finale musical number. So all in all, I was only in one sketch apart from a very tiny walk-on part in another where I only had to say three words. But I was doing that duo with Grant, 'Me and my girl' - a rather romantic song. We took alternative verses and ended up miming getting married. As we rehearsed, I kept getting the giggles. At first, Grant stared at me as if I was mad, but then he started laughing as well.

'Oh, for goodness' sake, you two!' George said with an edge in his voice. 'We'll get on with something else while you two get control of yourselves.'

'I'm going to get a glass of water,' I said. Embarrassment caused my giggles, and I knew I was red in the face. Grant made to follow me but Madge, rotten Madge, glared at me as if she smelled something long dead. She tugged at his arm.

'Come on, Grant, we need to practice our sketch.' She looked at me. 'You're not in it so you can go away.'

He laughed again, put his arm round her shoulder and walked off with her, leaving me to go to the kitchen area to get a drink. I leaned against the sink, all giggles gone. Bronwyn came over and put her arm through mine. 'Perhaps he's not for you, Cariad. Looks like he's one of those very polite blokes who never takes it any further. Plenty more fish in the sea. Now come on, back to work.'

Next it was my sketch, which was about sweet rationing. Me and Beattie were supposed to be old ladies moaning about not getting their favourite sweets. Although we'd had the script for a while, we all still held them in case we forgot our lines. I had to pretend to lift my bosom up with folded arms and say, 'And it's not fair on me and my Ernie. He likes a sweet before he gets frisky, you know what I mean.'

'No! Stop!' George shouted as I said the words. He was tugging at his hair. 'I know your line isn't funny. It's up to you to make it funny.'

I went cold, ashamed at my lack of skill. 'Um, how do I do that?'

He looked around. 'Anyone?'

Nigel spoke first. 'You try to look as if you think you're really important and sexy, and you could pretend you have no teeth.' He looked around, checking his suggestions were okay.

George smiled. 'That's the spirit, listen to what he said.'

It took me three attempts before George was happy with my line. If everyone was as slow as me, we'd be here practising for years.

As we went on, some people got it right first time, and others were as useless as me. But we all knew what to do to get better. What did go well was singing Chattanooga Cho Cho and the number Grant and I did. I swear he looked into my eyes as he sang as if I was something special.

We had to practice George's two songs several times, with Carolyn bashing away at the piano to help us. One song was funny, and one nostalgic. I was sure they'd go down well. Our final finale song was Flanagan and Allen's 'Are you having fun?' Everyone would know that and be able to sing along.

CHAPTER TWELVE

'Hey, you've been to the Savoy before, haven't you?' Bronwyn asked as we walked towards the hotel. I had, what seemed like a lifetime before. Edward, who had been my fiancé, bought me to the hotel for afternoon tea two or three times. It was such a contrast to Lyons Corner House, where I usually went, that I felt like a fish out of water each time. I was sure all the posh people would know I was just Lily Baker from a corporation house in Sunbury.

'Hmm, I hope I won't feel so uncomfortable this time,' I said, wrapping my coat tighter over my long dress. They didn't match at all, but it was the best I could manage.

'You know what my ma always says, "They've

all got bottoms the same as us."' Bronwyn laughed. 'Well, she didn't put it quite as politely as that.'

I smiled. My mum would say the same, but nonetheless she'd be scared to talk to anyone in any sort of authority.

'We're here. Come on, shoulders back and chin up!' Bronwyn said, obviously trying to convince herself. The hotel front had space for cars to drop people off. Many came in taxis, but the ones who came in their own cars handed their keys to the doorman for someone else to park it. All were treated like royalty.

Above the entrance was a huge sign saying SAVOY and on top of that, a gold statue of a medieval knight holding a jousting pole in one hand and a shield in the other. A uniformed man helped people out of cars, bowing each time. Even though we arrived on foot and must have looked a bit wind-swept, he held the hotel door open for us just the same as for the others.

We stopped halfway across the hall, 'This is lush,' Bronwyn said with a low whistle. 'Talk about luxury, and it's all spotless too.' I smiled as she ran her fingers along a side table, checking for dust. We handed our coats in at the cloakroom and held up our long dresses as we walked towards the ballroom where the party was being held. From the entrance lobby, we could hear a Big Band number being played.

Bronwyn nudged me. 'Right, we may not know many people, so it's up to us to introduce ourselves, or we'll be wall-flowers the whole night.'

But before we went in, we were dragged away by a photographer. 'This is your chance of a momentoe of this wonderful party.' He pushed us closer together. 'Now, smile Girls!' There was a flash, and he quickly pushed us to one side so he could photograph the next guests. His assistant took our details so the photo could be sent on to us.

'That'll cost an arm and a leg,' Bronwyn said, 'but we can give the photo to Mrs W for lending us the dresses.'

It did cost a fortune, and we had to hand the money over without even seeing if the photo was any good. 'But what if my eyes are closed or I look stupid?' Bronwyn asked, but she didn't get an answer.

Carolyn was at the door with her parents. Her hair was up in a fabulously elaborate style that must have taken a hairdresser ages. And her dress! It was straight off the cover of Vogue. I'd never seen anything like it in my life, and especially with clothes and fabric rationing. It was bright cherry red, with a fitted bodice and a very full skirt that swirled as she moved. What made it even more striking was huge puffy sleeves that came down to her elbows. Her lipstick was a perfect match and her earrings were diamonds. We'd been happy with our dresses until we saw hers. 'Lily! Bronwyn!' she cried, and would have hugged us if her skirt didn't stick out so much. 'Mummy, Daddy, this is Lily and Bronwyn who I share with. What a pity Peggy couldn't come,' she said. It was, she'd have loved every minute of seeing how the other half lived.

Carolyn's parents were very polite, but understandably too busy greeting other guests to give us much time.

Carolyn grabbed a man standing nearby. 'Jonathan, take care of my friends, will you? I've got to say hello to others.'

He smiled the sort of polite, upper-class smile I'd seen with some of Edward's friends. Edward's mother had a smile just like it, and she was a horrible person, but at least this man's smile reached his eyes.

He guided us towards a group of six people who were all holding champagne glasses and laughing at something one of them said.

'Gang!' Jonathan said. 'Quiet a minute, this is...'

He looked at us.

'Lily.'

'And Bronwyn. I'm the Welsh one.'

They raised their glasses. 'Welcome, come and join us.' As we moved nearer, a waitress appeared at our elbow holding a tray with champagne glasses. We took one each and soon began to feel more at home. The gang knew each other well, but were kind enough to try to involve us in their conversation.

Half an hour flew by, and then we heard a gong.

A man in an evening suit stood next to it. 'Ladies and gentlemen, your buffet is ready in the dining room. Please follow me.'

From the sumptuous spread laid out on several long tables around the room, you would never have known food rationing existed. There was a massive variety of breads, cold meats, pies, pates, fish, potatoes, and salads. My mouth watered just looking at it, and I wondered if I could slip some into my handbag for the next day.

'Hello, Ladies,' the voice made us jump. We turned and there was Nigel, the man who worked with Bronwyn backstage for the Review.

'Nigel!' she said. 'Wow, how come you're here?'

He grinned. 'Nice to see you too, Bronwyn. This is my sister Harriet, she's a good friend of Carolyn's and invited me to come with her. Harriet, this is Bronwyn and Lily. They are involved in the Review I told you about.'

When we'd met him at the Park, he was always dressed casually, but now in a dinner jacket and bow tie, he looked very distinguished. And rather handsome. Harriet wore an off-the-shoulder deep blue dress. It was figure-hugging, but flared at the bottom. She had a warm smile and was soon chatting about our dresses, asking where we'd bought them.

'We were given some very old ballgowns and I played around with them,' I said.

She gasped. 'You remodelled them and made these lovely gowns? You could make a living doing that!'

'That's what I keep telling her,' Bronwyn said, giving my shoulder a quick hug.

We'd been shuffling forward and reached the end of the nearest food table. Spoilt for choice, we picked up plates and began helping ourselves.

'This spread is tidy, I gotta say that,' said Bronwyn, helping herself to some salmon and beef. 'If my ma could see me now!'

'Do you know the law says no-one can spend more than five pounds on a meal in a restaurant?' Nigel said.

'Five pounds!' I gasped. 'I think I've overdone it if I spend one pound, no, ten shillings. But people who come here must order meals for more than that!'

Harriet looking up from choosing which salad to have. 'They get round it, of course, charge extra for things they usually include, like bread rolls. And the price of wine! I'm glad I'm not an alcoholic.'

We found a table near the double doors we'd come in. Like all the other tables, it was covered with a starched tablecloth so white they must have used gallons of bleach on it. Cutlery was already laid out, as well as linen napkins and condiments.

The noise level rose as people chatted, clinked glasses, and used their silverware. We learned a lot more about Nigel, not just from him, but from the little sister-like comments Harriet made.

The double doors opened once more, and three women took a couple of steps into the room. They were probably in their twenties and wore fur coats and hats. I assumed they'd arrived late and expected them to take off their coats and find a table.

But no.

Picking up a glass and fork from the nearest table, the tallest women tapped it to get attention. The room hushed and everyone turned towards the group.

They took off their coats.

But they weren't wearing ball gowns.

Far from it. Instead, they had posters over their everyday clothes. They held them up for all to see. They read:

RATIONS FOR THE RICH!

Then they chanted those for words over and over, getting louder and louder. They held their banner with one hand while shaking a fist with the other. One or two men seated at tables began to stand up, but most of us just sat and gawped at them open mouthed.

'Hear, hear!' Bronwyn shouted. There was a tiny smattering of applause, but I glanced around, and most people looked anything but happy. I even heard someone say 'String them up!' Suddenly, I hated being part of all this. I looked again at the expensive gowns, the glittering jewellery, the immaculate hairdos, the beautiful perfumes, and the opulent food, and had a bitter taste in my mouth. I doubted if any of them ever had to worry about paying bills or putting food on the table for their children. Yet here they were, disapproving of three women who had a very good point.

The protest didn't last long. The Maitre'd and two waiters hurried towards them, grabbed their arms and pulled them back into the hall.

There was no sound at all for a minute, then the dining room exploding with conversation. I looked at Nigel and Harriet, who hadn't said anything.

'What did you think of that?' I asked.

Nigel raised an eyebrow. 'I can't say I approve of that type of behaviour, but... well... you can see their point of view. There are better ways to go about it though.'

'Better ways that won't inconvenience you, you mean!' his sister said.

He went pink and picked at his napkin. 'Hmm, I suppose that does make me sound a bit selfish.'

She lightly stabbed his hand with her fork. 'Well then, think on that!'

Before they got too heated, a bell rang at the other end of the room and Carolyn's father stood up to speak. 'Well, that was unexpected, but I hope it doesn't stop you from enjoying your evening. I want to say a few words about my lovely daughter, Carolyn. Doesn't she look gorgeous?'

He went on to tell us a couple of funny stories about her childhood and how he hoped she would find a wonderful husband and give him and his wife several grandchildren to spoil.

'Carolyn's in no hurry for that,' I muttered to Bronwyn.

'Me neither,' she said.

When he'd finished, we got caught up in conversation with the other couple on our table. They were friends of Carolyn's parents. They asked where we worked and all we could say was Station X because the Park didn't seem to have any other name.

'But surely it can't be called Station X,' the woman said, putting down her knife and fork. 'You're making it up.'

'We're not, honestly,' Bronwyn said, but the woman didn't seem convinced.

As usual, we were vague when asked what we did, 'Just office work, nothing interesting.' That was the truth, but we still hoped in the great scheme of things it would help the war effort somehow.

By now, we'd finished eating, even getting through a mountain of delicious deserts and cakes. I could feel my stomach expanding by the minute.

The gong sounded and the Maitre'd called, 'Ladies and gentlemen, the ballroom awaits you!'

~

Feeling far too full for dancing, Bronwyn and I stood talking at the edge of the ballroom with a glass of wine. Nigel and his sister had drifted off to chat to friends, but we were quite happy on our own.

The band struck up a swing number, and the floor was quickly full of dancers. The glorious colours of the dresses swirled to the music and jewellery sparkled as the glitter ball twirled. Ten minutes later, Nigel came back and asked each of us to dance. He and I had a slower number, and he was good company, chatting about nothing in particular as he gently guided me round.

'I told Grant I was coming tonight, and he asked if you'd be here. When I said I thought you were, he said he was sorry he couldn't come.' His words made the evening even more special.

Studying the people around me, it was like I was in a different planet, but I couldn't deny I was enjoying the luxury, even if it did make me feel uncomfortable.

Then the air-raid siren screamed.

I tensed, ready to run, but to my surprise, most people ignored it. The number we'd been dancing to had just finished and the Maitre'd took the microphone from the singer.

'Ladies and Gentlemen,' he shouted over the siren noise, 'our very comfortable air raid shelter is in the basement. You are very welcome to use it, but if you choose to stay, the band will of course continue, as will waiter service.'

I expected a rush, but no. Only a few people headed towards the door.

I looked at Bronwyn and we nodded understanding. 'We're going down to the shelter, Nigel. Are you coming?'

He looked flustered. 'I... most people aren't... '

'Have you ever seen bombing?' I asked, picking up my bag.

He shook his head.

'Well, we have. A lot more than we'd want to remember. I'm not staying up here. Come with us or not, it's your choice.'

In the end, about twenty of us followed the waiters downstairs. My jaw dropped open when I saw what the basement was like. It was divided into three areas, each painted a different pastel colour. Each section had cubicles kitted out with narrow beds, complete with pristine matching bedding. Deck chairs and a variety of armchairs were scattered around too.

Bronwyn turned to me. 'Blimey, Lil, this is better than some of the places we've lived in!'

Nigel looked surprised at that comment, but followed us in to choose somewhere to sit.

Waiters hovered around, ready to take our food

orders. They were as calm as if nothing out of the way was happening. But that was probably true for them with the number of air raids they'd have worked through.

We read the small menu, but before we could give our order, there was a tremendous kerfuffle. Loud voices and the sound of running feet made us turn towards the door.

It was flung open and a crowd of people who were definitely not guests of Carolyn's ran into the room. They wore everyday clothes that showed they wouldn't be the Savoy's usual clientele either.

'Go on in, make yourselves comfortable!' A man in a cloth cap shouted from the doorway in an educated voice. Waiters paused, looking at each other, unsure what to do.

We'd already settled on a small group of chairs, and some of the newcomers joined us. ''Cor, love a duck. This is a bit of all right,' one of them said, taking off his hat and putting it on his knee. He looked at us. 'I'm Ted. You toffs from that do upstairs?' He shook hands vigorously with each of us.

It was understandable that he thought we were toffs when you looked at our clothes, but I couldn't bring myself to own to the name. 'I'm not a toff, but I was at the party. All three of us were.'

'How come you're all down here then, Boyo?' Bronwyn asked.

The woman with the man, poverty thin, looked up. Her coat was so threadbare it couldn't have kept her warm, even on a summer evening. 'We're with them Commies,' she nodded to the man who had called them in. 'They're trying to get the rotten government to do something about the shelters. 'ave you seen the state of 'em?'

Nigel looked blank, but Bronwyn and I had used them more than once and some of them were awful. Flooded, insanitary and overcrowded.

'Yes, we have... so...?' My question hung in the air.

'So, like I said, these Commies are tryin' to get the government to do somethin' about it, ain't they!'

'Yeah,' her husband said. 'They tried it with some other posh hotel, but the press didn't report it enough, so 'ere we are. Not complaining, mind.'

He sat back and folded his arms, looking like someone who's settled down for an evening in front of the fire. Not that there was one.

A waiter came over to us. 'Can I get you anything, Sir? Madam?'

The man's mouth fell open. 'You talking to us, mate?'

'Yes, Sir, all of you.'

'Well, in that case I'll have a pot of tea and a couple o' slices of bread and butter.'

'That'll be two and sixpence each.'

Ted stood up. 'What! 'Arf a crown for tea and a bit of bread. I should cocoa.'

He waved to the Communist leader. ''ere, Brian, this waiter says it's two and sixpence for a pot o' tea an' a bit o' bread an' butter.'

By now, we could hear heavy footsteps and loud voices upstairs, competing with the band and the siren.

Brian ignored the commotion and spoke to the waiter. 'We'll pay you what we pay in Lyons Corner House. Two pence for a pot of tea and two pence for a plate of bread and butter. Okay?'

The waiter's bottom lip trembled. 'One moment, Sir,' he said, and went over to two other waiters who looked as shocked as him. They had a lively conversation, but then walked away, looking surprisingly calm about it. I wondered if they were secretly pleased. After all, they probably came from similar backgrounds to the newcomers.

While they talked, I took in the room. Many of the party goers were looking either frightened of the newcomers or amused.

''Ave you been down one of them shelters,

then?' the lady, whose name was Annie, asked Nigel.

He shook his head. 'No, I don't live in London.'

'Well, let me tell you a thing or two. Them shelters is so bad that, d'you know what some people do?'

Nigel shook his head again. 'No, what do they do?'

'After work, no matter what the weather, some of 'em walk all the way to a bit of London what's not bombed and sleep under bridges and things. Then they 'ave to get up next morning and walk all the way back. What do you make of that, then?'

Nigel had gone pale. 'I had no idea, that's awful.'

'An' that's not all. Some people get a charabanc to the countryside and sleep in ditches! What do you think of that? The likes of you wouldn't 'ave to do that.'

He blinked hard. 'They sleep in ditches? Are you sure?'

'I'm bloody sure an' worse still, they get charged two and six for the ride! I ask you, 'alf a crown just to be dropped in a ditch.' She folded her arms over her skinny chest. 'Ought to be a law against it.'

Just then the law appeared. Four policemen

thundered down the stairs, truncheons raised. The Communist, Brian, and two of his colleagues stood in their way, rigid, refusing to move. To add to the confusion, the waiters appeared with trolleys of teapots and plates of bread and butter, and began handing them out and taking two pence for each item.

'And who might you be?' the lead policeman asked Brian in a loud, and very important voice.

'I'm a man of the people, here to protect the rights of these people to have a decent air raid shelter.'

The policeman smacked his palm with his truncheon. 'Well, they can't stay here. They have to leave. Now!'

A few of the newcomers began getting their coats on, but Brian held up his hand and stopped them. 'Stay just where you are. Enjoy your tea and bread while I sort this out.'

He turned back to the policeman. 'Now, I happen to know there are some gentlemen of the press upstairs. They've come to report on what's happening. I'm sure you wouldn't want to make women and children go out in the middle of an air raid, would you? It'd look very bad in the papers. Not good for the reputation of the force at all. Or the hotel.'

We watched the conversation going backwards and forwards like a tennis match. Brian kept calm, and all around us, people kept an eye on the police while they had their tea and bread.

After several minutes, the policeman gave in. 'I accept your point that the air raid is still going on, but I want everyone out of here as soon as the All Clear sounds. Got it?'

But the All Clear didn't sound.

Instead, there was the most almighty bang, and the building shook as if had been hit by a bomb.

It had.

~

Bronwyn and I had heaps of experience of bombing. We'd been bombed out of our homes twice, though luckily we weren't in either time. I'd been an Air Raid Warden, and she'd been an ambulance driver. We'd both been exposed to unbelievable horror that continued to haunt our dreams. But we'd never been inside a building when a bomb actually dropped on it.

There was silence inside the basement as we all looked around in fear, searching the ceiling for signs it would fall on us. Dust fell like motes in the sunlight, but the ceiling held fast. Two children cried, and some women sobbed quietly, and all at once there was lots of terrified chatter. Several people stood up, ready to run.

I got to my feet. 'STOP!' I held up my hand, my ARP training flooding back to me. The people who'd been about to run paused, looking at me for reassurance. 'We're safer here than upstairs or in any other shelters. It doesn't seem like a direct hit, so sit tight for a while until someone comes to get us or the All Clear sounds. This is the safest place.' I remained standing until everyone was sitting.

'Well done, Lil,' Bronwyn said when I joined her.

There was plenty of noise from elsewhere - bricks falling, people upstairs running, screams, yells, thuds and, thankfully, sirens from the emergency services.

'My boy!' one woman sobbed. 'What if 'e's been killed? We live near 'ere! I gotta go!'

I stood and put my hand on her arm. 'Stay here with Bronwyn, and I'll go to see if it's safe yet.'

The atmosphere is the room, already tense, became even more strained as every single person watched me walk to the door. My hands were clammy and my shoulders tight. I knew it was crazy to leave the basement with the bombing still on. My heart raced, and I had a sudden urge to empty my bladder. But people were depending on me, so I pushed myself forward, one heavy footstep in front of the other. I forced my legs up the stairs and took a deep breath as I looked at the door to the upper floor. It was painted blue and scratched around the handle. Attached to it was a poster of Churchill, planes overhead, saying 'We shall go forward.'

The handle squeaked as I turned it, and I pulled it tentatively as if a monster were on the other side.

Then, at that very moment, the All Clear sounded. My shoulders dropped and my cheeks relaxed.

But there was still the worry about damage to the building.

'Hang on, everyone, let me check it's safe,' I shouted.

The stairs to the basement were at the end of a corridor past the kitchen, so a little distance from the entrance hall. I walked a few steps and saw pandemonium. There was no major damage there, so the bomb must have fallen on another part of the building.

But party goers, no doubt afraid the roof would fall in, were frantically calling for their coats or taxis or their loved ones. I could see a crack in the ceiling, and as I watched, there was an ominous creak that made people stop and look up. Another crack, then one of the grand chandeliers crashed to the floor, making a tremendous noise. People scattered and one man fell, crashing into another, making him fall too. He swore and clutched his knee. Glass drops from the chandelier flew across the tiles, tripping people up and cutting women's ankles.

I looked through the front door and could see the Savoy sign had fallen to the floor, narrowly missing the line of taxis waiting for business.

Amazingly, the band was still playing. Just like the Titanic, I thought, but it was hard to recognise the tune over all the chaos.

I ran back to the basement, cursing my high-heeled shoes. Half way there I met people who were too impatient to wait for my say-so. I could hardly blame them. Some still clutched their bread and butter. 'Go ahead, get out as fast as you can!' I called. Soon I was struggling to get past them and back to Bronwyn and Nigel.

Bless their hearts, they were still in the same seats, waiting anxiously for me.

'Come on!' I said. 'Let's get out of here.'

We had to queue to get our coats despite the cloakroom being staffed by three times the usual number of people.

'I'm going with Carolyn when I find her,' Nigel said. 'Are you two okay for somewhere to stay?'

I nodded. 'Yes, we're all fixed up.'

'Got a place in a women's hostel, haven't we. We're all right,' Bronwyn said, tension beginning to leave her face.

As we spoke, firemen pushed their way into the hall, took one glance round and ran outside again. Two ARP wardens appeared and started to direct people, sounding as bossy as I used to.

Taxis came and went, two police cars and an ambulance arrived. Other ARP wardens were putting out fires caused by incendiary bombs.

'Like old times, isn't it.' Bronwyn said, putting her arm through mine. 'Think we should go and help?'

I looked down at our long dresses and silly shoes. 'I don't think we'd be much use. Anyway, it looks like the bomb only flattened a bit of the hotel.'

We managed to get past all the other guests pushing their way out, and crossed the road where we thought it would be safe.

'Shall we go straight to the hostel?' I asked. Nigel had already gone to find Carolyn and his sister.

Bronwyn blew air out of her cheeks. 'I don't know about you, Cariad, but I'm too wound up after all that to sleep. Shall we find a cafe open and get a cuppa?'

We felt a bit overdressed for the greasy Joe cafe we went to and we got a few sniggers. One man said, 'Slumming it, ain't you?'

'Tell you the truth,' Bronwyn said. 'I come from the slums. Don't judge a book by its cover!'

We got tea, strong enough to stand a spoon up in, and sat in the corner.

'Our clothes are going to smell of egg and chips,' I said, wondering if our lovely dresses would wash.

Bronwyn laughed. 'That's the least of our worries. Let's hope the hostel keeps the door open late and hasn't been bombed as well.'

'Poor Carolyn, this is one birthday she won't forget in a hurry.'

'You're not kidding. Protests for rations for the rich, a load of people gate crashing the air raid shelter, and then a bomb drops. You couldn't make it up!'

The hot tea almost burned our mouths as we sipped it. 'Do you ever wish we could do more at...' she looked around, 'that place where we work? Typing and clerical work has to be done, but surely we could do something more important.'

I thought back to the conversations I'd heard in the last few days. 'I did hear they might be looking for more French speakers. I don't know if our French is up to it though.'

Her eyes looked brighter at the news. 'Come on, we managed in France and we can learn more if we need to. Mind you, from what I've seen, most of those interpreters are like Carolyn - learned the language by living abroad or on skiing holidays with Mummy and Daddy.'

I blew my tea and sipped it again. 'Let's talk about it some more, and if we think it's a good idea, we can ask around.'

'Let's start now,' she said, 'from this minute on we speak to each other only in French until we get back to work.'

She looked at the menu. 'Je veux des œufs et des frites,' she said with a grin. 'If we're going to stink of egg and chips, we might as well eat them.'

So, despite stuffing ourselves silly in the hotel, we sat down to another meal and enjoyed it just as much.

CHAPTER THIRTEEN

I needed three outfits for the Review. The dance dress for the number with Grant. In another song I was a canteen worker because the song, not surprisingly, was about the awful food. That was an easy outfit to organise. Mrs W loaned me a wrap-around pinny. I planned to use one of the jumble sale dresses I hadn't altered yet underneath it and that, combined with rollers in my hair and a scarf over the top would do.

My other outfit needed more work, so my sewing machine was at the ready. It was mid-evening, and I'd soon have to close the blackout curtains so I could put on the light. Doreen has been round earlier for an hour with some hand-sewing, but said she had to get back to help her landlady prepare the meal.

I needed to dress up as a land girl for my sketch, so I was busy making some dungarees with a dyed sheet. I was threading my sewing machine when I saw Peggy walk towards the house. Her head was bowed and she was crying, her hair all over the place. She came in the house and rushed up to the bathroom, but I heard her sobs as she went.

She didn't come out for ages. I could hear her hiccuping sobs and water splashing, and stood outside unsure what to do. Should I knock and go in? It sounded as if she might be having a bath. After a few minutes, I tapped lightly.

'Arc you okay, Peggy?' I wasn't sure she'd hear me over her sobs.

'Go away!' she shouted.

I didn't. I had no idea what had upset her, but whatever it was, she seemed like she needed a shoulder to cry on. So I waited and waited. Eventually, I heard the bath water going down the drain and the toilet flush. Then the door was flung open, and she ran past me, wrapped in just a towel. She dashed into her room, but didn't close the door. I took that to mean she didn't want to be alone. I gently tapped on the open door and took a step inside. She was curled up in a ball on the bed, with only the bedspread over her. Her face was blotchy and red, and her blond curls stuck wetly around her face.

She didn't shout at me to leave, so I slowly moved towards the bed and knelt beside her.

'What is it, Love?' I asked, putting a hand on her arm.

My answer was another sob.

I waited without saying anything as she gradually stopped crying.

'What's happened, Sweetheart? Has someone died?'

She blew her nose and wiped her eyes, but wouldn't look at me.

'I... I... 'ad a date and…' She started sobbing again, so I gave her time, trying to ignore the fact that I'd have to be up sewing into the middle of the night to get those dungarees finished.

'What's happened, Peggy? You don't have to tell me if you'd rather not.'

She half glanced at me, and the pain in her face made my chest squeeze. I held out my hand, and she gripped it as if it was a lifeline.

Still looking down, she whispered, 'Shut the door, Lily.'

I did and came back to hold her hand again.

'I 'ad a date... it was the lad from the butchers' shop, Melvyn. 'e seemed okay. We...'

She stopped and buried her face in her hankie.

'But what about Ken?' I asked.

She dried her eyes. 'I think he's being unfaithful. I 'aven't dumped 'im yet, but this lad asked and I thought I might as well…'

I waited.

''e... We went to the pub and I only 'ad two halves of shandy so I wasn't drunk. 'e... 'e had three pints, but 'e seemed sober.'

I overheard Mrs W talking to the neighbour outside, something about how awful bread was these days, but I ignored their conversation. Peggy needed my full attention.

'What happened then?' I asked, tucking her curls behind one ear.

''e said "Let's go for a walk." It's nice tonight, so I thought it was a good idea. We could walk around the park and go to the river. But we went down a road I 'adn't been down before and, before I knew what was 'appening 'e pushed me into an alleyway between two 'ouses.'

My heart leapt, imagining what was coming.

'Did he...?'

She blew her nose again. ''e pushed me against the

wall. 'e's a lot bigger and stronger than me. ''e put 's 'and over me mouth and pushed against me. I couldn't move or even scream. I tried to bite 'is 'and or knee 'im in the you-know-what, but I just couldn't move.'

Her face crumpled, and she began sobbing again, but less violently this time. I waited. Outside, Mrs W was still comparing the prices of food with her neighbour, and I was glad Peggy was unaware of them.

'Did he...?' I asked in a whisper.

She shook her head, ''e would 'ave, that's for sure. 'e put his hand up my skirt right up to my knickers. Then... then someone came along. I don't know who 'e was, but 'e saw what was going on straight away. 'E shouted and ran towards us. Melvyn let me go and legged it fast as fast can be.' She had sat up as she spoke and I put my arm round her shoulder, feeling the sobs still moving her body.

She looked up at me. 'Did I do something wrong? Do I seem like that sort of girl? I like a laugh and a joke, but I never... well... 'e couldn't know.'

'Know what?' I asked, frowning.

'Nothing. Was it my fault, do you think? They says girls what get molested are asking for it.'

I pushed her away from me and held her by the shoulders, looking directly into her eyes.

'Let's get this straight, Peggy. It's not your fault. Get it? It's not your fault. It's his fault, the dirty bugger.'

She sniffed and wiped her nose. 'You're just saying that to be nice.'

I shook her shoulders just a bit. 'No, Peggy, I'm not. I'm saying it because it's true. It's all his fault, not yours.'

'I've 'ad a bath and washed and washed meself, but I still feel dirty, like I can feel 'is 'ands on me. I know I'm no innocent, but I've never 'ad anything like this happen before.'

My heart went out to her. 'Oh, Peggy, you didn't deserve this. You really didn't.'

She grasped my hand again. 'Lil, will you make me a cup of cocoa? I'll drink it and try to sleep.'

My steps heavy, I went to the kitchen and put some milk on to warm up. Mrs W walked in as I put the cocoa powder in the cup.

'Did I hear someone else come in?' she asked. 'I was talking to next door.'

I poured the milk into the cup. 'Yes, it was Peggy, but she's not feeling well. She asked me to make her some cocoa then she's having an early night.'

She reached for the biscuit tin. 'Go on, give her a biscuit as well. Make her feel better.' She pulled her cardigan closer round herself. 'I'm off now. Toodle pip!'

I went back upstairs to find Peggy in her nightie and a net on her curls. She took the cup from me. 'You're so kind, Lil. I dunno know what I'd've done without you.'

'Do you want the others to know?' It was an awkward question, but needed asking.

She bit her lips. 'Let me think about it. Don't tell 'em now.'

We sat in silence while she drank her cocoa. 'I'll try to sleep, Lil, thanks for being 'ere for me.'

I hugged her. 'Remember, the fault is all his. You're completely innocent.'

Outside, Mrs W was chatting to the neighbour again, this time comparing how useless their husbands were.

Next morning Bronwyn, Carolyn and I were eating toast in the kitchen when Peggy appeared. She had dark rings round her eyes, but looked fine apart from that. Without speaking, she put the kettle on.

'You okay, Cariad?' Bronwyn asked. 'Not like you to be quiet, even first thing in the morning. Proper chatterbox you are, usual like.'

Peggy topped up the teapot and sat down, looking up at me. ‘I’m going to tell 'em,’ she said, a tremble in her voice.

There was a long silence as the other two looked at her. Then Carolyn spoke. ‘Tell us what?’

‘You tell 'em,’ Peggy said, looking at me again.

‘Sure?’

She nodded, her bottom lip trembling.

I took a deep breath. ‘Last night Peggy had a date with the lad from the butchers’ shop. He pushed her into an alleyway and molested her. Luckily someone saw what was happening and saved her just in time.’

There were a few seconds of stunned silence. Bronwyn got up and hugged Peggy, who began to cry. ‘Oh, Peggy, that’s just awful, you poor thing.’

Carolyn reached over and touched Peggy’s hand. ‘Did you tell the police?’

Peggy shook her head. ‘No, they wouldn’t do anything.’

‘But surely...’ Carolyn began.

‘She’s right,’ Bronwyn said. ‘Worse happened to my friend, and they weren’t interested. It’s like they think all girls are gagging for it and leading boys on. In any case, it’d be Peggy’s word against his.’

‘But what about the man who saved her? Surely he’d be a good witness.’

Peggy bit her lip. ‘'e didn’t get a good look at 'im. ‘e told me that. ’e was very kind.’

Bronwyn sat down again and folded her arms. ‘Well, if the cops won’t do anything, why don’t we? Bet we can think of some way to make him pay. If he tried this on Peggy, you can bet your life he’s done worse with others. Probably will again unless he’s stopped.’

‘But what can we do?’ Carolyn said, frowning, ‘I don’t want to go to goal otherwise we could kill him.’

I looked at her in surprise. ‘Crikey, Carolyn, I didn’t know you were so violent.’

‘No more than he deserves!’

Peggy was listening to this closely. ‘I’d like to do something,’ she finally said. ‘We just need to think of the right thing.’

Bronwyn’s eyes sparkled at a memory and she gave a wicked smile. ‘I can tell you what I heard some girls did to a lad in Swansea.’

It was perfect, and we began to plan.

CHAPTER FOURTEEN

The officer sat at his desk and looked at us. 'So you want to be French translators. How much do you know about it?'

I blinked hard. 'Well, nothing really because no-one talks about their work, but we realize there are translators so we thought perhaps we could be of use. We've worked in France with the BEF.'

He shuffled some papers on his desk without looking at them. 'I'll look into it and you'll have to have a test to check your fluency.'

Bronwyn coughed. 'If we're nearly good enough, can we have a bit of training to get us up to scratch?'

He shook his head. 'I'm not sure. The officer who does the tests is away for a week. He'll be in touch to arrange an evaluation date when he gets back.'

~

We grabbed Carolyn when we were next at home at the same time. 'Carolyn, you're a translator, aren't you?'

She looked shocked. We never discussed our work. 'I'm afraid I can't tell you that. Why do you want to know?'

We were in the kitchen making our meal and I was peeling potatoes. 'We pay as much for the mud on these spuds as we do for the spud itself.' I muttered, scraping it off and turning the water in the bowl brown.

'Me and Bronwyn are applying to be French translators, but we're not sure we're up to it. Can you help us?'

She began laying the table. I'd never seen her cook. I don't believe she knew how. 'I suppose so, as long as I don't have to give away any secrets. I thought you lived in Paris for a while.'

Bronwyn stopped cutting up cabbage and looked at her. 'We did, but we've got a bit rusty and there's sure to be some words we don't know, anyway.'

Carolyn looked in the kitchen drawer-of-all-things and found a sheet of paper and a pencil. 'Right, what terms might you need?'

We looked blank. 'No idea,' I said, feeling stupid.

'Well, consider the job. What might any French communications be about during wartime?'

Bronwyn and I stopped what we were doing and sat opposite her.

'Something military, I suppose.'

She nodded, 'So... '

'Um... tanks, guns, troop movements...'

'Ships? Food? Casualties?'

Carolyn smiled. 'You're on the right line. Let's make a list of as many of those words as you can think of and I'll translate them for you. That's not giving away any secrets. And I suggest you go to the library and see if they have an English-French dictionary. And make sure we all speak French all the time between now and then. You'll be up to the mark in no time.'

We began immediately and ten minutes later Mrs W walked in and stopped suddenly just inside the door, glaring as she heard us speaking. 'What's all this then, what language is that? You three spies?'

Of course, we couldn't explain what it was all

about, so we pretended it was some sort of game to improve our French. 'Oh, that's okay, then, I thought it might be German.' She shrugged her shoulders and went out without another word.

'I meant to say,' Carolyn said, looking at me. 'I saw that friend of yours, Doreen. I went for a bike ride, and she was standing by the side of the road near RAF Cranfield. I said hello, but she either didn't hear me or pretended not to.'

I frowned. 'Perhaps she was waiting for someone, or a bus somewhere.'

'I didn't say but last time she was round here and you two were sewing, she waited until you were out of the room and then tried to get me to talk about our jobs. The way she asked put me on edge somehow.'

Ten days of speaking French non-stop at home meant we felt confident when we got called up for our tests, which were going to be one after the other. We didn't speak French when Peggy was home because she'd never learned it.

'Have you noticed she goes out once a week and never says where?' Carolyn asked one day when Peggy was out.

'I assume she goes to Bedford. I saw her getting off the bus once. She said she was sight-seeing, but then she said she had a friend there.'

We looked at each other. 'I wonder why she's being secretive?' Bronwyn said. 'Maybe she's carrying on with a married man.'

'Or robbing banks.'

'Or on the game. She's always broke.'

I laughed. 'She wouldn't be so broke if she was. She'd get plenty of customers, someone as pretty as her.'

We were no nearer unravelling her secret.

We were taken to one of the upstairs rooms in the big house for our translation tests. We knocked on the door and waited a minute before we heard 'Come in!'

To our surprise, our tester was none other than Grant. My stomach did a little flip at the sight of him, especially as he smiled warmly and held my eyes for a second longer than necessary.

'Ah, I should have recognised your names. Lily, Bronwyn. I can only check one of you at a time. It takes about half an hour. Who wants to go first?'

Bless her heart, Bronwyn immediately volunteered to wait, leaving me with Grant and his assistant.

'It's lovely to see you Lily, but I've got a packed day, so let's get straight on to it, shall we?' he said. 'There is a written vocabulary section, then I'll get you to listen to a recording in French and write down what you think they're saying. In English, of course.'

Wishing he wasn't a distraction, I took the first test from him and forced myself to concentrate. I had to guess a few words, but didn't think I'd done badly. I didn't appreciate how easy that was compared to what was to come.

He walked round the desk and put some headphones on me, brushing my shoulder with his hand. I tingled all over, even if it was probably an accident. Then he sat on the desk, ankles crossed in front of himself. 'This is a simulated recording of the type you'll have to listen to if you become a translator. It's scratchy and you won't be able to catch everything. Do your best.'

He put a pencil and pad in front of me and went to sit out of my line of sight. I was relieved because I had to listen to the recording with absolute single-mindedness. It was exhausting. The volume level went up and down and I wasn't used to the accent, which must have been from a different part of

France. Certainly not from Paris. Sometimes whole words were missing or impossible to guess or got scrambled by interference. I scribbled what I could make out as fast as I'd ever written anything. I found I could get the gist of the message which was about German troop movements, although I couldn't really have said more than that. When I finished, I sat back and looked at what I'd written and found I could guess one of the missing words. I wrote it down and turned to Grant. 'I've finished.'

He looked up from what he was doing and gave me that heart-melting smile I loved so much. Taking the paper from me, he glanced at it. 'It looks as if you've managed to write quite a bit.'

'Do I get the job, then?' I demanded, feeling very forward.

'I can't tell you that yet. I need to test your friend and then I'll look at the results.' He checked his diary. 'Come back at the same time tomorrow and I'll have the results then.'

~

Bronwyn and I returned next day towards the end of our shift. My mouth was dry, and I had butterflies in my stomach. I wasn't sure if it was because of the test results or seeing Grant again.

'Come in!' he called in response to our knock.

His assistant wasn't at her desk, and Grant was busy writing something in a large diary on his desk. He finished and sat back, smiling. 'I expect you girls are waiting for your results.'

He paused. We fidgeted.

'Okay, Boyo, did we pass?' Bronwyn said, trying to sound calm.

Grant tried to suppress a grin. He moved a couple of pieces of paper on his desk and found what he was looking for. He waved the papers around like a parent teasing a child. I reached for it, but he pulled it back. I growled.

'Okay, okay, I'm delighted to tell you you've both passed. Only just, mind you, but you'll get better quickly. I hope you're ready for the job, it'll require a lot more concentration than what you're currently doing.'

'When do we start?' I asked, excitement making me breathless. At last, doing something really useful.

'Tomorrow. I hate to leave Miss Abbott without two of her assistants, but our need is greater than hers, I'm afraid. On a different topic, have you remembered it's the dress rehearsal tonight?'

'Lily's been singing in the bath non-stop, practising her number. We'll be there.'

He nodded and looked at the clock on the wall. 'Well, there's only about an hour between the end of our shift and the rehearsal. What say we meet in the Beer Hut for some fortification?'

My heart leapt. I'd seen Grant at other rehearsals and he was always attentive, but not so much that I could make anything of it. With any luck, we wouldn't be too surrounded by people he knew in the hut.

'Not for me,' Bronwyn said. 'I've got some bits and pieces to do. I'll meet you at the rehearsal.'

It was still afternoon, and the days were getting longer. I stood for a few minutes watching the sunlight shining on the lake and stretched my arms up to the blue sky. It was only now, when my tension dropped, that I realised quite how much I wanted this change of job. I walked round the lake, my favourite part of the Park, and by the time I got back to the beer hut Grant was waiting outside for me, smoking and leaning against the wall. He could have been on holiday instead of working on highly secret stuff.

'Ah, there you are!' he said with a smile, then kissed me on my cheek very lightly. 'Glad you could come. We never get a chance to talk at rehearsals.'

I smiled. 'I guess we need some more moonlight rendezvous.'

'Mmm, that sounds ideal. Now let's go in so I can buy you a drink.'

Peggy was on duty. She gave me a big grin and pushed a tin in front of me. 'You'll be very pleased with me, Lil. I thought about what you said about the school needing money for books.' She rattled the tin. 'Beer costs eleven pence a pint, and most people give me a shilling. I ask 'em to put the penny change in the tin.' She glowed with pride at her initiative.

'Gosh, Peggy, that's brilliant. Do they usually give it?'

'They do. Some of the blokes what come in 'ere are loaded. So are some of the girls - got real plums in their mouths, they 'ave. Worked that out listening to 'em. You 'ear all sorts in 'ere.'

Grant fished in his pocket, took out a shilling, and put it in the tin. 'Here you go. It sounds like a very good cause.'

Without thinking, I stood on tip-toes and kissed him on the cheek. He grinned and asked me what I wanted to drink.

I opted for lemonade, too scared I'd forget my

lines if I had any alcohol. Or forget myself and kiss him again. Grant had a beer. He put the change from our drinks in the tin.

'Feeling ready for the rehearsal?' he asked with a smile.

'If I'm not ready now, I'll never be. I've read it through and practised it in my mind over and over again.'

He touched my arm. 'Don't worry, if you forget your lines, someone will prompt you. There isn't a performer in the world who hasn't died at some time.'

I took half a step back. 'Died? What do you mean?'

'Sorry, theatrical jargon. It means dried up. Forget your lines. But enough of that, what made you join up?'

I nudged him. 'I told you that on one of our lake walks.'

He nudged me back. 'So you did, but there must still be a lot about you I don't know.'

We'd walked back outside and stood against the side of the hut.

'I don't know anything about you,' I said.

He took a sip of his pint and wiped away the beer moustache. 'I told you, I'm boring.'

'I don't believe you,' I said. 'You must have

done something interesting. Spied for king and country, committed bigamy, murdered someone… And sometimes you work in a hut and sometimes in the big house. That's got to be unusual.'

He laughed. 'No, my life's been very boring. I've got a sister close in age to me who has a wonderful little girl, May. I go to see them every chance I get. That's about it.'

A group of drinkers laughing nearby stopped our conversation for a minute or two.

'Were you in Paris when the Nazis invaded?' he asked when we could hear each other.

I sighed and groaned. 'That's a very long story, and we should be with Bronwyn when I tell you. She was involved, too. Let's talk about something else. What do you want to do when the war ends?'

'I suppose it depends who wins the war. If we get invaded, who knows what life will be like.'

I blinked hard. 'Never say that! Churchill will never allow that to happen.'

He shrugged. 'I hope you're right.'

I went quiet for a minute, wondering if his job gave him some knowledge about how the war was going. More than we read in the papers.

The time flew past and as we left the hut to go to the rehearsal, I realised I didn't really know Grant any better than I had before. He had a way of giving me attention, but not disclosing much about himself, however hard I tried. I vowed that if we ever had a chat like that again, I'd ask him more direct questions.

As we walked towards the rehearsal room, he turned to me. 'I'm glad we'll be working in the same hut sometimes, Lily, even if it's not in the same room.'

It was strange seeing everyone at the dress rehearsal in different clothes. Like me, Beattie had a land girls' outfit on and a long gown for one of her numbers. Bronwyn and Nigel were behind the scenes. Carolyn was already seated at the piano wearing an elegant royal blue evening gown. Not even the same one she wore to her party.

There was a lot to remember - our lines, the timing, where to stand, how to act and goodness knows what else. I was glad I'd only had that lemonade. George had to correct us all a lot more times than I'd expected for a dress rehearsal.

'No, no, no! How many times do I have to tell you to stand here where the red dot is!' 'Keep upright while you're singing!' 'Pause after the punchline of your joke to give people time to laugh, don't go straight into the next joke!' And a hundred other instructions to get right. Inevitably, one or two things went wrong. Someone sat on a chair as part of their sketch and it collapsed under them, luckily doing no harm. A singer had a coughing fit in the middle of her number, and one of the few pieces of scenery fell over.

'How on earth will this all be okay next time?' I asked Grant when we'd finished.

He grinned. 'Trust the magic. It'll be alright on the night as they say.'

CHAPTER FIFTEEN

At eight o'clock sharp the next Monday morning, Bronwyn and I presented ourselves at our new workplace - one of the huts.

'This is a come-down after the big house,' Bronwyn said, and she was right. We'd already been warned the huts were freezing in winter and stifling in summer. They were really just big sheds.

We went to the first door on the left like we'd been told and stood in the doorway. Six girls were sitting in absolute silence, headsets clamped tight. Four were busy writing, but two didn't seem to have anything to do except twiddle knobs on their receiver and listen. I presumed they couldn't hear anything. They looked up and gave us a little wave.

'Are you Lily and Bronwyn?' A voice behind us said, making us jump.

'We are. I'm Bronwyn and this is Lily,' Bronwyn said. 'Are you our new boss?'

She signalled for us to leave the room and walked us down the corridor, looking for somewhere quiet. Most of the rooms were occupied by men in tweed jackets. Several men were smoking pipes. They were concentrating hard on whatever it was they were doing. In one room, four desks had been pushed together and three men and a woman studied a map spread over it.

'I'm Dorothy Johnson,' our new boss said. 'Most people call me Dot. We're pretty informal in this hut about that type of thing. Come in here and sit down while I explain what you'll be doing.'

There were three other desks in the room, and charts I didn't begin to understand on the walls. Dot sat behind a desk and told us to sit. 'You've just seen where you'll be working. I believe you've had two hours training on tuning in to messages?'

She looked at us for confirmation. 'You listen to messages from France and write down what you hear. You'll be with other girls who may be listening to a different language. Sometimes you won't hear anything, but you still have to keep searching on the tuners. You can't leave your station, but it'll give you some rest. This job is mentally exhausting. Is there anything else you want to know?'

I hesitated. 'What if we can't catch some words?'

'That's going to happen, and quite a lot. Leave a space and occasionally the rest of the message makes the missing word or number obvious. You do understand it might be numbers? And, don't expect to know the importance or otherwise of your message. You probably won't even understand what they mean. The messages get passed on to the brainy bods who collate them and try to make sense of them.'

'What about if we need to visit the WC?' I asked.

'Try to go in between messages if you can. Just do your very best. Remember, the lives of brave servicemen may depend on what you're doing.'

That was such a daunting thought. With my ARP work, I sort of had responsibility for people's lives when I got them safely to a shelter or got them to stick to the blackout. Even more responsibility if I was first on the scene after an accident or bombing and had to apply first aid. But this was different. My work could affect many lives. Perhaps changing jobs wasn't such a good idea after all.

Would I ever sleep at night wondering if I'd missed something important?

For the first morning, I was convinced I'd failed to make out more than half of what I heard. That's despite concentrating so hard I was sure I'd get deep frown marks. But by mid-afternoon I was doing better, although I could see other people, including Bronwyn, were writing more. Someone came round often to collect all our papers and took them goodness-knows-where.

At the end of our shift, at four o'clock, our replacements arrived and with no more than a quick greeting, took over our headsets. I stood up and stretched my back and shoulders. Joining Bronwyn and another girl, we left the hut.' I don't know about you,' I said, 'but I fancy a walk before getting on my bike. Anyone else?'

The other girl couldn't stop, so Bronwyn and I headed to the lake. It was a warm day for June. Wood anemones circled the trees like a fallen white skirt, and the young leaves in the trees waved us a greeting.

But that's not what got our attention. The sound of splashing and laughter made us look at the lake. To our amazement, there were men swimming in there. I couldn't believe my eyes. They didn't appear to have any swimming trunks on. Or anything else come to that.

'Well, I never,' Bronwyn said, pretending to peek through her fingers. 'There's a sight for sore eyes and no mistake. It's been a while since I've seen one of them.'

I giggled. 'I don't know where to look.'

Pretending we weren't looking, we carried on our walk, enjoying the fresh air after the closed in atmosphere in the hut.

'Good afternoon, Ladies!'

The voice made us jump.

It was Grant. 'May I escort you on your perambulations?'

'Get you,' I laughed, 'perambulations indeed. Think you're in a Jane Austen novel or something?'

He grinned and pushed his way between us, linking his arms through ours. 'It's only a couple of days 'til the Review. Are you feeling ready?'

We were interrupted by more shouting and splashing from the lake. 'Excuse me, I can resist anything but temptation,' Grant said with a grin. He stepped behind some bushes and the next minute he was jumping in the lake, naked as the day he was born.

Bronwyn nudged me. 'Well, there's a sneak preview of what you'd be getting if you and him get it together.'

I raised an eyebrow. 'That's not likely to happen. I heard he was a Ladies' man, but he seems more like someone who doesn't actually go out with anyone.'

Sidestepping some geese who were stretching their wings, we sat on the grass trying to avoid obviously looking at the men in the lake.

'How did your date with the fruit and veg man go? You never said.'

Shc pulled a face. 'He's a nice bloke and he'll make someone a good husband, but not me. No chemistry between us. Pity. It's not as if there's a lot of choice around here.'

'What about Nigel? You spend time with him getting stuff ready for the review.'

'Maybe. He seemed interested in you, to be honest, but he's being more attentive now. I'm going to ask him out.'

My jaw dropped open. 'You'll ask him! That's brave! I'd never have the nerve to do that.'

'Well, why don't you try it with Grant, then? One thing my granny used to say...'

'Your drunken wise old granny?'

'The very one. She wasn't all bad. Anyways, she said always ask yourself "what's the worst that can happen?" Seems to me the worst that can happen is we both get turned down for a date. We'll get over it. By the way, have you heard there's a rumour that there's a spy in the Park somewhere?'

I frowned. 'A spy? Here? Crikey, I hope not. I wonder how they'll check who it might be. No good just questioning everyone. Spies don't own up, do they?'

She plucked a blade of grass and rubbed it between her fingers. 'My guess is we'll never know. They'll be quietly checking up on us and our work. Still, not like we've got anything to worry about.'

I thought back over the last few days. 'I've noticed the atmosphere is slightly different in the canteen. Come to think of it, Peggy said the same about the beer hut. What a pity if we've all got to be wary of each other.'

Bronwyn shrugged. 'Tell you the truth, it's not that hard. It's not like we give anything away, anyway. Talking of Peggy, she seems to be back with that Ken. I don't know what it is about him, but I don't trust him somehow.'

I remembered when I'd seen him around the Park. Sometimes he'd stop for a quick chat, other times it was as if he'd never seen me in his life. And when he did speak, he often seemed to be checking out my body in a way that made me feel uncomfortable.

‘I’ve seen the way his eyes follow the girls around. A bit creepy somehow,’ I said.

Bronwyn shook her head. ‘Poor Peggy. It looks like she might have a bad 'un there.’

CHAPTER SIXTEEN

'So,' Bronwyn said, 'you all ready for our revenge for Peggy's attack?'

We all nodded, although I suspect Carolyn and Peggy felt as nervous as I did. Bronwyn carried on. 'I've got the date with Melvyn, the butcher's boy, the attacker, tonight. When I spoke to him, I wore a wig and put some powder on my face to make me look paler. He won't recognise me in the future.'

Thank goodness for the props we borrowed from the AmDram group.

Peggy's bottom lip trembled. 'Are we really gonna do this? Really? What if it doesn't work and 'e attacks you an' all?'

Bronwyn smiled. 'It's like this see, me and Lil

have had army training. We can look after ourselves.'

'But he's bigger than you.'

'And I'm more cunning. Anyways, it won't go wrong, we've got it planned exactly.'

Carolyn grimaced. 'Let's go over it again. I'm not used to this sort of thing.'

I laughed, 'You were for killing him!'

'Not seriously!'

Bronwyn clapped her hands. 'Stop squabbling, you two. Concentrate.' She opened up a bag and scattered the contents on her bed. We were in the bedroom because we didn't want Mrs W to hear us planning revenge. Mind you, she'd probably want to join in.

'So, I go with the scumbag Melvyn to the pub and you three follow me.' She picked up another wig I'd got from the AmDram props box. It was black. 'You wear this, Peggy, and put on your most boring clothes and no make-up. He'll never recognise you.'

Peggy put the wig on and we all laughed, it looked so unlike her. 'So we're following you... all in disguise...'

'But you mustn't drink alcohol. You all need to be on top form. Then you follow me and the ratbag...'

'And then comes the fun part,' I said, smiling.

It didn't quite go to plan. Disguised, we left home soon after Bronwyn intending to follow her to the pub, but Mrs W came out of a neighbour's house just as we went past. Bronwyn was now ahead of us.

'The very girls I want to see,' Mrs W said, then she took half a step back. 'Hang on, why are you all dressed up like that?'

I caught my breath. 'Rehearsal. I'm sorry, Mrs W, but we're in a hurry. We've need to catch up with Bronwyn.'

She looked around and turned back. 'She hasn't gone far, you'll soon catch her up. It's about what I charge for food...'

I hated to be rude, but couldn't stop. 'I'm really sorry, but we just have to go.'

'But, it won't take a minute!' she called after us.

'Tell us later!' I shouted.

Carolyn blew the tension out of her cheeks. 'Phew, let's hope we get no more hold ups. My nerves won't take it and I won't have Nanny to calm me down.'

I laughed and nudged her. 'You and your nanny. Most of us have to make do with a real one.'

'She was real!'

Most grannies weren't on staff, I wanted to say, but decided it was better to keep quiet.

Peggy dragged my arm. 'Come on, they're going in the pub.'

It was a different one from the one Melvyn had taken her to. 'I'll never go in that one again as long as I live,' she said with a shiver. She was bearing up well. She'd decided the horrible incident would not ruin her week, much less her life. Having a revenge plan helped a lot, too.

The White Horse Inn was a step up from the other pubs we'd been in. The bar was made of dark wood, as highly polished as the matching tables. A rail over it held sparkling beer glasses hanging from hooks, and above that, pictures of film stars of yesteryear. The carpet was a red pattern, and the colour matched the fabric on the stools. It smelled better than most pubs too, because the side door was open, letting in fresh air.

Bronwyn was sitting at a table while Melvyn was getting the drinks. She was wearing one of Peggy's low-cut blouses, and I saw her hitch her bosom up so more was exposed. She saw me looking and raised an eyebrow. We hid behind a group of four who were waiting to be served and watched what was going on.

Melvyn was at the bar buying their first round. Bronwyn asked for lemonade, but it horrified me to spot Melvyn order a vodka and poured it into her drink. He was careful to keep his back to her so she couldn't see what he was doing, the rat. I decided one wouldn't hurt her, but determined he wouldn't repeat that sneaky trick.

'Four lemonades, please,' I said when it was our turn.

Peggy's mouth turned down. 'By rights, I should pay for this, but I'm a bit boracic.'

We sat so her back was to Melvyn, just in case he recognised her despite the wig. Carolyn and I could see Bronwyn without much trouble. Waiting while they had their drinks was nerve-wracking. What if something went wrong and Bronwyn was assaulted? For all her brave talk of our army training, being up against someone a lot bigger and heavier was nothing to make light of.

Chatting when two of us were constantly looking over towards Bronwyn was difficult. Then I saw Melvyn doctor Bronwyn's drink a second time, and I had to take action.

Whispering to the others to tell them what I was going to do, I walked towards the Ladies', caught

Bronwyn's eye, and indicated to follow me. I must have only been in there a minute when she appeared.

'He's putting vodka in your drinks,' I said. 'You've already drunk one. Don't drink the second. We need you sober.'

Her eyes narrowed. 'I thought it tasted strange. The cunning rotter. I'll find a way round it. Leave it to me.'

I went back to our table ahead of her, giving the others a thumbs up. Two minutes later we heard glass smash and looked round. Bronwyn had 'accidentally' knocked her drink on the floor. We heard Melvyn trying to insist on buying another as a member of staff cleared up the mess. Bronwyn was having none of it and bought her own lemonade, giving us a quick smile. She drank it and acted slightly tipsy. I wondered if she should be onstage in the Review, not behind the scenes.

Melvyn encouraged her to have another drink, but I heard her saying she'd rather go for a walk. He shrugged, pushed his greased hair off his forehead, and pulled his jacket on.

We hurriedly finished our drinks and followed them out. The first thing Melvyn did was grab Bronwyn's hand and pull her arm through his, bumping her hip with his own.

As we watched, he attempted to get her to walk towards the alleyway where he'd attacked Peggy, but Bronwyn insisted on going towards the park. Occasionally, she glanced over her shoulder to make sure we were following. I lifted our bag of props to reassure her.

'I'm so scared.' Peggy said. 'What if we can't stop 'im?'

I was scared, too. Truth was, my hands were clammy.

Carolyn gave a little groan. 'Scared? I'm terrified! What if someone sees us?'

'We'll pretend it's all a game. We're girls, no-one will think we could attack a boy. Anyway, we're not going to hurt him.'

'Not his body, anyway.' she said. 'His ego is going to take a battering though.'

'Jolly good job, too,' I muttered.

We followed them round the park and then back to the road. It didn't take long before Melvyn guided Bronwyn into an alley. Breathless, we hurried to catch up with them.

They were the only people in the alleyway. From the corner where we hid, we could hear Melvyn attempting to persuade Bronwyn to kiss him. He was pushing her against the wall, and had one hand on her breast. She pushed his hand away, but he kept trying.

We tip-toed towards them as quietly as we could. True to plan, Bronwyn didn't look at us at all. If she had, she'd have given the game away. So Melvyn didn't hear us, and the first he knew was a gun poking him in the back. Hard.

'This is a gun. Keep still and you won't get hurt!' I said, doing my best to disguise my voice. He wasn't to know it was a world war one stage prop.

He froze, and Bronwyn pushed him away. 'You can't do this!' he shouted.

'Say another word and you'll get it!' I hissed in his ear as I pushed the gun even harder. I'd seen too many detective films.

Bronwyn yanked a dirty rag out of her pocket and stuffed it into his mouth. Then Carolyn, who was the tallest, tied an old scarf round his head to keep the rag in place.

He made as if he'd make a run for it, but I threatened him with the gun again. We'd practiced the next bit over and over, so we were sure we could get what we needed to do quickly.

In no time at all, the others had him bound as right as a chicken at Christmas. The rope cost a fair bit, but it was worth every penny. We tied his wrists together behind his back, his arms to his side, and his knees together.

'Will those ropes hold?' I wondered out loud.

'Trust me, I know ropes. I wasn't a Brownie leader for nothing,' Carolyn said.

A car backfired somewhere, and we all jumped, wide eyed, as if the police had blown a whistle in our ears.

Then came the pièce de résistance.

We pulled down his trousers and underpants.

'Yuk!' Bronwyn said, looking at his private bits. 'who'd want that? Call yourself a man?'

He tried to shout at her through his gag. Laughing, she pushed it further in his mouth.

We froze as a couple went by the end of the alley. I thought my heart would burst out of my chest. If they saw us, it would be hard to convince them it was all innocent fun. Struggling again, Melvyn tried to get their attention, but Bronwyn stood on his feet so he couldn't kick, and Carolyn pulled the gag tighter still. Thank goodness the couple didn't look down the alley and were soon gone.

We turned to Peggy. 'The last bit is for you.'

Peggy got a tiny bottle of black paint and a thin paintbrush out of her bag and, standing on tip-toe, wrote RAPIST in big letters on his forehead. All the time he was struggling and attempting to shout. She stepped back and grinned. 'Don't you dare molest any more girls, or we'll know and we'll cut off your bloody pecker and stuff it in your mouth!'

His eyes widened, he went pale, and his knees sagged a little.

There was one last thing. Tied up and with his trousers and pants round his ankles, we pushed him towards the street. He struggled some more, but we'd done too good a job for him to escape.

'Keep moving,' I said, prodding him in the back again with the pretend gun.

He could only do a penguin walk. It was likely nerves, but seeing that waddle seemed like the funniest thing we'd ever seen, and we all had to stifle our giggles.

When Melvyn got to the road, we prodded him until he stepped onto the pavement.

Then we high-tailed it as fast as we could the other way.

~

We sprinted into another pub, out of breath from running and laughing. 'His little winkie!' Carolyn said, doubling over.

'Winkie?' Bronwyn said, slapping her arm. 'how old are you then? How about prick, w...'

I stopped her. ‘Bronwyn, none of your Swansea slang here. Come on, let’s get ourselves a stiff drink. We deserve it.’

First, we hurried into the Ladies’, threw our wigs into a bag and changed our look. Then we each ordered our favourite drink. Carolyn insisted on buying Peggy’s.

We lifted our drinks. ‘To you, Peggy, and to revenge!’ Carolyn said, ‘I’d love to see Mummy’s face if she ever heard about this. She’d never speak to me again.’

We were high from our success and couldn’t stop talking, our words tumbling over each other. Thankfully, there was a noisy darts match at the other end of the bar that covered our conversation.

Five minutes later, the door was flung open, and a red faced man rushed in. His tie was crooked and his face was dripping with sweat.

‘You’ll never guess what!’ he shouted. ‘There’s only a bloke in the High Street all tied up like a Sunday roast.’ People turned to stare at him, open mouthed. He could barely speak for laughing. ‘It gets better. His trousers were down his ankles and his tiny little pecker there for everyone to see! Funniest thing I’ve seen in years.’

CHAPTER SEVENTEEN

Next time we were in the beer hut, luck favoured our goal to get a double date. Nigel and Grant were there, chatting about the review. They insisted on buying us drinks, and put their penny change in the book collection tin, earning a big smile from Peggy. There was talk about performing the review in Leighton Buzzard at a later date as well.

'I hope you'll be at the after-show party on Saturday night,' Nigel said, wiping his beer moustache away.

'Try to stop us!' Bronwyn replied. 'And while we're talking about going out, how's about us all going out for a meal one evening?'

'You mean a double date?' Grant asked.

She laughed. 'If you want to call it that. Up to you.' The tiny twitch on her cheek told me she wasn't as casual about it as she made out.

'Sounds like a great idea,' Nigel said. 'Okay with you, Grant?'

Grant nodded. 'How about tomorrow night? After that, we'll need our sleep if we're going to be at our best for the show.'

A few minutes later he went to the Gents' and Peggy called me aside, whispering, 'I 'eard you fixing a date with that Grant. He's a good 'un. I learn a lot about people 'ere and can weigh 'em up. You'll be alright with 'im. 'e's a looker, too. Hope you get lucky.'

Bronwyn and I were in the bedroom getting ready for our double date. 'You nervous?' I asked Bronwyn.

'Nah, I've got to know Nigel quite a bit. He's a nice bloke, even though there're no fireworks when I see him. But this is my chance to get him to see me in a different light. Maybe I'll see him in one too.' She paused. 'No sarky comments if I flirt, either!'

We wore the dresses I'd made with the things I

got at the jumble sale. Mine was pink with tiny green spots, and Bronwyn's was plain blue. Both had sweetheart necklines. Bronwyn looked at herself this way and that in the mirror. 'You'd never know this wasn't new. You're a genius, Lil, I look a million dollars.'

Neither of us had any decent stockings, so we drew lines up the back of our legs with eye pencils, and headed out the door. We were going to see a film first, then on to a restaurant.

I was thrilled when Grant sat next to me in the cinema. He smelled of Imperial Leather soap, and faintly of pipe tobacco. As we settled down to watch the beginning of the B film, a really corny horror, I wondered whether to act like Madge would have done. She'd have pretended to be terrified and clung on to Grant like a two-year-old. I considered it for two seconds, but couldn't bring myself to do it. Anyway, the door kept opening with late comers, ruining what tense moments there were. It squeaked and let in fresh cool air that helped clear the smoky atmosphere and broke any tension from the film.

The main film was a thriller, *Suspicion,* with Cary Grant and Joan Fontaine, and it had me on the edge of my seat. Would the Joan Fontaine character see through the wicked Cary Grant one, or would he succeed in murdering her? As always, there was a tall man in front of me. Grant saw me dodging my head from side to side, trying to see, and whispered to change seats. Our hands touched as we did, and I got that familiar tingle. I wished I could see if he had it, too. I wanted him to hold my hand or put his arm round me like blokes do in the pictures, but no such luck.

The more times I saw him, the more baffled I was. He always seemed pleased to see me, even seeking me out, yet he never took it a step further. I glanced over at Bronwyn and Nigel. They were holding hands, and I felt a pang of jealousy.

We were full of the excitement of the film as we left the cinema and headed to the little hotel nearby. Its restaurant was bright and cheerful, with gingham tablecloths in red, white, and blue. Grant held my chair out for me with a smile.

The menu was in French and I was ridiculously pleased that I could not only read it, but I'd had most of the meals when we were in Paris. I didn't think I could eat three courses, but chose from the four dishes on offer for a main course. I rejected the fish and chips, even with French names - we could have them any time. Instead, I chose Carre d'agneau de nouilles which I knew was lamb and noodles, a rare treat indeed. For dessert, I planned to have ice cream. At the bottom of the menu was the usual warning 'Only one dish of meat, game, fish, poultry or egg may be served at a meal.'

Nigel and Grant both spoke French too, but were keen to learn more about our time in Paris.

'What did you get up to there?' Nigel asked. He probably expected us to say we'd spent our spare time shopping or visiting museums.

'Bronwyn killed someone,' I said, aiming to shock them. It worked. They both looked at her with dropped jaws.

Nigel laughed and moved his chair further away from her. 'You didn't really, did you?'

Bronwyn gave me a death look, but before she could answer, the waiter came to take our orders. The men ordered the meals, and a bottle of wine, which still felt very sophisticated despite having it often in France.

'Come on, tell us all about it, Bronwyn,' Nigel said, 'or is Lily having us on?'

'Not telling a lie, nor nothing, but it was us or him. A German soldier. It's a long story, but we were running away from the invasion of Paris and came across him on a quiet road...'

'He had a gun,' I started.

She looked at me and shook her head. 'Is this my story or yours? As Lil said, he had a gun, and he was about to molest our friend. Then he'd probably have killed us all. He didn't see me creep up behind him. I whacked him with a branch of a tree. I didn't mean to kill him. I just thought if I could knock him out for a while we'd have a chance to escape. But he hit his head on a stone when he went down. Dead in a minute. Couldn't believe it.'

They sat back, stunned. 'I had no idea,' Grant said, looking at me. 'I assumed you had an easy time in Paris.'

'Most of the time it was great, but we uncovered a spy who worked with us, which was awful. Then getting to the coast when the Nazis marched into the city was a nightmare.'

Grant looked at me as if weighing me up. 'So you've found a spy and negotiated your way through enemy territory to escape.'

'Not just me. There were four of us.'

Bronwyn did indeed flirt with Nigel, who seemed to treat it as a joke. Grant was more serious. 'Forgive me if I'm not much fun. Lack of sleep again.'

The waiter appeared with our meals. He was well past retirement age with sparse grey hair, and a small saggy stomach that pushed his uniform maroon waistcoat forward.

'Excuse me,' he said, as he went to put Nigel's

plate in front of him. His hand shook, and he spilled a little gravy on the tablecloth.

Nigel turned on him, eyes blazing. 'Be more careful, damn you!' he said, moping up the tiny spill with his napkin, which he then thrust at the waiter. 'Bring me another napkin double quick.'

The rest of us were silent at this outburst, but he was oblivious. 'Now, what were we talking about? Oh yes, Paris. When I was there in '35...'

I decided I didn't need to hear his story and turned to Grant. 'I'd still like to know something about you. Just one thing. No, two.'

He gave a little sigh. 'What would you like to know?'

'Where do you come from?'

'I was born in Egypt, but I grew up in Kingston-upon-Thames with my very kind parents and my sister. It's a pleasant town close to London. You'd like it. Next!'

I blinked. 'Next question?'

He nodded. 'Yes, what else would you like to know?'

I'd have loved to ask him why he seemed to hold back from me, but I was too scared. A dozen other questions went through my mind, but eventually I asked, 'What is your greatest fear?'

He answered without hesitation. 'Being captured by the Nazis and tortured to death.'

My head jerked back. I hadn't expected that answer. 'But that's not likely to happen here, is it?'

He fiddled with his spoon and fork. 'Not in this country, no. Not unless we're invaded, and then who knows?'

He'd never told me what his job was, of course, but that didn't stop me wondering. A few times since we'd started at the Park, he'd vanished for a week or more. No-one asked why, and I'd assumed he had some leave or been to the London office. But what if he went to France? Would that be possible? If so, what could he do there?

Although much of what I heard on the headset at work made no real sense to me, I guessed some messages were from, or about, resistance workers. Maybe the numbers were co-ordinates for drops of people or supplies. But I was taking wild guesses, because I had no idea what they did at all. Whatever it was had to be dangerous. Was Grant's answer about the Nazis torturing him a sign that he was involved somehow?

CHAPTER EIGHTEEN

For days before the review, Bronwyn had helped me rehearse my lines and even sang with me. She twirled me around and stared into my eyes as she did so, pretending to be Grant, overacting so much we always collapsed in fits of giggles.

'Hey,' she suggested with a wicked grin. 'Why don't you kiss Grant at the end of your number? It might get him going.'

'I couldn't do that!' I said, feeling breathless at the idea.

She placed her hands on her hips. 'You're such a wimp! I'm not talking about a big, tongue and all, kiss. Just a quick peck on the mouth. The audience will love it!'

It did sound tempting. 'But what if he's horrified and backs away? That'll spoil the romantic ending.'

She scoffed. 'He won't do that. He may never make a move, but I've seen how he looks at you.'

My heart beat faster. 'Really? Have you? Does he?'

'He looks like he can't keep his hands off you, you daft thing. I wonder why he doesn't ask you out. Perhaps he's married.'

I gasped. 'Surely he can't be.' My stomach dropped to my feet. 'He doesn't wear a ring.'

'Loads of married men don't wear rings. Doesn't prove anything.'

'Do you think I should ask him?' The mere idea made me tremble.

She folded her arms. 'You could, but if he chooses to play away, he won't tell you the truth, will he? Anyway, it could be some other reason why he's keeping you at arms' length.'

I sat down on the armchair. 'I can't imagine what. Maybe he's been hurt in love and scared to try again. Will you go out with Nigel again?'

She sneered. 'I am not. He was rude to that waiter, and that's always a warning sign. If they're rude to waiters, they'll be rude to their wives once the honeymoon is over. Pity, but better to know now.'

We were interrupted by a shadow passing the window. It was Ernie, Donnie's brother, walking round to their flat. He had a bag over his shoulder that bounced as he strode along. 'If it was night time, I swear that bag would be full of nicked stuff,' Bronwyn said. 'I bet he's the local thief.'

I clapped my hands. 'Enough of him. Why else would Grant be holding back?'

'Hmm, let me see. Perhaps he knows he's being posted somewhere else and doesn't want to love you and leave you. Or he's got some incurable disease. Or he can't do you-know-what.'

She really wasn't helping. 'Come on,' I said, standing up, 'let's go to the British restaurant for a cuppa. My treat, I'll buy you a bun for helping me practice.'

We headed towards the restaurant where you could get a cup of tea and a bun for sixpence.

We hadn't gone a hundred yards before I heard a voice behind me. 'Hey, Miss! Miss! Miss Baker!'

I recognised that voice. It was Tommy, the lad I listened to reading.

'This is my mum,' he said proudly, pulling his mother's hand. 'Mum, this is the lady what listens to me reading. She says I'm doing good.'

His mother appeared worn out. Even with her bulging stomach, she was far too thin. I held out my hand. 'It's lovely to meet you, Mrs Gibson. Tommy talks about you all the time.'

She smiled. 'He talks about you as well. And his reading is coming on a treat. He still gets some words wrong though, don't you?' her tone was harsh with him.

I touched Tommy's shoulder. 'With the way he's getting better, you'll soon be very proud of him. And he's a lovely boy, a credit to you.'

'Excuse us, please,' she said, pulling Tommy towards her. 'We've got to be off. Thank you for what you do.'

We said goodbye and wandered on.

'Not kidding, that woman needs a long rest and a slap-up meal. Should we have suggested she come for a cuppa and a bun with us?'

We stopped to look either way before crossing the road. 'It's hard to know. Tommy always seems hungry. Each time I go, I take something for him to eat while we're together. I wonder what she'd say if I gave him some to take home.'

Bronwyn shrugged. 'Hard to say, Cariad. You can only try, but some people are right funny about taking charity. By the way, has Peggy said anything else about how her romance is going now they're back together?'

'She's mentioned it a bit, although she seems quite secretive about it. But he's around her so much it's like he doesn't want her out of his sight.'

'Perhaps he's head over heels in love,' Bronwyn said with a laugh. 'Seriously though, it's more like he wants to be in charge of everything she does. She's had to stop him getting on the bus when she goes to visit her sister in Bedford.'

We were on four til midnight that week, and two surprising things happened when we cycled back in the dark after our shift. Because of the blackout, the roads were dark and the shielded lights on cars and our bikes threw little light. Sometimes we'd spot a chink where someone hadn't pulled their blackout curtains right across, or the glow of a cigarette as someone walked to the pub or home. Mostly, we relied on the light from the stars or moon to help us find our way. That didn't work on cloudy nights, though.

On this particular night it wasn't a full moon, a bomber's moon, but it was almost full with only light cloud so we could tell where we were going. Carolyn, Bronwyn, and I had all fallen off our bikes in the dark more than once. Cycling down the dark country lanes, we heard an owl hooting, crickets sawing, and frogs croaking. Then we reached the outskirts of the town. Petrol rationing meant there were never many cars on the streets, and there were less at nighttime.

We paused at a junction to let a horse and cart go by, the clip-clop of the horse's hooves echoing in the empty streets. Then a movement caught my eye. A man was coming out of the side of a house without using a torch, as most people did.

'He looks dodgy,' I said, and they all followed where I was looking.

'That looks like Donnie's brother Ernie,' Bronwyn whispered. 'I'd recognise that walk anywhere.'

We stood where we were for a minute or two and watched him until he turned into a side street.

Then another bike passed by. A cloud moved away from the moon and there, clear as day, was Doreen cycling along as if her life depended on it. She didn't seem to notice us, probably because she was on the other side of the road.

'Wasn't that your friend Doreen?' Carolyn asked.

'It was. Blimey, if they'd come from the same direction, I'd think she and Ernie had a thing going. It's odd she's out this time of night.'

An owl hooted nearby, making us jump. 'I understood she had cleaning jobs. They're not usually at night. I wonder where she's been.'

I shook my head. 'Goodness knows. Perhaps she had a date.'

When we arrived at Happy Days, we pushed our bikes into the garden and went into the kitchen. I put some milk on to heat for our Ovaltine. 'Do you reckon Ernie was up to mischief?' I said, as the other two settled themselves in the chairs.

'It's hard to think of any other reason,' Carolyn said, combing the tangles out of her hair.

'I'm not sure about that,' Bronwyn said. 'He could be going out with a married woman, and had to sneak out before her old man came home.'

I grinned. 'Trust you to come up with a dirty idea!'

I heard the milk boil and hurriedly took the saucepan off the heat.

We sat unwinding as we drank our Ovaltine. We all found that after a stressful shift at work and the bike ride home, we were far too wide awake to go to sleep immediately.

'Do you think we could drop a hint to Mrs W that we saw him out late?' Carolyn asked.

'I'm not sure it would do any good,' I replied, getting up to wash my cup. 'She's going to defend him even if she believes us. And, let's face it, we could have been wrong.'

But then we heard the telltale sound of footsteps on the gravel at the side of the house, followed by the sound of their front door opening and closing.

We glanced at each other. 'Doesn't prove anything,' Bronwyn said. 'What we saw would never stand up in a court of law. I'm going to bed before I fall off this chair.'

The next week's local paper had more stories about robberies from local houses. But we couldn't prove it was Ernie who'd done them.

~

It was the big day. The Review.

The show started at seven, but we had to be at the village hall at five to make sure everything was in order. All the cast and backstage people were in their normal clothes, and laughing nervously at silly things. It was like no-one could remember how to be themselves. That was true for me too. We were all on stage, the old maroon velvet curtains closed, and it felt like a small exclusive club. We opened a side door to let some air in. It had been a hot day, and as evening approached, it was still warm enough to make the stage area muggy.

We prepared the stage for the first act and organised everything else for when it was needed. George had cleverly written sketches that needed little in the way of props, so it didn't take long.

The hall was ready with rows and rows of chairs. Peeking through the curtains made me nervous, despite the seats being empty. I gave myself a stern talking to. After all, I'd done a solo once in a picture house that held a lot more people. As I stood there, head through the curtains, Grant came up behind me and lay his hand on my shoulder.

'Feeling confident? Fancy a last-minute practice of our number?'

Of course I did.

There was no room on the stage, so we walked to the back of the hall. Carolyn hadn't arrived yet, so we had to make our own music with words.

The number started with me in his arms, and he held them out ready. I stepped into them, wishing I could stay there forever. But we sang, and we swayed, I whirled, we gazed into each other eyes at the right moment, and when the number finished Grant kissed my cheek. Maybe I could be brave and give him a peck on the lips on stage, I decided.

There was a tapping noise, and an elderly man we didn't recognise had his face pressed to the window. 'Well done!' he shouted and gave us the thumbs up sign. Our first audience member - he made us smile.

'I think we're ready as we'll ever be, and we'll wow them,' Grant said with a grin. He took my hand and led me back to the stage. 'Let's find out what everyone else is up to.' Sadly, he let go of my hand as we went up the steps to the stage and didn't hold it any longer.

Carolyn had arrived, and Bronwyn and Beattie made us all hot drinks and found some biscuits from somewhere. George lifted his cup. 'Here's to us and a great performance tonight!'

The hall filled up quickly, and backstage we could hear plenty of chatter from our audience. We knew it would be people from the Park and local people. George, who was stage manager as well as writer, had been very careful not to write anything that would give away the type of work we did. He did a last minute check everything was as it should be, then came round to speak to each of the performers, checking us off his list on his clipboard. It was only then he realised one of the cast was missing. A man called Archie, who was due to tell some jokes.

George glanced around wildly. 'Has anyone

seen Archie?' he asked. 'Where the heck is Archie?'

His question was soon answered. The external door, which we'd closed, swung open and crashed against the wall, making us all jump.

'Whashs 'appening, then?' A drunken voice said, loud enough to be heard by all. It was Archie, drunk as a Lord, his hair all over the place and a dirty mark on his jacket that might have been vomit.

He staggered over to George. 'Ish it time for me to go on yet?' he asked.

George's nostrils flared, and he grabbed Archie's arm roughly. 'Out!' he hissed. 'You are leaving now and don't come back!'

We all gaped in silence as he marched Archie to the door and forcibly threw him out. There was a brief pause, then we could hear Archie cursing as he picked himself up. I held my breath, wondering if he'd try to come in again. Thankfully, his voice got quieter and quieter as he staggered away, still muttering to himself.

George peered at his watch. 'Damn, we've only got five minutes to curtain up. Can anyone do his act?' He looked around. 'Anyone?'

'I can,' Bronwyn said, stepping forward. My jaw dropped open. I knew she was a talented story teller, mostly about the wrong-doings of people she knew in Swansea. She usually had us laughing.

'Quick, tell me one of his jokes,' George said.

She put her shoulders back. 'The train was full, and a German soldier, on leave, shared a compartment with an elderly lady, a beautiful French woman, and a young French man. The train entered a tunnel. It was too dark to see anything.

'A kiss was heard, then a hollow slap. When the train emerged from the tunnel, the German soldier was clutching his face. He had a horrible black eye.

"That's not fair," the German soldier thought. "The French man got the kiss, and I got the blame!"

"Well done, my girl!" the old lady thought. "You stood up to that brute!" The beautiful woman was puzzled. "Why would that German kiss that old lady?"

'The Frenchman, meanwhile, smiled, "How clever I am! I kiss the back of my hand, hit the German and no one suspected me!"'

Bronwyn paused for effect, then stepped back, looking smug. Her timing had been perfect. George leaned forward and kissed her. 'You're a star. Sure you remember them all?'

'I've heard them plenty at rehearsals,' Bronwyn said. 'Do I get the job?'

He hugged her. 'You certainly do!'

She still had to do backstage stuff with Nigel until it was her turn, though.

George looked yet again at his watch. 'Show-time, folks! Break a leg!'

Not daring to move, we all hid in the wings as he stepped in front of the curtains to introduce the show.

The audience hushed. 'Ladies and gentlemen, welcome to the latest Bletchley Park review. Thank you so much for coming this evening. As you may be aware, monies made this evening will be used for a very worthwhile cause. With advice from the Head Mistress, we'll be buying new books for the primary school. A superb cause. There will be buckets near the door when you leave in case you want to make any additional donations.

'We've got some great acts to keep you entertained, so I won't keep you waiting any longer. Curtains open please!'

I'd suggested giving the money to the school, but hadn't realised he'd taken me up on it. Tommy and his school friends would have a much bigger library in the future.

There was a drum roll, made by Nigel on an old tin tub, then Bronwyn opened the curtains. Considering we had had little time to rehearse, and the dress rehearsal was far from perfect, all went well. At least at first. The sketch I was in went like a dream and we got a lot of laughs, but the story was different when it came to my number with Grant. We stepped on stage as the music started and sang and swayed. Next was the part where Grant twirled me round, but at exactly that moment there was a loud noise outside and he jumped, taking a step forward. We were already near the edge of the stage and his movement meant that as I twirled I had one foot and leg hanging off the edge. My upper body leaned dangerously towards the front row.

The audience gasped. My hand was at the back of his waist, and as I swung round it slid down his arm and he caught me hand to hand, taking my full weight. He took my arm with his other hand and pulled me back onto the stage, getting a smattering of applause. The music continued. He nodded to me and we picked up where we should have been and tried to act as if nothing had happened, but my breathing was all haywire. I even forgot I was planning to give him a quick kiss. I didn't need to. He kissed me instead. On the lips. Briefly, but sufficient to get a cheer from the audience.

The after-show party was at the Green Man pub next to the canal. We had all mucked-in and cleared away everything in the village hall after the show, then strolled through the town. It was still light and there were plenty of people out walking their dogs or simply taking the evening air.

We were high on success after a standing ovation, and George glowed with happiness. Walking along the canal side, we sang songs from the Review, acting drunk despite having no alcohol yet. Even those people who didn't normally sing joined in, for once not too embarrassed about their voices being heard. Bronwyn and I walked arm in arm, skipping now and then like kids.

'You were brilliant tonight, Bronwyn. I'd never have been able to tell jokes that well without a load of practice.'

She grinned and pretended to polish her halo. 'Natural talent, that's what I've got.' She paused as she looked ahead. 'Hey, look,' she said, 'Grant's walking with that awful Madge. He should be with you.'

'I've noticed,' I said. 'But that's because she won't leave him alone. He's a grown man. He can get away from her if he wants to. Seems like he doesn't.'

We reached the pub and ordered our drinks. As well as local people, there were men from the RAF base at Cranfield nearby. A couple of them had been at the Review and kept telling us how much they'd enjoyed it.

But it was hot and stuffy in the bar, so we all went outside, enjoying watching the ducks and swans on the canal as we sipped our drinks. A spindly tree clung on in a crack on the opposite side, and below it was a smart house-boat decked in bright green and yellow.

George tapped his glass to get attention. 'Before we're all too squiffy to talk sense, I want to thank you all again for making this evening such a success. We raised a great amount for the school, and because it was Lily's idea, I'm asking her to present it to the head teacher.'

'Teacher's pet!' someone joked.

I laughed. 'I will be, that's for sure.'

Nigel began singing. 'For he's a jolly good fellow,' and before George could object, he was being lifted off his feet, still waving his beer glass around.

Grant came up to me, smiling, 'Well done, Lily, you've done something really useful for the school.'

He grabbed my arm and twirled me around as he had in our dance. 'Let me get you another drink. What would you like?'

He went back to the bar to get my order, and I continued chatting to Bronwyn and a couple of other people.

Then, as if out of nowhere, Madge sidled over to me and acted as if the others weren't there. She tossed back her hair and rocked on her heels. 'You see,' she said. 'He's got fed up talking to you already. I told you, he's mine. You may be able to dance with him when you got a chance. But that's all it was, only a dance. He was only acting. So you can leave him alone.'

'Hey!' Bronwyn said. 'Back off. You out of your tiny mind, or what? Leave Lil alone.'

Madge turned to her. 'You keep your stupid black nose out of it!'

Bronwyn gasped and drew back her fist. I thought she'd punch Madge in the nose, and no-one would have blamed her. But she took a deep breath, gritted her teeth, and lowered her arm.

Madge was out of her mind. And I was sick of her stupid attacks. Not to mention her being rude to Bronwyn.

I glared at her and, without thinking, stepped

forward and pretended to trip. Some of my beer went over her low-cut blouse and her bosom.

'Oh, so sorry...' I started to say, but didn't get any further.

She turned to me with fury in her eyes as she tried to wipe herself down.

'You bitch!' she hissed. Then, without warning, she strode forward and pushed me.

Into the canal.

My glass flew out of my grip, and I went under, swallowing a mouthful of dirty water. My first thought was I was going to drown. I opened my eyes, but the canal was so muddy I couldn't see anything beyond the dim light from above. Then I bobbed back up, coughing and spluttering. My hair clung to me and there was ringing in my ears. My skirt and shoes weighed me down. I could swim, but it was hard with that extra weight. I looked around, trying to work out where to swim to so I could climb out. The sides of the canal were too high for me to pull myself up.

Then I heard the loud splash nearby, and my head was drenched again.

It was Grant. He'd dived in to save me.

He came to the surface and swam towards me, only then realising I could swim too. Paddling to keep upright, he laughed. 'So much for me being your knight in shining armour!'

I swam over and kissed him right there in front of everyone. Not the best kiss. We were both kicking our legs to stay near each other, hair stuck to our heads, and aware of the smell from the canal. It was only a tentative kiss, but Grant put his arms round me and kissed me harder. My stomach contracted and my heart sang. Silly thing that I am, I hoped this kiss in the canal would be a story to tell our grandchildren.

Cheers and a loud round of applause from the others watching from the safety of the canal bank brought us to our senses.

'Put her down,' a voice shouted, 'you don't know where she's been.'

He laughed. 'Same place as me from the look of it.'

'Come on,' he said. 'Let's find the nearest steps and get out of here. It seems like there's no current worth speaking about.'

The steps were only about twenty yards away, thank goodness. Grant climbed them ahead of me and helped me up.

To my embarrassment, my clothes were clinging to me, and my white blouse had become almost transparent. If Grant noticed, he pretended not to. We weren't far from the rest of the group. Laughing, we stayed where we were and rung our clothes out as best we could.

We looked at each other and grinned. 'You look a sight!' he said.

'No more than you. What shall we do? Brave it out or call it a night?'

'Why don't we just sit here, and dangle our feet over the side of the canal? Our feet won't touch the water and we can dry off a bit.'

Of course, several people from our group came over and poked fun at us, but it was all in good humour. 'Take your shoes off,' Bronwyn joked. 'they'll dry off and we'll never smell your feet over the smell of the canal.'

We did, tipping what seemed like a pint of water out of each one.

Bronwyn squatted down beside me. 'Gotta say, Girl, you do get yourself in some scrapes.'

I laughed. 'No need for you to kill anyone with this one, though. Mind you, I thought Madge was a gonna there for a minute when she insulted you.'

Grant turned and looked at us as if he were weighing us up.

'What?' I asked. 'Why are you looking at us like that?'

He raised an eyebrow. 'I was just thinking what brave girls you are.'

Bronwyn pretended to show off her muscles. 'You have my upbringing, you learn to fight for yourself.'

I looked round. 'Where is Madge?' I asked.

George stepped forward. 'I saw what she did and I've sent her away with a flea in her ear. Told her we never want to see her again.'

'Gosh! I...'

I looked at Grant to see his reaction, but he just shrugged his shoulders and took a sip of the beer someone had put into his hand.

Suddenly I felt light and had butterflies in my stomach. Grant's reaction showed he didn't have any feelings for her after all.

After another drink, I shivered. My clothes were still damp, and I longed to soak in a bath and then get into bed.

'I'll head home now,' I said. 'Bronwyn, you don't need to come. I'll be fine.'

'If you're sure. I won't be long, just finish my drink here.'

Grant stood up, his clothes still wet and clinging to him. 'Come on, I'll walk with you, it's not far out of my way.'

If I was hoping for a romantic walk, I was to be

disappointed. Grant put my arm through his as we walked, but that was as close as we got. He kept the conversation light, mostly about the Review. You'd never have known we shared a passionate kiss in the water. When we got to my door, he turned to me. 'You're a very special girl,' he said, then kissed me on the cheek and wandered off with a cheery 'Goodbye.'

I stood, still dripping, and watched him walk away, baffled as ever about his feelings for me.

CHAPTER NINETEEN

It hadn't taken me long to get used to being a translator, and I soon got better at making sense of what I heard over my headset. But it needed constant concentration and I was always ready for a break to clear my head. Unless the weather was dreadful, I usually went for a walk - the fresh air was the best tonic. Added to that, the grounds and lake were always a pleasure, and sometimes I'd bump into people I knew for a chat.

But I wasn't expecting what I saw when I went to lunch one day.

There, standing in front of the lake, was Prime Minister Winston Churchill. He wore a black suit with a navy spotted bow tie and a Homburg hat. He held a fat cigar in one hand and waved it around as he spoke.

I thought I was hallucinating.

There was a small crowd listening to him, and I hurried over to hear what he had to say. Disappointed I'd missed the beginning, I heard him thanking us for all our hard work. He said he was certain it would bring the war to the end sooner than it would have done otherwise. It was a brief speech, but bucked us up no end. Churchill had come to visit us at Bletchley. A busy Prime Minister found time to thank us.

When he'd finished, he waved goodbye and climbed into a waiting car. Most of us stood and waved him off. Then I overheard two of the boffin types speaking. 'We need more people if we're going to win this war quickly,' one said. 'No harm writing to him,' the other one said. 'He's well disposed towards us.' Then they walked off, and I couldn't hear any more.

Only then did I realise Carolyn was among the other listeners. 'Well, that was unexpected,' she said. 'What a pity they didn't give us warning. I'm positive heaps more people would have loved to hear him.'

'I presume the more people that know, the more

his visit might get leaked out and someone might want to assassinate him.'

Her shoulders sagged. 'You're right, I hadn't thought of that. How ghastly, but if there are any spies here, I suppose it could happen. It doesn't bear thinking about. I'm going to the canteen, are you coming?'

'No, I'm having sandwiches today. Best of luck finding something worth eating.'

She laughed. 'I'll need luck. See you later.'

I rushed to my hut, longing to tell Bronwyn about Churchill. But she had her headset on and was busy scribbling away. Disappointed, I returned to the lake to eat my sandwiches. There was a watery sun, just enough to keep the chill off, and I sat on the grass enjoying being out of the hut. As I unwrapped my cheese sandwich, a man ran past me, his feet slapping the grass. A bird chirped in a nearby tree, and a fish jumped out of the lake, landing back in with a gentle splash. In the distance, I heard the sound of a cricket ball being hit and the occasional groan or cheer.

Sitting back, I reflected that Churchill's visit was a wonderful pick-me-up. It made me feel I was doing useful work for England to help stop the wretched war.

Armed with the money we'd raised at the Review, I knocked on the Head Mistress's door at Tommy's school.

She looked up and smiled as I went in. 'Hello, Lilly, come to hear Tommy read? You've done him the world of good listening to him. His teacher is very pleased with his progress.'

I stepped towards her desk and handed her an envelope. 'I have come to visit Tommy, but I wanted to give you this.'

She took it from me, looking puzzled.

'You probably know some of us from the Park had a review...' I began.

She nodded. 'I do, and I was very sorry to miss it. I heard it was excellent.'

She indicated to sit in the chair opposite her. 'So what's in this envelope?'

'It's the proceeds from the Review. It's customary to give them to charity, and I put in a word for your school library. So there it is!'

She tore open the envelope and her jaw dropped when she realised how much was inside. 'Miss Baker! Lily! This is wonderful. It will make such a difference for our pupils. I can't thank you enough.' Breathless, she came round the desk and gave me a massive bear hug. She was as soft as my grandmother, and smelled of lavender. Still smiling and clutching the envelope, she sat down again.

'Actually, there was an issue I needed to talk to you about. Do you have a minute? It's about Tommy.'

'Of course, I'm not at work today.'

She took a deep breath. 'We teachers hear a lot about our pupils' lives one way or another as you'd expect.'

I wondered what that had to do with me.

'I've been hearing about Tommy's home life,' she went on. 'You may know his mother is expecting a baby and has had several miscarriages. I've heard that she really needs total rest if that is not going to happen again.'

'So... is there anything I can do to help?' I expected her to ask me to do some shopping or cleaning, but no.

'As I was saying, she needs complete rest. She told one of the other mums that ideally Tommy would go and stay with her sister Jean, who lives on a farm in Essex. Trouble is, she has no-one to take him and she's not up to the journey. Between you and me, I doubt she has the train fare either.'

She paused, and I blinked hard, not understanding.

'So, would you be willing to take him? You know Tommy well, and I understand that as you are in the forces, you can get a free travel warrant so it wouldn't cost you anything but your time.'

She noticed me hesitate. 'Perhaps I shouldn't have asked. I'm sorry.'

A few days later, I stood at Tommy's front door, waiting for him to put on his coat.

'Are you certain you don't mind doing this? It's asking a lot of you,' his mother said. She was pale and her hair was limp and drab.

'I'm very happy to do it. I always enjoy seeing Tommy, and we can practice his reading on the journey. Does he know your sister?'

She sighed. 'He's only met her once, about a year ago when she came here because I lost... well, you understand. But she's got three children around Tommy's age, so I hope he'll be happy.'

Tommy came up behind her and wrapped his arms round her legs. 'I don't want to go, Mum. I want to stay with you. Don't make me go.'

She bent forward and gently unpeeled his arms. 'I know, Love, and I don't want you to go, but I'm not well and you'll have a lovely time with aunty

Jean. I told you, they live on a farm so you'll see sheep and cows and pigs and all sorts. You'll love it. Go on now, get your case and gas mask or you'll miss your train.'

His bottom lip trembled and tears rolled down his cheeks. She held out her arms, and he hurled himself into them for a goodbye hug and kiss. 'I know you'll be a big boy and do me proud,' she said. 'It's not for ever. You'll be home before you know it.'

I picked up his things and passed them to him. 'I've got a new book for you. It's about a dog who's a spy. We can read it on the train. I might even have a little something special for you to eat.'

'Sweeties?'

I ruffled his hair. 'That would be telling. You'll have to wait and see.'

I bid his mother farewell and took Tommy's hand. He held it, his gas mask on his other side. I picked up his cardboard suitcase, it didn't weigh much.

'You go in,' I mouthed to his mum.

'Right, off to the station, young man. Have you been on a train before?'

He swung my hand back and forwards. 'No. Is it big? Does it make a big noise? Will I be scared?'

The rest of the walk was filled with his lively

chatter about the journey. I knew it would be short lived, he'd miss his mother terribly, but I was glad he had something to look forward to.

As we neared the station, I looked back to where I thought Doreen's room must be. It was quite easy to work out because it was only the second house from the next street. My intention was just to wave to her. But what I saw surprised me. She was at the window, looking at the trains through binoculars.

'Hang on a minute,' I said to Tommy and watched her. She stopped regularly and looked down, apparently at her lap. I guessed she was writing. Puzzled, I took Tommy's hand again and continue into the station. Then I saw something I'd seen many times before but never taken much notice of - men standing on the bridge over the tracks writing down train numbers. I wasn't sure that was allowed in war time, but no-one seemed to stop them. Of course, I thought, Doreen must be a train spotter. They were usually men, but there was no reason why they had to be. She'd be able to see them with her binoculars.

As usual, there were men, and some women, in uniform, going in and out of the station. All had kitbags over their shoulders. When a rush of soldiers came through because a train had just arrived, I glanced up again at Doreen's window and saw she had moved her binoculars and was instead looking at the troops.

Tommy tugged at my hand. 'Miss, what did you buy me, Miss? Is it sweeties?' And with his question, the moment was gone.

He was excited and overwhelmed by the number of people waiting for the train; by the noisy announcements and the smoke from the engines. 'Cor, Miss, they're ginormus!' He was bouncing up and down, anxious to see everything.

We were lucky and got seats on the train straight away. 'We have to change trains in a while,' I said as we sat down.

He peered around, frowning. 'Why? Don't you like this one?' he said, making the woman opposite smile.

We settled down and he snuggled close to me. 'Do you think aunty Jean really has all them animals Mum said?'

'I'm sure she does. Your mum wouldn't say it if it wasn't true. What do you think you'll like best?'

Talking about the animals took ten minutes, and then I got out his new book. 'This is an adventure book about a dog who has to solve a mystery and find a thief. He's a spy.'

His eyes widened. 'Cor, that sounds smashing.

Some books they give me at school are a bit young for me 'cos I can read so good.'

'Go on, read the title,' I suggested.

With only a brief hesitation he did, and the woman opposite said, 'Very well done, young man.'

He gave her a shy smile. 'Miss helped me, I can read good now.' But for the first part of the journey, he was too engaged staring out of the window at the passing countryside. He regularly pointed, 'Look, tractor! Look, cow! I wonder if it's like aunty Jeans'? Look, some sheeps!'

After a while, he calmed down. 'Miss, I'm hungry. Are we there yet? Have you got any food?'

I got a pack of sandwiches out of my rucksack. 'We're not there yet. We have to go to London first, then get a different train.'

His eyes were enormous as saucers. 'London! Will we see any bombing? They said on Mum's radio there was heaps of bombing in London.'

I hoped to disappoint him.

There were the inevitable mysterious delays on the train and I was relieved I'd brought the book with me because Tommy got fed up with looking out of the window.

He read beautifully, only hesitating over a few unfamiliar words. 'Cor, that dog was clever, finding all that out. He was a spy, wasn't he? I read about them in my Rover comic.' He looked around and seemed to notice for the first time that I was in uniform. Usually I wore civvies when I visited his school.

'Are you a soldier, Miss?'

'I am, and look, there are three other soldiers in this carriage.' The men grinned at him.

'But she's a lady soldier,' one said. 'God bless 'em.'

'So are you all spies?' Tommy asked.

The men all shook their heads. 'No, we're just soldiers, we don't do anything so exciting.'

The corners of Tommy's mouth turned down.

'I found a spy once,' I said, 'a long way away.'

They were all looking at me, but of course I couldn't tell them any details even though it was in Paris and I couldn't see what harm it would do. Secrecy was drilled into me.

'Blimey, was he a dangerous spy?' Tommy wanted to know.

'It wasn't a man, it was a woman. I knew her and she was very nice.'

He laughed. 'Spies can't be nice, they're horrible. In my comic they're all big mean men with guns and things.'

One soldier spoke up. 'Some spies pretend to be nice to get information out of you. But you don't need to worry, fellow-me-lad. You'll never meet one.'

Tommy looked relieved. 'I suppose they won't want to know much about cows and sheeps, will they? I expect I'll be safe.'

'You definitely will.' I got the sweets out of my bag and his eyes lit up.

The train slowed and pulled into Euston Station. As we got off and walked towards the bus stop, Tommy was overwhelmed with everything he saw. The station had half the roof missing.

'Cor, Miss,' he said. 'Did a bomb do that?'

I nodded. 'Yes, that will be a bomb. The bombs ruin loads of places. We might see some more from the bus.'

I had to keep a tight hold on his hand because he pulled this way and that keen to see everything.

'Do you know,' I said, trying to keep his attention, 'some children came to this station to get away from London and all the bombing. They had to leave their mums behind and go to live with people they didn't know in the country where it was safe.'

He looked at me as if not sure whether to believe me. 'Not kidding? They left their mums just like me?'

'That's right. Their mums loved them so much they wanted them to be safe. Just like your mum.'

'I think we have some of them at my school, but we don't have bombs.' By now, he was pulling me towards the station exit.

'No, you don't, but you'll have a gorgeous time with your aunt Jean on the farm.'

As the bus took us towards Liverpool Street station and our train to Colchester, we passed several bomb sites. Tommy was almost jumping up and down in his seat with excitement at seeing it all. I was grateful there was no sign of very recent damage. I'd have hated him to see the dead and injured.

We were in plenty of time to get the second train and again were lucky to get seats easily. In the past, I'd always had so much trouble I was thinking Tommy was my good luck charm. To my relief, once the train started moving, he nodded off. I'd forgotten how tiring kids were when you look after them all day.

While he slept, I got to thinking about what the future held for me. I could keep doing what I was doing. It was important work, but I enjoyed performing and wondered if I could do more of that. We'd already decided to go to an ENSA concert coming up. The Entertainments National Service Association was sometimes known as Every Night Something Awful, but their shows cheered up the troops in the UK and elsewhere. Another thing to think about.

My breathing slowed and my last thought before I nodded off was I'd ask Grant if he knew anything about it.

We had to get a third train, a local one, from Colchester to Debden where Jean lived. It was a short journey, and she was there to greet us. She looked like a better fed version of Tommy's mum, soft and cuddly. She gave Tommy a big hug and turned to me.

'Would you like to come to the farm? I'd like to give you a cuppa and some cake after your journey.'

I was tempted, but a look at the station clock told me to resist. 'I'd love to, but I'd better get back. Journeys take so long now. Tommy has been an angel all the time, and he'll have a lot to tell you about.'

She smiled and ruffled Tommy's hair. 'If you're sure. Thanks again for bringing him. We'll take excellent care of him.'

Tommy was already chatting, asking her about animals and tractors.

His aunt frowned. 'How come you sound like you come from London, young man?'

He looked blank, but I smiled. 'Some of the

kids at school are evacuees from London, and they try to copy the accent!'

With that, I said a sad farewell to Tommy, then his aunt led him off to her battered car. It was hard not to shed a tear as I waited for my train back, but I was happy he was going somewhere where he'd be cared for. And I hoped his mother would have her baby safely this time.

CHAPTER TWENTY

Bronwyn, Carolyn and I were getting our breakfast prior to an eight o'clock shift. Peggy was still in bed.

'Does Peggy still see that boy?' Carolyn asked, getting out cups and saucers.

Bronwyn nodded. 'She told me she does, and I sometimes see them around the Park when she's about to go on duty. I expect they can't go out much because she works most evenings.'

'And she goes to Bedford on her day off, don't forget,' I chipped in.

Bronwyn took the boiled eggs off the heat, put them in egg-cups and smashed their heads in. 'I think that's a mystery, visiting her sister every week. Do you think she's got another bloke in Bedford or something?'

'No, I haven't,' Peggy said, making us all jump. We hadn't heard her come downstairs. I felt my face go red with embarrassment.

I stood and went over to her. 'I'm very sorry, Peggy, we're not being nasty. It's just that you're such a lovely chatty person, but you never let on a thing about what happens in Bedford.'

Before she answered, there was a strong smell of burning toast, and Bronwyn jumped up to retrieve it. 'I'll give it a good scrape,' she muttered, going over to the sink.

'You don't have to tell us anything you don't want to, dear,' Carolyn said to Peggy.

Peggy's face dropped, and she sighed heavily before sitting down with us. 'Make us a cuppa, Bron, while you're up, will ya?' she asked, over the noise of the toast being scraped.

There was an awkward silence while Bronwyn finished with the toast and poured some tea for her. She had a sip as if it would give her strength for her story.

'It's like this, see,' she looked at us, 'you gotta give me your word you won't repeat any of what I'm gonna tell you.'

She looked at each of us, and we nodded.

'Cross your 'eart and 'ope to die?' she said, staring at at each of us.

We nodded again.

'When I go to Bedford, I go to see my sister, that's true. But… she's not the only one. She's married, and she's got two kids and… well… one of 'em's mine.'

There was a stunned silence.

'How do you mean, one of them's yours?' Carolyn said.

Sometimes her naivety was amazing.

Peggy frowned. 'She's mine, my little girl.'

'Oh, Peggy,' I said. 'It must break your heart not being with her.'

She pulled out her hankie and wiped her eyes. 'It does. Thing is, I was only fifteen when I 'ad her. Old story, boyfriend ran a mile when 'e found out and me dad threw me out. Worse still, me mum didn't stand up for me and I 'appen to know she was up the duff when they got 'itched. Bloody 'ypocrite! I'll never speak to 'em again as long as I live.'

Bronwyn handed her a slice of toast. 'Not being funny nor nothing, but I've heard that story so often in Swansea. Wicked, it is. Them lads need their bits cut off.'

I lay my hand on Peggy's arm. 'So your sister is

looking after your daughter. Does your little girl know she's yours?'

She shook her head. 'No, we decided it was best if she thinks me sister is her mum. Lucky 'er 'ubby's a good bloke. 'E loves kids so 'e's okay with it all. My little one calls 'em Mum and Dad, and she thinks I'm her auntie.'

She absentmindedly looked for the margarine and marmalade, which were slightly out of reach. 'You must've noticed I've never got a penny to spare. Now you know why. I give my sister as much as I can every week. It's the least I can do.'

'That's such a sad tale,' Carolyn said. 'In my circle at home, if a girl gets in the family way, she gets packed off somewhere abroad and the baby is usually adopted. I'm not sure they ever get over it. Actually, one friend of my mother's went away as well, and they came back pretending the baby was the mother's. No-one would have known, although I always thought it sad the little lad didn't look like any of them. I never found out who the father was.'

'How on earth did you know about it?' I asked.

'It was my friend. I was her confidante. Does your boyfriend know about your child?'

Peggy shook her head. 'I don't know if I should tell 'im. You know what blokes are like. They all want to be the first you do it with. Even though they want to have done it with other girls.'

Bronwyn gave a low whistle. 'So you're not going to tell him? That's tricky.'

'Lots of girls do it. I wouldn't be the first. And I think 'e might be going to propose. I'd have to decide whether to tell 'im then, I suppose.'

I noticed the time. 'Oh, Peggy, this is awful, but we'll have to go or we'll be late for work. I'm so sorry. Perhaps we can talk about this later.'

She bit into her toast. 'Go on, you go. I'll be okay now. I feel better now I've told you.'

The three of us cycled along the country roads to the Park, unable to talk more about Peggy's child because the lanes weren't wide enough to ride three abreast. It was a lovely early morning ride with the sun up, but not yet hot. Grass and wild flowers grew on the road's shoulder and ditches. A barbed wire fence leaned at a crazy angle and a stone post told us we had a mile to go was nearly lost in the weeds. We whizzed past crows sitting on a wooden fence and cows happily munching grass in the field behind them.

My morning was routine, although the tension

of getting the messages just right meant I never relaxed. Instead, I sat listening through the headset, shoulders raised and back rigid. No wonder I always stretched when I stood up.

That lunchtime, Bronwyn finished the same time as me for a midday break. The sun was high in the sky, so we took our sandwiches to the lake. Once we got to the grass, we took off our shoes with a relieved sigh. 'That grass is so cool on my feet after that stuffy hut,' I said, wriggling my toes. Faintly, we caught the inevitable smell of cabbage from the canteen and, nearer, the smell of algae on the lake.

We sat on the grass and unwrapped our sandwiches. I had to keep pushing my hair behind my ears as the welcome breeze blew it about. We sat contentedly eating and chatting about nothing in particular when,

'I've got you now, you bitch!'

I spun round, and there was Madge. At first I didn't see what was in her hand because the sun was in my eyes.

It was a bottle of ink.

Before I had a chance to move, she flung it all over me.

'Serves you bloody right!' she screamed, and smacked me round the head.

My head jerked back and I let out a squeal, holding my hand out to ward her off. Breathless, I struggled to get to my feet, but Bronwyn was there before me. She shoved Madge away, the ink bottle falling to the grass, staining it black.

'Bugger off, you nutter!' she shouted, shoving her again. Madge's arms windmilled as she struggled to stay upright.

By now I was standing, but we weren't alone. People nearby had seen what happened and rushed to help. Two men grabbed Madge, one on either side and, without a word, marched her off to the big house. Her feet barely touched the ground.

'Where are they taking her?' I asked, trying to wipe ink off myself.

No-one seemed to know, but a kind WREN dipped her hankie in the lake and handed it to me to clean myself with.

I felt so shaky, I was too confused to know what to do next.

'Come with me,' Bronwyn said. 'We need to get you to a bathroom to clean up. But I don't think that will all come off your clothes.'

A couple of people walked with us to the WC in our hut. One of them was a man who appeared very sure of himself. 'What she did to you is assault. You could have her charged.'

Did I want to? She must have had a screw loose to behave as she had. Having a police record wouldn't help her at all. But I wasn't thinking clearly enough to decide just then.

In the WC, I saw the full impact of what she'd done. Where I'd tried to wipe the ink off my face, I'd left black streaks that made me look like a badger. I shook my hair and ink splattered onto the mirror, the floor and the wash basin. Bronwyn, bless her heart, got some toilet paper and wiped it up while I attempted to get it out of my hair.

'There must be a proper bathroom here somewhere,' she said. 'It used to be someone's home. Let's see if you can wash your hair.'

I did my best to blot the ink on my clothes and we left the WC and headed for the big house. Our old boss, Miss Abbot, was on reception. When she saw me her jaw dropped.

'Good heavens, Lily, what on earth has happened to you? Make sure you don't drip ink on anything!'

'Is there... a bathroom... where I can wash my hair?' My voice sounded shaky and child-like.

'Some mad woman did this to her, and we should get back on duty soon,' Bronwyn said.

Miss Abbot blinked rapidly. 'Well, this is most

unusual. We're not supposed to use the bathroom here.'

Before she spoke again, Bronwyn leaned over, hands on her desk. 'Where's the damn bathroom?' she hissed.

Miss Abbot backed away as if someone had hit her. 'No need for language like that, young lady. It's upstairs, last door on the right.'

I let Bronwyn come up with me, but once we'd found the bathroom, I insisted she leave and go back to work. Helping the war effort was too important to need two of us to clean me up. Added to that, she could explain why I was late back.

I glanced around the bathroom. It was less luxurious than I'd have thought for a big house like that. The walls were tiled to shoulder height, white tiles with a pale green paint above. The big wash basin stood on four metal legs. The bath had seen better days, with a few brown spots where the enamel had worn through. But I was relieved to see a drinking glass and, on a chair, a small pile of neatly folded towels.

I stripped off my blouse, glad to find the ink hadn't gone through to my bra. Using the drinking glass and bar of soap, I washed and washed my hair, rinsing it repeatedly. Finally, I wrapped my hair in one towel while I struggled to make my blouse more respectable. I didn't have much luck with it, but remembered my mum telling me to soak the stain in alcohol might work. Mrs W would have some, but I wasn't sure she'd own up to it.

Running my fingers through my hair, I put my damp blouse back on and stared in the mirror. My face and hair were clean. It would have to do.

As I walked through the house on my way to my hut, I got a lot of curious looks from people. When I went into our room everyone looked up, even the girls who were listening and scribbling. The boss came over to me. 'Lily, you poor thing. Bronwyn told us all about it. I'd love to say take the rest of your shift off, but we're already one short. Do you mind carrying on?'

'Of course not,' I said. As I sat down and put my headset on, I was glad it was a hot day. My blouse was already drying.

At four o'clock, Bronwyn and I finished our shift. She looked me up and down. 'Your hair has dried and your curls look like you spent an hour on them. Fancy going to see Peggy and having a lemonade?'

Peggy had just come on duty and was wiping down the already clean bar. She smiled and put her finger to her lips to remind us to keep her secret. Only then did she notice my state.

'Oh, Lil, what's happened to your blouse?' she asked. As she spoke, she was pouring two lemonades.

'Someone threw ink at me,' I said, taking the glass from her.

Her eyes widened. 'That was you! Someone told me about it just now, but I didn't know it was you. They said the girl who did it has left the Park. She'll never be coming back, apparently.'

'I wonder if she has been taken to a doctor or a hospital,' Bronwyn said. She sipped her drink and wiped her mouth. 'I reckon she's had a breakdown. As well as how rotten she's been to you, I've heard she's behaved strangely at work a lot, too. She'll probably end up in the loony bin.'

I gasped. 'That's such an awful thing to say. It makes me shudder to think about it. Let's hope she gets sent home to recover.'

'Want some crisps?' Peggy asked. 'If she's been taken to the police, you'll have to give a statement, I suppose.'

A customer approached the bar, so Peggy had to leave us to serve them. We took our drinks outside to enjoy the fresh air after hours concentrating in the hut.

We hadn't been there over five minutes when Grant came hurrying toward us, red in the face.

'Lily,' he said. 'I just heard what happened. I'm so sorry. That Peggy has been acting strange for a long time.'

I gave a half-hearted smile. 'Well, she was certainly your biggest fan. From the sound of it, she won't be bothering you again.'

He let out a groan. 'I hope that's right. It's been awkward trying to keep her at bay without being rude. I'm sorry you've had such a rough time with her.'

CHAPTER TWENTY-ONE

Bronwyn was spreading margarine on her second slice of toast. 'I swear this bread tastes worse every day. This…' she waved it around, 'has got a weird texture as well. Full of sawdust, I reckon. It doesn't seem worth getting out of bed for.'

Carolyn, who'd at last learned to make tea and toast, was putting the kettle on again when Peggy came into the kitchen. She had red rings round her eyes and was blowing her nose. Carolyn peered at her. 'Are you okay, Peggy? You look like you've got hay fever.'

Peggy pulled out a chair and sat down heavily. 'Can I 'ave a cuppa when it's ready please?' Then she faced us all. 'I worried a lot about what we was talking about yesterday. You know, should I tell Ken or not about my little one.'

We all froze, knowing nothing positive was coming.

Peggy blew her nose again and wiped her eyes. 'What 'appened was, he 'ung around at the Park 'til I had my break then 'e got down on one knee and proposed. Right there, in front of the beer 'ut. Some people saw 'im and cheered.'

I didn't know what to say. If the story had a happy ending, she'd look more cheerful.

'What happened, Cariad?' Bronwyn asked. 'I thought that was what you wanted.'

She was about to reply when we heard Mrs W shouting at the rear of the house, 'GET THAT FENCE MENDED NOW, YOU APOLOGY FOR A MAN!' She sounded ready to kill, and we heard a thud that made us jump. But then she came in the back door, fag in hand, calm as calm can be.

'Men! Who'd have them!' she replied with a grin, then stopped and sniffed the air. 'I thought I smelled toast. Can I cadge a slice?' Never usually a sensitive soul, she sensed the atmosphere after a few seconds. 'What's wrong with you lot then? Never known you so quiet. Someone died or something? Bump my old man off if you want. Useless lump of lard, he is.'

I tried not to look at Peggy, but her sniffles gave the game away. She got up and turned the toast over, avoiding Mrs W's eye. 'It's me what's miserable.'

Mrs W sat down and knocked her cigarette ash into a saucer. 'What's up then, girl? Tell Mrs W, I'm excellent at solving problems.'

Peggy passed her a slice of toast. 'It's difficult…'

'You wouldn't be upset if it was easy, would you!'

I sat next to Peggy, linking my arm through hers. I didn't speak - she'd tell the story in her own way or perhaps decide not to.

Mrs W took another long drag of her cigarette, squinting through the smoke. She reached into her pocket and pulled out her packet. 'Anyone want one? All they had left in the shop were these Spanish Shawls. Made of wood chips, I wouldn't wonder. Stink to high heaven.'

We'd already noticed.

She twisted back to Peggy. 'Well, you gonna tell me, or do you want me to leave you to it?' Mrs W said, her voice kinder than her words.

Peggy sat down. 'My boyfriend proposed last night…'

Mrs W waved her cigarette around excitedly.

'That's wonderful!' she paused. 'Oh, I suppose it's not or you wouldn't have red eyes. What's the problem?'

Peggy pushed the marmalade towards her. 'It's like this. I did something before I met 'im, and I don't know if 'e'll choose to break it off with me when I tell 'im.'

Mrs W sat back in her chair and took a bite of toast. We all waited to hear what she'd say.

'Already lost your cherry?' Is that it? More common than you think, I can tell you.'

Peggy went red. 'It's more than that.'

Mrs W held up her palm. 'You needn't tell me any more, but do you have to tell him? That's the point. Often what people don't know won't hurt them.' She spread more marmalade on her toast, and I wanted to shout that she was eating too much, considering our food rationing.

Peggy chewed her thumb nail. 'That's it, see. I don't, but it would mean living a lie. I don't think I can do that. It's no way to start a marriage. My family already 'ave a ton of secrets.'

'Better tell him then, if he's a decent bloke and he loves you enough, he'll forgive you for whatever it is. If he doesn't, he's not worth bothering with.'

With that she swallowed the last of her toast,

called, 'Toodle pip, all.' and left without another word.

'Well, she doesn't mince her words, does she,' Carolyn said.

'Truth to tell, what she says is right,' Bronwyn said. 'you'll be seeing your little one growing up. She might even look like you as she gets older, and that might mean awkward questions. It's a tough choice you need to make there, Cariad.'

'I've been wondering whether to move to Bedford to be near her. There's jobs in the Filling Factory there and the pay's not bad.'

Carolyn frowned and turned to her. 'What's a filling factory? What do they fill?'

I butted in. 'Munitions. My mum works in one. It's dangerous work, but she has nice mates to work with and enjoys it. They haven't had any explosions so far.'

Carolyn's eyebrows raised up. 'My goodness, that makes Mummy's Women's Institute work sound very tame.' She spoke to Peggy. 'And you'd be happy doing that sort of work? It would be dull after bar work.'

Peggy shrugged. 'As long as I got people to talk to, I'll be alright. But look, you lot better get going or you'll be late for your shift.'

As we three were getting our bikes out, Carolyn

spoke. 'I meant to tell you, I have two friends from home coming for the day next week. I've arranged it so it's a day when we're off so you can meet them if you'd like to.'

Little did we know what they would be like.

Their names were Felicity and Christabelle. I'd never met anyone with either of those names before. Felicity was a carbon copy of Carolyn - perfect skin, shining hair and teeth that spoke of good nutrition and health. Christabelle was darker, with sleek chestnut brown hair and lovely eyes. Both wore day dresses that must have cost more than everything in my wardrobe.

'Come in, come in,' Carolyn said, ushering them into the living room. 'Come and meet my friends.'

They peered around as if they were in an alien world. 'I suppose you get little choice of accommodation when you're in the forces,' Felicity said, putting down her handbag. Her voice sounded, if anything, even posher than Carolyn's.

She brushed the seat of the armchair before she lowered herself gently onto it. Then she sat demurely with her back perfectly upright and legs crossed at the ankle. I'd read about finishing school and decided she must have been to one.

'These are two of my house-share girls, Bronwyn and Lily,' Carolyn said.

Christabelle shook hands with us and looked as if she needed to wipe her hands on her dress after shaking hands with Bronwyn. 'You never told us you shared with such… interesting gels.'

But Carolyn had spotted a ring on Felicity's finger. 'Flis! You're engaged! I had no idea. When did all this happen? Who's the lucky man?'

Smiling widely, Felicity held out her left hand, turning it this way and that, all the while admiring the enormous diamond. 'It only happened at the weekend. And the very lucky man is Gussy Courtenay.'

Carolyn blinked twice. 'What, old Gussy, the Viscount?'

Felicity's smile faded a little. 'He's not so old, only fifteen years older than me.'

Christabelle raised an eyebrow. 'Bald as a coot though, you've got to admit.'

Felicity turned on her. 'You are so shallow, as if that's the most important thing. Anyway, he'll be an earl one day, and he's worth a bomb.'

Carolyn admired the ring. 'Never mind his hair.

Congratulations, you must be thrilled. Where will you live?'

'On his parents' estate. The house is massive so we can just take over one wing.'

Just then Peggy walked in, dressed in her barmaid clothes. 'Watchya,' she said, seeing Christabelle and Felicity. 'You gotta be Carolyn's friends. Nice to meet ya.'

She walked over to them, holding out her hand. After a second's surprised hesitation, they shook hands with her half-heartedly. 'Surely you're not in the army as well,' Fclicity said.

'Nah, I'm the barmaid over there. Most important job in the place.' She stepped backward. 'Like your dress. That's classy, that is.'

Felicity seemed pleased and smoothed down the fabric of the skirt. 'Yes, it's my favourite.' She looked over at me. 'That's a pretty dress you're wearing. What designer is it?'

I couldn't resist. 'It's an Elle Baker special.' It was actually a jumble sale dress I'd remodelled.

She raised her eyebrows. 'I've never heard of her. I'll look out for her work in the future.'

Then she spoke to Carolyn, who was trying to hide a smile. 'You never informed us what work you do.'

Peggy laughed. ‘She’d 'ave to kill you if she did!’

‘What do you do?’ I asked the newcomers.

‘We’re typists at the Home Office,’ Christabelle said, ‘very important work. Totally confidential, of course, so we can’t say more. Thank heavens we don’t have to wear a uniform.’ She looked at Carolyn. ‘What on earth made you join up, Carolyn? You’re looking very good on it I must say, but the army is so, well, unsuitable for gels.’

Carolyn had been excited about her friends’ visit, but she was looking uncomfortable. ‘What do you mean, unsuitable, Chrissie?’

Chrissie simply smiled. ‘Nothing, forget it. Shall we find somewhere for some refreshments? This is a small town. Is there a pub where the Hunt meets? Those pubs always have people like us.’

Bronwyn and I glanced at each other. ‘I think I’ll give it a miss,’ I said, not wanting to spend any more time in their company.

Carolyn stood up. ‘No, Chrissie, no Hunt pubs that I know of. We usually go to the British Restaurant, it’s excellent value there.’ I knew she could well afford much more, but came with us to the British to keep us company.

Felicity picked up her handbag. ‘Never mind

that, my car's outside, let's find a nice country pub. You've always loved those, Carolyn. We can have a proper catch up there.' She glanced at the rest of us. 'So sorry, but there wouldn't be room for everyone in the car, although we would love to get to know you further, of course.' Her tone dripped with insincerity.

Carolyn bit her lip, looking from her friends to us as if there was a magic way out of the dilemma. Then, 'Okay, I'll come,' she turned to us. 'See you all later. I hope you don't mind.'

Several hours later, we saw her friends drop her off outside Happy Days. She waved them a jaunty goodbye, then turned and saw us looking out the window. She made the universal sign for cutting your own throat then joined us in the living room, pulling a face. 'I can't believe I once liked those two. They haven't got an entire brain between them.'

She buttoned up her cardigan and sat down with a sigh. 'Worse still, I sat listening to the pair of them, and realised I used to be as shallow as they are. I've got you three to thank for that. You and my army training, not to mention the work, means my eyes are well and truly open.'

'Not being funny nor nothing,' Bronwyn said. 'but do you think you'll ever fit in with your set again after the war?'

Carolyn shrugged her shoulders. ‘Not a chance. What shall I do? I’ll have no friends I want to be with, and it’s been a long time since I’ve been keen to spend much time with Mummy.’

Peggy went over and put an arm round her shoulders. ‘We’ll always be your mates, and you’re good at making friends. I’ve seen you in the beer hut chatting to people. People like you.’

‘Yeah, and we’ll tell you if you’re turning into a shallow idiot like them, don’t worry!’ Bronwyn said laughing. ‘Come on, let’s go to a common people’s pub and have a drink.’

It was early evening and still warm, so we strolled to the pub by the canal. ‘You gonna keep an eye out for Madge?’ Bronwyn joked.

We walked past the park where a few parents were swinging their children and a small group of youngsters hung around smoking. All the time, they keep looking around in case they got caught.

On the way there, Carolyn regaled us with snatches of the conversations she had with her friends. ‘Flis is going to have an absolute monster for a mother-in-law. She and Gussy might have their own wing, but they’ll have to build a strong wall to keep Gussy’s mother from walking in and interfering. I’ve met her twice and I shudder at the memory.’

As we walked, an elderly lady in front of us stumbled and fell, her stick hitting the pavement with a bang. We hurried over to her, and were relieved to find she was conscious and able to talk.

'I'm glad you're here, Girls. I'm all right. That's a bit of luck. Break your hip at my age and you'll be dead in a month, that's what they say. Can you help me up?'

Bronwyn and I put our forearms under her armpits and gently pulled her upright. Carolyn passed her her stick. The lady looked down at her knees and frowned. She had a hole in one stocking and her knee was bleeding. 'Better get home and sort myself out,' she said sighing.

'Shall we come with you?' Peggy asked.

The lady shook her head. 'I only live a couple of doors along. Stocking darning for me tonight.'

We watched her until she went into her house. 'It's tough getting old, isn't it?' Bronwyn said. 'I try not to think about it.' Then she clapped her hands. 'But let's think about something more cheerful.'

Sitting down with our shandies, we reminisced about our revenge on Melvyn, the man who'd attacked Peggy. 'Do you remember,' Carolyn said with a smile. 'he got arrested for indecent exposure! Like he'd have chosen to show off his man bits like that!'

Peggy let out a gentle cheer. ‘We did it, Girls, didn’t we! I only wish I’d been a fly on the wall when 'e was put in the Black Maria and taken down the nick. 'alf the town was watching by all accounts.’ She stopped and looked at us. ‘You’ve never 'eard what ‘appened to 'im, 'ave you?’

Bronwyn raised an eyebrow. ‘Word is, he was never seen again. I’ve been in the butchers’ shop a few times and tried to find out, but it’s like he never existed.’

‘Good riddance to bad rubbish, is what I say,’ I said.

‘Well, let’s hope he’ll think twice before attacking a girl again,’ Carolyn said. She turned towards Peggy. ‘Hey, you haven’t said what you decided to do about telling Ken your secret.’

Peggy put her hand to her mouth. ‘I’ve been putting it off.’

‘But doesn’t he want to know if you’ll marry him?’

She nodded. ‘Yes, 'e does and 'e can’t understand why I’m keeping 'im waiting. But I’ve decided. I’m gonna tell 'im tomorrow. If he dumps me, well, 'e wasn’t the right one for me.’

Carolyn hesitated for a minute. Then, ‘I have some news to tell you. When I was in the pub with Fliss and Chrissie, we bumped into someone they knew, George Arundel. He's an officer and home on leave for a few days…'

She paused. We waited.

'And?' I said.

'And I've got a date with him tomorrow. It might not go anywhere, but he seems a nice chap and guess what! He's going to be working at the Park!'

CHAPTER TWENTY-TWO

'So, how did your date go?'

Bronwyn and I were preparing our evening meal. Lord Woolton Pie and Bread Pudding with custard. The custard wouldn't be very sweet, we'd used up most of our sugar ration.

'You got all the veg we need there, Lily?' Bronwyn asked, looking at the recipe. 'We should have potatoes, carrots…' she paused. 'Silly recipe, let's chuck in any veg we've got.'

I passed her the sharp knife and began making the pastry as she peeled and chopped the veg. 'That Lord Woolton might be the Minister for Food, but I bet he's never had to eat one of these pies.' She cursed as her knife slipped. 'He probably has beef in his pies, not damn Bovril.'

The back door opened and Ernie, the landlord's brother, sauntered in. 'Hello, my lovelies,' he said with his slimy smile. 'Got any of whatever you're cooking for me?'

I stared at him and wondered, as I had before, how he made perfectly good clothes look so scruffy. He sat down on a kitchen chair and slumped, legs apart as if he wanted to show off his private bits.

'Did you hear me?' he asked. 'I know you two are decent cooks.'

I stopped rubbing the fat in the flour and gestured to him. 'No, there's not enough for you. In case you didn't know, there's rationing on.'

He reached into the bag by his side and produced a tin of bully beef. 'This change your mind? It'll pep that pie up no end.'

Bronwyn put down her knife and looked at me. We'd been in this sort of dilemma before. Do you stick to the law and turn down the extra food, or have it and be grateful? The trouble was the creepy git sitting at the table would feel we owed him something and be smug about it. I had just decided to turn down the offer when Bronwyn spoke. 'We'll take it. You can have one slice of the pie. But you've got to go back to Mrs W's place to eat it. We don't want you eating with us.'

He hesitated and half withdrew the tin of beef. I

guessed he was weighing up whether we'd be talked round. He sighed and passed us the tin. 'Okay then, but I want gravy, mind. Thick gravy.'

I took it from him and opened it as he lit a ciggie. 'You don't want to use all that in one meal,' he said, like he was a master chef, 'stretch it out for another night. Corned beef hash or something.'

I raised an eyebrow. 'Thanks, brain box, I'd never have thought of that.'

Carolyn walked in, looking tired. 'You okay, Carolyn?' I asked.

She nodded. 'Yes, the shift work is getting to me, but no more than it does for us all.'

I saw she'd spotted Ernie, but ignored him. But he wasn't willing to be ignored.

'What exactly goes on over there at the Park that needs you working round the clock? It sounds fishy to me.'

'It's fishy you're not fighting for king and country,' she replied. 'Why aren't you?'

'Too old to be called up yet, but I've gotta keep an eye on that. Might need to make myself scarce.'

Carolyn got a second knife out of the drawer and began peeling carrots.

'Did you ever hear anything from the police about your bracelet?' Bronwyn asked, tossing a lump of potato into a saucepan.

'Funny you should ask,' Carolyn said. 'I called into the police station yesterday. They're no nearer to finding the thief, although they have their suspicions. I wish they'd give it back to me, they've kept it for ages.'

'It was excellent quality, wasn't it?' Bronwyn asked.

'Twenty-four carat,' Ernie muttered. We turned and looked at him, open mouthed. He had his nose in a newspaper, apparently not noticing our conversation, yet he definitely knew something about the bracelet he shouldn't have known.

Eyes narrowed, Carolyn took a step towards him and knocked his paper out of his hands. 'How would you know that, then?'

He folded the paper up. 'Donnie must've mentioned it,' he said, and bolted from the room without another word.

We watched him walk past the kitchen window, too stunned to chase after him.

'It's him,' Bronwyn said. 'He nicked your bracelet.'

'And knickers,' I said. 'Did you ever tell Donnie or Mrs W it was 24 carat?'

'No, never.' Her lips were pursed. 'I'm going to the police station once we've eaten. Anyone coming with me?'

'I will,' I said.

We had to wait ages at the police station. A tired looking man in a flat cap was reporting some money he'd lost. 'I'm skint, Officer, that was me pay packet. The wife'll kill me. What're we going to do with no money for a week?'

The desk officer took his details. 'I don't hold out a lot of hope, I'm afraid,' he said, 'but come in and ask every day. If someone is honest, they'll probably bring it in soon.'

As the man walked past us, Carolyn tapped him on the arm. 'Excuse me, Sir, but I couldn't help overhearing what happened to you.' She reached into her purse and handed him a pound note. He looked at her in amazement. 'Thank you, Miss, thank you!' He had a tear in his eye as he walked towards the door.

The policeman coughed and called to us. 'How can I help?' He looked as weary as the man he's just dealt with. He had dark rings under his eyes and his shoulders slumped.

Carolyn spoke up. 'I need to speak to someone about my stolen bracelet. I'm pretty sure I know who the thief is.'

That made him perk up. 'Hmm, how do you know? Tell me all about it.' Carolyn gave him the short version, and he listened attentively and took notes. 'Hang on there, I'll get the sergeant.'

A couple of minutes later, he was back with another officer. The police officer, Sergeant Brown, took us to a small room and asked us to sit. He got out his notebook and pen and lined them up precisely. Opening the notebook, he wrote down Carolyn's story, asking several questions to be sure he understood completely. Then he sat back and folded his arms.

'We've had our eye on him for some time, but we have to have a reason to search where he lives. A brief conversation such as you had isn't proof, of course, but it may well be enough to persuade my boss we can take this further.'

'If you're looking for him, he's got a room at Happy Days, in the annex where his brother- and sister-in-law live.'

He nodded. 'I know where you mean.' He paused and tapped his teeth with his pen. 'Leave it to me and don't say a word. We don't want him running off. But trust me, we will take action. Thank you for reporting this. It's tough on you, but this might be just what we need.'

'You're still holding my bracelet as evidence. Will I get it back if you catch him?'

He thought for a minute. 'I'm not sure, but we'll let you know as soon as we have made a decision.'

The next morning early, we heard a lot of banging and swearing. Looking out of the front windows, we saw the police dragging Ernie towards a police car. He was shouting his innocence and struggling to get free, but his hands were handcuffed behind his back and two officers were holding his arms so tight he had no chance of escape. Minutes later, a third officer came out carrying a heavy bag.

'That'll be the rotter's loot!' Peggy said. 'Loads like 'im where I come from.'

Then we spotted Mrs W standing to one side, ciggie in her mouth, arms crossed, looking on as if it was nothing to do with her.

'I don't suppose he'll ever own up to stealing my bracelet,' Carolyn said. 'I hope the police give it back to me soon.'

~

At the town park, we spread the old blanket down on the grass, careful to avoid the ducks who were waddling all around us. The blanket must have been ancient. It was a faded grey and coarse and scratched my skin. All of us wore shorts and blouses, making the most of the first fine day for a week. Needless to say, Carolyn looked the most elegant in hers.

'This is a rare treat,' Peggy said, sitting beside me, 'all off duty of an afternoon. And a nice day, too.'

Bronwyn put down the picnic basket and sat guarding it. 'Can't trust all these kids,' she muttered.

Carolyn laughed. 'I think we'd notice if they ran off with that! It weighs a ton.'

We took out our bottles of water and settled down. In the distance we heard the sound of a cricket match and nearer, a mother calling her child to 'come back right now!' The air smelled of freshly cut grass and, faintly, from the nearby road, petrol and horse droppings.

'How did your date go?' Bronwyn asked. 'What was his name again?'

'George, George Arundel. It went well.' Carolyn didn't look at us. She fiddled instead with the bright green scarf round her neck.

We all waited.

'And… come on, spill the beans!' Peggy said.

Carolyn sighed. 'You lot are so nosy. Okay, we went for a walk, then saw a film, then had a drink in a pub.'

We waited some more.

'And...'

She smiled and her eyes shone. 'We had a lovely time. We have a lot in common, our backgrounds are quite similar...'

'Unlike you and the rest of us!' Bronwyn said with a laugh. 'So, are you meeting him again?'

'I am, in a couple of days. It will be good to get to know him better.'

'Oh, look over there!' Peggy interrupted.

A wedding couple were standing in front of the fountain, ready to have their photo taken. The bride wore a beautiful long white dress. It was damask silk, with a high V neck, long sleeves and a ruched waistline. As she turned, we saw it became a big floppy bow at the back.

The chief bridesmaid was arranging the hem of the dress to best effect while the groom stood patiently waiting. Smaller bridesmaids and a little page boy chased each other, and were constantly pulled in line by the adults in the group.

'That's so lovely,' Peggy said, a dreamy look on her face.

'Do you think you'll have a wedding like that?'

Bronwyn asked.

The corners of Peggy's mouth turned down. 'Well, there's something I 'aven't told you all. Me and Ken, we've split up.'

My jaw dropped open. 'You kept that quiet. What happened?'

She put her head down, got out her hankie, and wiped a tear from her eye. 'I did it, like I said. I told him about my little girl. He looked at me as if I was trash, called me a name I will not repeat and walked away without another word. I 'aven't seen or 'eard from 'im since. The rotter. But I suppose I can't blame 'im.'

I put my arm round her and Bronwyn held her hand. 'I'm so sorry. You can blame him, you know, he should love you just as you are. He's scum behaving like that.'

'I would say you've had a lucky escape,' Carolyn said, a deep frown on her brow. 'Any man who acts like that isn't worth having. You'll find someone much kinder, I'm sure.'

'But will I ever find one who'll want me after what I did?' She wiped her eyes again and blew her nose.

'Tell you the truth,' Bronwyn said, 'it makes my blood boil that not a word gets said about the blokes in situations like this. Oh no, they just walk away and get on with their lives. It's us girls who have to live with the consequences every single time.'

We talked about it for a few more minutes, then Peggy blew her nose. 'Let's drop it now and 'ave something to eat. I don't want 'im ruining my day, never mind yours.'

Carolyn leaned over and patted her arm. 'That's the spirit, you're made of tough stuff, Peggy.'

I opened the picnic basket again. 'Come on, let's enjoy our food.'

We had egg and salad sandwiches, sticks of carrot and cucumber, scones and jam.

Peggy perked up. 'That lot looks a treat, just what the doctor ordered.'

We were helping ourselves when I heard my name called. I look round and there was Doreen, pushing her bike.

'Fancy seeing you here. Can I join you?' she asked with a smile.

'Of course, we can stretch this to another one if you haven't already eaten.' I looked at the others, who nodded agreement.

She sat down on the grass near us - there wasn't enough room on the blanket for her. 'I haven't got long,' she said. 'Off to my next cleaning job soon.'

She took a little sandwich - we'd cut them into four, so they were dainty triangles.

'When I was at the station recently, I saw you looking at the trains,' I said.

She finished her sandwich and nodded. 'Yes, I'm a real train enthusiast, probably because I grew up near a railway line. That's why I got the rooms I did. When I was a child I used to spend a lot of time dreaming of getting on a train and going on adventures.'

'I still do,' Bronwyn said with a laugh. 'Where would you go?'

Doreen pointed to half a scone. 'May I have that?'

We all nodded. 'I don't know where I'd go,' she said, nibbling the edge of the scone as if she wanted it to last a long time, 'somewhere hot where there's no war, I suppose.'

A horse neighing as it walked along the street edging the park caught our attention. 'Poor old horse,' she said, 'even more prisoners than we are.'

Before I could ask her what she meant, she was hit in the back by a ball thrown by some lads. She jolted forward and muttered something I couldn't catch before getting upright again and throwing the ball back to the boys.

'No harm done,' she said.

As she spoke, the church bell rang the hour. She looked at her watch and jumped up. 'Goodness, is that the time? I'll be late! Sorry, must dash.'

And she jumped on her bike and rode off furiously.

Carolyn watched her go, then turned to the rest of us, her face very serious. 'You're probably going to tell me I'm going mad, but do you think Doreen could be a German spy?'

There was a moment's silence. I too stunned to take in what she was saying immediately.

'Doreen? A spy? You for real?' Peggy said.

'What's put that into your mind?' Bronwyn asked.

Carolyn started counting points off on her fingers. 'One, she often asks what we do at the Park. Two, I heard what she muttered when that ball hit her in the back. It was a German swearword. Three, you've just said she was watching trains, Lily.'

'Yes, she was using binoculars. She was studying the soldiers as they left the station, too. I thought it was strange.'

She pursed her lips and ticked off another finger. 'Four, and Bronwyn and Peggy may not know about this, but she started her monthly when she was at Happy Days recently. She needed a… well… a sanitary towel. She told Lily that Aunt Rose had come to visit and she needed a present for her. Not surprisingly Lily had no idea what she was talking about, but that's a German expression for starting your monthly and needing a towel. And lastly, I saw her near an army base watching what was going on.'

I remembered visiting her room once. 'Actually, that's not the last thing. When I went to her room, she had a book of poetry. She went to the WC and I looked at it. The poems were written on strangely, some letters were circled or underlined. I couldn't make head or tail of why. I'm not much into poetry, so I thought it must bc something I've never learned.'

'Or code,' Bronwyn said, giving a low whistle.

We all sat back for a minute, taking in what all this meant.

'But she's not snooping round the Park,' I said.

'I wondered about that. Those rumours about a spy were soon forgotten. There are other sorts of spies, though. She could be reporting on troop movements or morale in Britain. The Germans would need that sort of information as well. From what you've told me, Lily, she's always been vague about her family background, too.'

I watched some sparrows splashing in the fountain while I considered what she was saying.

'How would she tell the Germans what she's found? She wouldn't be able to send letters.'

Bronwyn side-swiped me. 'You daft thing. She'd use a radio, of course.'

Of course. How did I not realise that when we spent our working days listening to radio messages from France? Just as they messaged us, she might message to somewhere in Germany.

'If she's got a radio, she must have it in her room,' Bronwyn said.

'Her bedroom's upstairs. I bet there's a hatch into the loft just outside her room on the landing.'

Peggy spoke up. 'She couldn't use that. Too dodgy. Anyone could come along when she's going up and down, and anyway, she'd need a ladder. No, if she's got a radio, it'll be in 'er room.'

We looked at each other and I guessed we all had the same thought in mind. I was the one to voice it.

'We need to search her room.'

~

I'd met Doreen quite a few times, but I'd only been to her room the once. If I wanted to search for it, I had to get inside without her knowing.

'Tell you what,' Bronwyn said. 'Get her key and

press it into some wax. Then you can get a copy cut.'

I thought about it for a minute. 'I think you've been watching too many films. And if I had a key, then what? I've still got to get past her landlady. If she sees me, she'll tell Doreen and the game will be up.'

'We can climb in through the window,' Peggy suggested.

Carolyn laughed. 'It's upstairs and on a busy road. I think we'd get noticed.'

Peggy bristled. 'Wc can dress up as window cleaners.'

'Hmm, that's not a bad idea. But we'd still have the problem of breaking into her room, not to mention making sure she was out and wouldn't come back.'

Carolyn clapped her hands. 'Let's do the most obvious thing. Lily, she's your friend, suggest you go and have a cup of tea with her.'

I shook my head. 'I don't think that will work. She's been very reluctant to invite me in again.' I paused. 'There must be a way round it.'

We were speaking quietly because we were in the garden sitting on a low wall, enjoying the warmth of the sun. At the other end of the garden was Donnie's pride and joy - his shed. We heard sawing and nailing and the occasional swear word coming from inside. The noise competed with the songs on the radio coming from the next house. A rusty swing sat on the edge of the lawn on the left, creaking as it gently swayed in the breeze. A squirrel caught our eye as it climbed along the fence and jumped onto a neighbour's walnut tree.

I was glad of my hat to stop the skin on my face burning and fanned myself with a page from a newspaper. 'How about if I invite her round again, and see if I can find out any more about her schedule. I think she has two or three part-time jobs.'

Bronwyn swatted a fly away from her head, 'You mean so we know when to go into her room?'

'That's right. I can snoop into her handbag and pockets as well while she's here.'

Carolyn scoffed. 'No spy would be silly enough to leave incriminating documents in their bag or pocket, surely. And she'd need a suitcase to carry a radio around if she uses one of them. They're heavy, too.'

I turned to her. 'How on earth do you know so much about them?'

'I couldn't possibly say, my dear,' she said with a grin, pretending to zip her mouth.

A week later, Doreen came to the house to help me with an invented dress-making problem. We made some tea and went into the living room where my sewing machine was. I'd been changing a collar and pretended not to know how to do it. Seeing where she'd put her handbag, I nudged it behind her chair.

I poured the tea and handed her a cup. 'Where are you working now?' I asked.

She stirred the milk into her drink. 'I've got several cleaning jobs, here, there and everywhere. It's a bit of a bother when I have to hurry and cycle from one to the next.'

'Aren't they near each other then?'

'I wish they were. It's such a nuisance and my customers keep changing when they want me to call. It makes it very difficult to organise my time.'

I remembered us seeing her cycling along at night. 'Do you ever do cleaning jobs in the evening?'

She shook her head. 'No, thank goodness. It's tiring enough cleaning all day.'

I handed her a biscuit. 'You must go into some posh houses. Most people can't afford a cleaner.'

We were interrupted by the milkman, who whistled as he walked past the window, no doubt on the way to collect his money from Mrs W.

'I didn't tell you,' Doreen said. 'I've got one regular cleaning job. At the station. It's such a relief to have some regular hours, and I can look at the trains. I love that.'

Inside, I sighed with relief. This was just what I hoped for. 'That's good. What hours do you do?'

She sneezed and got out her hankie to blow her nose. 'Sorry, it's hay fever. I do early morning. It's a drag getting up so early, but worth it.'

The door opened and Bronwyn came in. 'Any tea in that pot for me?' she asked.

We chatted for a few more minutes then, 'Hey, Doreen, can you help me with one of my dresses? Lil can't seem to work out what to do with it.'

Doreen looked surprised. 'Well, it must be something complicated if Lily can't do it.'

'Come upstairs, it's in my wardrobe. I can try it on and you can tell me how to get it to fit better.'

For a breath-snatching minute Doreen looked for her bag, but Bronwyn distracted her. 'I love that dress you've got on. Did you make it?' As she spoke, she led Doreen out of the door.

It was my chance. I grabbed her bag and looked inside. There were the usual things most women have in their bag, lipstick, a hankie, keys, a purse. And there were two pieces of paper. Hardly daring to breathe, I opened the first with clammy, shaking hands and gasped.

It was a map of the area showing all the military bases.

There was no innocent explanation for that, but I had no time to ponder on it. I stifled a cry as I reached for the other piece of paper. Holding my breath, I unfolded it and couldn't believe my eyes. It was a detailed plot for assassinating an American Colonel. Written in English, with no code.

I longed to look at it in detail, but didn't know how long Bronwyn could keep Doreen out of the room. Trembling, I put the map back, but shoved the other piece of paper under my seat. Then I wiped the film of sweat from my forehead and tried to calm down my breathing, hoping Doreen wouldn't notice the paper was missing before she left.

Seconds later, I heard Doreen and Bronwyn coming back downstairs. As she entered the room, Bronwyn raised an enquiring eyebrow at me. I gave the tiniest of nods in response. She had the dress she'd been consulting about in her hands.

'Look what Doreen suggested,' she said. Doreen took it from her and spent a couple of minutes talking me through her idea. I didn't take in a word, my mind too full of what I'd found.

Then Bronwyn, bless her, rescued me. She made a thing of looking at her watch. 'Gosh, Lily, we'd better be going. We've got to be at work early today.'

I could have kissed her. Instead, I thanked Doreen again, and we bid her farewell. As she walked down the garden path, we leaned against the front door in relief. Then, in a panic, I rushed back to the living room and looked out to make sure she'd gone, worried she might check her handbag.

Bronwyn turned to me. 'What did you find, Lil? You're white as a sheet.'

I pulled the piece of paper out of my bag and shoved it in my pocket. 'Come on, we need to get up to the Park now. Grab your coat and bike, I'll explain as we go.'

'But... but...' she began twice as we snatched our things and mounted our bikes. I didn't reply until we were out of town and on a quiet country road. 'She had a map of the area with military bases marked, and the bit of paper in my pocket is details of how to assassinate an American colonel.'

She stopped peddling and gaped at me. 'You're kidding. Surely she wouldn't be stupid enough to carry things like that in her bag.'

'Keep peddling! Apparently she was. We need to take them to the boss straight away. I don't think the local police would know how to deal with this information.'

We cycled faster than we'd ever peddled in our lives and threw down our bikes when we arrived at the Mansion house.

Dashing into reception, we were glad it wasn't Miss Timson on duty. 'Quick! We need to see the Commander!' we said.

The woman on duty looked up, startled. 'You can't just come in here and expect to speak to him. What's it about?'

Bronwyn and I looked at each other and shrugged. 'We have evidence of a spy in Bletchley,' I said.

Her eyes widened and without another word, she picked up her phone. 'Yes, two girls are here...' she looked at us. 'Do you even work here?'

We nodded. 'We're soldiers.'

She spoke into the phone again. 'They say they have evidence of a spy in Bletchley and want to see the Commander.'

She listened for a minute, then thanked whoever was on the other end of the phone and hung up.

'Go upstairs, the door at the end of the corridor on the left. Knock and wait to be asked in.'

As we walked up the stairs, I checked for the umpteenth time that the paper was still in my pocket. I clutched it while we knocked on the door.

As we waited for a response, I felt a surge of panic. What if the Commander didn't believe us? After all, it was hard to image any spy would be as stupid as Doreen had been.

My worried thoughts were interrupted when the door was opened by a woman wearing civvies.

'I'm the Commander's assistant. Come in and tell me all about it.'

She sat us down and poured us some water. 'Now, I can see you're in a state. Take your time, drink that, it'll cool you down.' Her face was grave as she listened. 'Show me the paper.' I handed it to her, aware it was crumbled and damp from my sweaty hand. She read it twice, then stood up. 'Wait here, I'll go and show this to the Commander. He'll almost certainly want to speak to you.'

'What do you think will happen?' Bronwyn said when she'd gone.

'I suppose they'll arrest her and they'll have to tell the Americans about the assassination plot.'

Before we had a chance to say more, the Commander's assistant came back into the room. 'The Commander will see you now.'

His office was, without doubt, the best in the building. It was big, with bay windows overlooking the road outside and the lake. Crammed bookshelves lined one wall, and filing cabinets another. His desk was enormous, with two piles of papers in metal wire trays. He was an unassuming looking man, slim, with wire-rimmed glasses and a receding hairline. He was holding the paper I'd given his assistant.

'Sit down, Ladies,' he said. 'My assistant has explained what this is about.' He waved the paper as if drying it. 'Now, tell me in your own words how you come to know this… Doreen, did you say? And how you came to have this piece of paper.'

We told him all our suspicions about Doreen - the slip-ups she'd made using a German word and a German expression, and looking at trains and army bases. He made brief notes on a pad in front of him. 'So you came up with this idea of looking in her bag. That was a long shot.'

I nodded, struggling to find my words. 'We wanted to search her room to see if she had a transmitter or anything, but we couldn't work out how to do it. This seemed the next best thing.'

'It amazed us she'd have something like that in her handbag,' Bronwyn said.

He sat back and steepled his fingers. 'So she doesn't seem to know what goes on here,' he said, looking at us for confirmation. We nodded.

'Well, I see you're not on duty at the moment. I think the best thing is for you both to go and get yourselves a cup of tea while I make some phone calls. Where will you be? My assistant will come and fetch you when I'm ready.'

We looked at each other, sharing a thought. 'We'll go to the Beer Hut, not that we'll drink alcohol. But we can get tea there.'

'Right, I am very pleased you bought this direct to me. Enjoy your tea and I'll see you a bit later. Meanwhile, I don't need to tell you not to say a word about this to anyone.'

We hadn't even left the room before he was picking up his phone.

An hour and a half later, we were called back to his office. This time we were much less nervous and were shown straight in by his assistant.

The Commander looked up and smiled as we walked in. 'Lily, Bronwyn, I want to update you about this situation. I can't tell you the details, but please rest assured you don't need to worry about it any more. I'd like to ask you to stay here until your next shift to avoid any possibility of this Doreen coming to your house. By the time your shift finishes, that fear will be over. Do you have any questions?'

I bit my lip. 'I have a hundred, but I don't think you'll be willing to answer them.'

'Probably not. But thank you again for being so observant and for reporting this matter. Besides the work you do here every day, you have helped us to win the war by acting so promptly.'

He stood up and shook our hands, smiling warmly. His assistant, who'd been in the room the whole time, led us out the door. 'Well done, Girls,' she said, and patted us both on the shoulder.

As we left the building, Bronwyn looked at her watch. 'We've got a bit of time before our shift, let's sit by the lake. If we sit well away from people we can talk about what's happened.'

We were lucky that it was another nice day, so we sat distant from the other people who were enjoying the sunshine. The gentle breeze rustled the leaves in the tree above us, and birds chirped nearby. The sound of another choir practice drifted across the water, making a perfect soothing sound we needed.

'What do you think will happen to Doreen?' Bronwyn asked, keeping her voice low.

'I dread to think. They execute them, don't they? I hate to think of that happening to her. I wonder if they hang them or shoot them.' I shivered. 'Either is too awful to think about.'

Bronwyn's bottom lip trembled. 'It's so like what happened in Paris, isn't it? We found a spy there. Do you remember?'

It was my turn to feel tearful. 'I'll never forget. It's crazy that we've met two nice girls who you'd never think would work for the Nazis. They must have been brainwashed.'

Two men walked by, talking about an upcoming cricket match. We waited until they'd gone past before we spoke again.

I thought back to the two spies. 'It makes you wonder if you ever really know anyone, doesn't it. You might be a spy for all I know.'

She slapped my arm. 'I think you'd have spotted it by now, Cariad. But I suppose the lesson is to realise you can never be sure about anyone.'

I didn't say, but I wondered if something like that was what held Grant back from taking our relationship further. If we even had one.

Then it was as if thinking of him conjured him up, and he was beside us. He looked as gorgeous as ever and smelled of a lovely woody soap.

'You two are looking very solemn. Has something happened?'

I gave a weak smile. 'Yes, you're right, but it's not something we can talk about.'

He hesitated. 'Would you rather I went away?' he asked.

'No, it's fine,' Bronwyn said. 'We need to think of other things.'

He moved so he sat next to me. 'Lily, I've got a day off at the weekend and I wondered if you fancied a trip to the country? I can borrow a car so we can explore a bit. The weather is supposed to be okay.'

I felt my tension drain away at the thought of a day spent with him, away from these unhappy memories.

'I can't think of anything I'd rather do,' I said with a stronger smile.

'Right, I know where you live. Okay if I pick you up at about nine-thirty?'

'Perfect. I'll look forward to it.'

He stood up. 'That's wonderful. I'll be off. Nice to see you Bronwyn.'

CHAPTER TWENTY-THREE

I spend ages deciding what to put on to go out with Grant, and Bronwyn enjoyed herself poking fun at me. 'Too sexy!' 'Too frumpy!' 'You're the spitting image of my gran in that!'

In the end, I settled for a red and white flowery dress with a scooped neckline, flared skirt and short sleeves. I tried half a dozen ways to do my hair, but in the end tied it up in case Grant had borrowed an open-topped car. Bronwyn loaned me a red scarf that finished the outfit perfectly.

'Do you imagine he's worrying about what to wear?' she asked with a laugh. 'I bet not.'

As I waited for him, I had butterflies in my stomach and checked the time every two minutes.

Would this be the day when he asks me to be his girl?

As if she read my mind, Bronwyn said, 'I wonder if you'll find out why he's so slow in coming forward?'

'Who knows? He's never said until now.'

We were in the living room by the bay window. The previous day was cloudy and dreary, but now the sun was promising to break through.

'Let's think of all the reasons,' Bronwyn said, ticking them off on her fingers. 'He's married, he's engaged, he's too scared to tell his mum he's got a girlfriend.'

I snorted at that one.

'He likes girls as friends but really prefers… well, you know.'

'You'll run out of fingers to count on at this rate,' I said with a laugh.

She poked her tongue out at me. 'Well, I can't think of anything else. Just as well.'

The doorbell rang before she could come up with any more alarming or stupid ideas. I ran to it faster than I'd ever done before.

Grant stood at the door, as gorgeous as ever. He wore grey trousers and a white, open-necked shirt. Smiling, he handed me a rose he'd been holding behind his back. Not a red one, but a pretty pink one with a gorgeous smell. 'A rose for a pretty lady,' he said with a grin. 'Ready for our day out?'

I certainly was.

Bronwyn came up behind me, and she handed me my jacket and handbag. 'Have a wonderful day, both of you,' she said, almost pushing me into his arms and squashing the flower. There was an awkward moment. Then he stepped aside to show me the car he'd borrowed. I had no idea what make of car it was. It was an open-topped two-seater, dark red with headlights on either side of the radiator that looked like massive insect eyes.

'I've had a word with a friend at the Park who predicts the weather,' Grant said, 'and he assures me it won't rain today. I hope he's right or we'll get drenched.' He opened the passenger door, and I almost fell into the low, red leather seat, looking very unladylike. I took Bronwyn's scarf out of my bag and tied it round my hair.

Grant got in the driver's seat and indicated behind him. 'I've got a picnic in the boot,' he said. 'I thought we'd go to Tattenhoe. Have you been there?'

I shook my head. I'd seen it on maps, but that was all.

'It's a very ancient village with some pleasant

woods and the remains of Snelshall Priory. Does that sound okay?'

I'd have been happy to agree with whatever he suggested.

The sun came out from the clouds as if applauding our decision to spend a day in the countryside. Grant started the car, and I was surprised how noisy the engine was. That was soon forgotten in the thrill of the air in my face as we raced along. It was strange to be moving fast and yet feel as if we were outside.

'Okay?' Grant said, glancing at me as he changed gear.

'Yes, I love it!' I shouted over the noise of the wind and a passing bus.

We took a road out of town I'd never been on before and were soon passing an orchard with row upon row of apple trees. The grass between the trees was long and waved gently in the breeze. An elderly farmer, his back bent, was pushing a wooden wheelbarrow full of the tools of his trade. We stopped at a roadside stall that was selling fruit and vegetables. 'Let's get some apples to go with our picnic,' Grant said, climbing out of his low seat. There was no-one with the stall and I watched him put money in the honesty box, a rusty old biscuit tin with a hole cut in the top for coins.

He got in the car and rubbed an apple on his sweater. Then he handed it to me, saying, 'For you, madam.'

Perhaps it was being with Grant in that lovely car, but the apple was the best I'd ever tasted, even if the juice ran down my chin.

It didn't take much longer to reach our destination. Grant stopped the car on the edge of the village.

'It's a pretty village,' he said, holding my door open for me. 'I thought you might enjoy walking through it and there's a teashop that does good rock cakes, I believe.'

After a moment's hesitation, he held my hand as if it was a natural thing to do. We walked past a row of lovely cottages with mansard roofs, and unusually tall chimneys. Their gardens were a delight with hollyhocks, delphiniums, Chillia, coreopsis and echinacea nudging each other for space. Bees buzzed from flower to flower, and the air was rich with the most wonderful scents. An elderly woman was dead-heading some flowers and called a cheery 'Good morning,' as we strolled past.

We walked behind a mum pushing her child in a Silver Cross pram. She chatted to him all the while, even though he was too young to respond.

We reached the small row of shops within

minutes. There was a butchers', a fruit and vegetable shop and an ironmongers' that had an amazing display of its goods hanging from its walls. Then we came to the teashop. It blended perfectly with the age of the houses and shops. It was a house with a small front garden with roses round the window. A rickety white table and chairs were in the small space. We went inside and it was similar to being in someone's living room, which it must have been once. There were three more small tables set up with embroidered table clothes, and shelves stacked with flowery crockery.

A plump woman with tightly permed hair smiled as we walked in. 'Good morning, my dears,' she said, brushing down her spotless apron. 'My name is Jenny. How can I help you?'

Grant replied. 'We'd love some tea, and we hear you do excellent rock cakes. Is that right?'

'They are good, if I say so myself. You choose a seat, here or outside, and I'll bring your tea and rock cakes right away. Make yourself comfortable.'

We sat outside in the sun, which wasn't uncomfortably hot yet. Grant sat down and gave a contented sigh. 'Having a day like this is so wonderful after being too busy at work. Having you with me makes it even more special.' He reached across and squeezed my hand, then stretched his arms over his head as if easing stress in his spine.

Jenny came out with a tray laden with a china teapot, cups and saucers and a plate with enormous rock cakes. 'Here you are, my dears. I hope you don't take sugar. We use all we have in the cakes, I'm afraid.'

I smiled at her. 'It's fine, and this all looks delicious.'

When she'd gone, I set about pouring our tea and putting the cakes on the tiny tea plates. Grant looked more relaxed than I'd seen him before, so I decided to be brave. Not brave enough to look at him as I spoke, though.

'You mentioned once that you had been engaged…' I left the sentence hanging, hoping he'd say more.

He stirred his tea and sighed once more. 'I was intending to tell you today. I was engaged to a wonderful girl. We'd known each other since school days. But she became ill and died. It was tragic.'

My heart skipped a beat. I hadn't been expecting this. 'I'm so sorry. How awful for you both, and for her family. Was this a long time ago?'

'Three years. It's taken me ages to get over it, but I realise I am now. Ready to face the future.'

I lay my hand over his. 'And it's difficult to

look forward when we can't tell how much longer this war is will last.'

He patted my hand and picked up his rock cake. 'That's always on my mind.' He took a bite of his cake, then said, 'This is delicious. I haven't tasted anything this good since I had my mother's baking.'

I was going to try asking questions then, but a couple of mothers went by holding their little ones by the hand and chatting about rationing. By the time they had passed, the moment had gone.

'Shall we head to the Priory ruins next?' Grant said. 'Then we can take our picnic and sit in the woods.'

He paid for our tea and cakes and we strolled through the pretty streets towards the car. I was pleased he drove slowly enough for me to enjoy looking around at the beautiful countryside and thought what good company he was. He stopped the car and helped me out. 'The priory was built in about twelve hundred, but I know little else about it. I love ruins though, there's something very special and peaceful about them.'

There was only one wall standing, and that wasn't completely whole. Most of the rest of the ruins were part walls. The weather-worn stone pillars were surrounded by dead clumps of grass, and the cracked blocks were broken up by meandering tree roots. A partial staircase was covered with ivy and caved in roofs were weighed down by vines. Dappled sunlight filtered through the windows of the remaining wall. I stepped cautiously over fallen stones, which made the floor uneven. A mouse ran over my foot, making me jump and my skin feel prickly. Then I touched a large stone, it was rough and cool, and I wondered how many hundreds of people had touched it in the past and what their lives had been like.

'Are you okay there?' Grant asked. He'd been exploring a different bit of the ruin. The breeze ruffled his hair as he spoke. 'Have you noticed the smell?' I hadn't, but realised it was a combination of mildew and earthy scents of moist soil and dead leaves. 'I've always been curious about why anyone would prefer to shut themselves away from the world and be a monk. Did they have broken hearts or was their belief in God so strong it was the only way to do his bidding?'

He came over and took my hand. 'Have you seen enough? Shall we go for that walk now?'

Feeling grateful for his hand, I got into the car and we drove a short distance to the woods. He glanced at his watch. 'Shall we walk, then have our picnic?'

The day had got hotter, and we were glad of the

cool shade in the woods. Tall trees seemed to brush the sky and splashes of sunshine forced their way through their leaves as if spotlighting special places. Sounds around us were gentle, the wind rustling the leaves, our feet crunching leaves and small twigs, birds chirping, and the occasional sound of small animals hurrying about their business. Dead logs had become beds for moss and strange shaped mushrooms, and birch trees had lost their bark in giant white curls.

We came to a path blocked by a fallen tree. ‘You okay climbing over this?’ Grant asked.

My legs were just about long enough to step over it, and when I got to the other side, he took me in his arms and kissed me on the forehead. Then, as if remembering himself, he let go and started walking again.

Confused, I caught up with him and took his hand. He squeezed it without comment. The path narrowed, and I stepped on a leaf covered stone and turned my ankle over with a yelp. I attempted to walk, but it was too painful.

Grant’s face was full of concern. ‘Here, let’s me help, don’t keep trying to walk if it’s painful.’ He put one arm round my back and under my arm and took the weight from my injured side. We hobbled slowly back towards the car, stopping only for him to carry me over the fallen tree. The entire time, I struggled to stifle cries of pain.

The return journey seemed to take forever, but finally we were back in the sunshine. Grant eased me onto the ground in the shade of a tree, took off my shoe and inspected my ankle. 'I feel useless. I know nothing about first aid,' he said.

'Don't worry. I do. Let me see if I can move my ankle.' Although it was painful, I could move it in all directions and wiggle my toes. 'It's not broken, only a sprain. But this is a good time to have our picnic so I can rest it.'

Looking relieved, he hurried to the car and was soon back with a wicker picnic basket. He opened it and I gasped at the food he'd got. Sandwiches, a pork pie, a salad, spiced biscuits, a fruit loaf and a bottle of lemonade. 'How on earth did you get all this? It's more food than I've seen for years.'

He grinned. 'I have special ways and means. If we don't eat it all, I want you to take the rest with you to your digs, and share it with your friends.'

We sat in silence as we ate, and it was a comfortable silence. We didn't get through half of the food, of course, and I wrapped up what we left carefully and got Grant to take it to the car in case ants got it.

He came back and sat close to me, our arms

touching. ‘Want to lie down?’ he asked, and when I did he put his arm under my neck so I snuggled up against him.

‘How’s your ankle?’

‘It’s still painful, but easing off a bit. I expect it’ll be fine by tomorrow.’

We lay enjoying the shade of the tree which kept the direct sun off our faces. The war seemed a million miles away. ‘Have you thought any more about what you want to do after the war?’ I said.

He hesitated for a minute. ‘As you know, I’m a civilian, so I’ll have to find a job. I suppose what happens will depend on where I end up working.’ He paused again. ‘I hope I can persuade you to be part of my future wherever it is.’

I held my breath, hardly able to take in what he was saying. Was this a proposal?

‘I’m not asking you to marry me,’ he said, and my heart sank just a little. ‘but can we be a couple? You’ll be my girlfriend?’

I snuggled closer to him. Once I would have been thrilled if he had proposed, but my growing independence and confidence meant I wasn’t ready to settle down to married life just yet.

‘I thought you’d never ask,’ I said. ‘Of course I’d love to be your girlfriend.’

He kissed me on the forehead. ‘I know I’ve

been slow, and I need to explain why. You'll say I'm crazy when I tell you.'

A car drove past, and the driver hooted his horn and shouted something at us we couldn't hear.

'I presume he's jealous of me being with someone as pretty as you,' Grant said, chuckling.

I grinned at him. 'You were going to tell me what took you so long. I promise not to think you're crazy.'

He sat up and took a swig of lemonade. 'I'm not usually a superstitious person, but…' he hesitated, 'it's that several people dear to me have died, and that's made me terrified it'll happen again.'

I blinked hard and sat up. 'Died? That's awful. Who was it?'

His face looked grim. 'My mother died when I was fourteen. It was a slow and painful death, dreadful to watch. You can imagine the impact that had. It's bad enough at any age, but probably worse when you're young. I've never got over it.'

'That's dreadful, especially when you were still a child.' I tried to imagine how that would feel for the whole family. 'How did your father cope with it?'

'It was difficult for him. Sadly, he couldn't cope with it all; swung from being in a rage against God to being very depressed. This was even before she died.'

'That sounds horribly difficult. Your mother must have felt she had to be his carer, even though she was the one who was ill.'

He nodded, and his shoulders were slumped. 'You're right, she tried to put on a brave face for him. I was at school, and they offered to let me have time off to help my mother, but she refused. She worried I'd get too far behind, and she wanted me to succeed.'

I felt so sad for the boy he had been. 'You must have spent all your time at school worrying about her.'

'I worried about both of them. But that's not the only death. I was with a friend, a girl my age, at the local park. She fell off the slide and died. She was twelve. It was just horrendous. I saw what was happening and ran to try to catch her, but I wasn't fast enough. All that blood and nothing I could do about it but run to find an adult. If only I could have saved her. People tell me I'm crazy but I feel responsible for her death even now.'

He got out a hankie and wiped away a tear. Then he rubbed his eyes with the heel of his hands. 'Then my fiancé, I told you about that.'

'That was tragic.'

'And my first landlady when I lived in London. Although she was my landlady and as old as the hills, she was like a grandmother to me. I've always wondered if I should have spotted that she had a weak heart.'

My heart went out to him. 'You've had a lot more than your fair share of tragedies, but it doesn't seem as if you're to blame for any of them.'

He shrugged. 'My logical side knows that, but… So if you want to go out with me, it's taking a colossal risk. I'd be scared for you to take me on.'

Secretly, I didn't believe he had some sort of curse on him. He had just been very unfortunate. I grinned and kissed him lightly on the lips. 'I'll take the risk,' I said. In return, he kissed me more passionately, taking my breath away with longing.

We kissed several times more and then lay down again, so close it was as if we were one. Looking up at the trees above us, I remembered when I first met Grant in the tea room. How as soon I saw him, I felt a spark that got stronger each time he sought me out. I relived our nighttime walks round the lake and our dance practice, as well as the excitement of the review. Mostly, I recalled how often he looked at me as if I was a special person, as if he wanted to be with me.

Although I was glad he hadn't proposed, I

hoped he would when the war was over, and I was ready, then we could start our lives together. Perhaps we would get married and have children. Two. A boy and a girl. My mind made wonderful pictures of our future that I longed to come true. I couldn't see myself being a timid wife though. Ours would have to be an equal relationship. I never wanted to live the life my mother had with my father.

'Penny for them,' he said, noticing my day-dreaming.

'My thoughts are worth much more than that,' I said with a smile and kissed him again.

THE END

But not the end of the series! (or indeed the beginning!)

The next Lily Baker book will be *Christmas with the Bletchley Park Girls*. Get ready to curl up with the heart-warming saga of friendship, love and courage at Bletchley Park.

. . .

If you sign on to Patricia's Facebook page, you will learn when it is released.

https://www.
facebook.com/patriciamcbrideauthor

Would you like the FREE prequel to the Lily Baker series? Simply go to patriciamcbrideauthor.com or email Patricia at patricia.mcbride1@icloud.com.

FACEBOOK - if you'd like to keep up to date with Patricia McBride's books you can follow her at

https://www.
facebook.com/patriciamcbrideauthor

Other books by Patricia McBride

Lily Baker Series

- The Picture House Girls
    - The Telephone Girls
    - The A.R.P. Girls
    - The Deptford Girls

. . .

Standalone books

- Murder, mystery and magic
- Winner Takes All

Non Fiction

- How to be Assertive
- Time Management for the Office
- The Assertive Social Worker
- The EI Advantage (with Susan Maitland)
- CVs and Applications
- Excel at Interviews
- Study Skills for Success

CAN I ASK YOU A FAVOUR PLEASE?

If you've enjoyed The Bletchley Park Girls, do please leave a review on Amazon or just a star rating if you're busy. It means the world to me as the author, and helps others to decide if they want to read the book.

ACKNOWLEDGMENTS

As always I would like to thank the many people who helped me with this book. My husband Rick for helping me with plot ideas, my friend Fran Johnstone (Smith) for ideas and masses of general support, and Maggie Scott for brilliant proof-reading.

Thanks also to my kind readers who offered opinions, spotted any last typos and offered invaluable help:

- Barbara Rozijn
- Margaret Smith
- Samantha Sherratt
- Fran Smith

- Jacqui Kemp
- Eve Sherratt-Cross